THIRST

NEW AND COLLECTED STORIES

KORY M. SHRUM

DEDICATION

For my mother,
who thought scary stories were good fun

I can't remember the *exact* moment I discovered and fell in love with vampires—as I would have been quite young—but I can certainly be sure of *why* I would have been interested in them in the first place.

We can blame my mother for that.

During her life, she'd been obsessed with all things fantastical and macabre. The darker the better. I have many memories of watching *The Twilight Zone* and *Tales of the Crypt* reruns late into the night with her. It didn't matter if I had school in the morning or not. We would stay up anyway, watching episode after episode after episode. These nights were likely my favorites because it meant I knew where my mother was, that she was safe, and for even the briefest of moments, we were happy together. Growing up with an alcoholic, bipolar mother did not guarantee such conditions.

So it's no surprise that I liked having her home, liked doing something as simple as watching television with her, listening to her scoff and laugh at the madness unfolding on-screen.

This is probably why I first picked up a vampire book in

my local library at the age of eight or nine. Instead of finding it weird that some creepy guy was running around in the night, sucking on people's necks and drinking their blood, I likely thought something more to the effect of *cool*.

The vampires I grew up with were not romantic. Before I discovered Anne Rice's The Vampire Chronicles, they didn't even have feelings. They were horror-movie monsters through and through. I think that's why I laughed so hard the first time I saw Edward Cullen *sparkle*. No, I'm not picking on *Twilight*. I enjoyed the first book. I'm just saying that Meyer's vampire vision is quite different from the throat-tearing, blood-lusting villains I knew.

There are a few vampire books that definitely shaped my own fiction and explain why my own novels tend to bend toward the darkness as they do, the most important being the Sonja Blue series by Nancy A. Collins. If you have read and loved any of my Shadows in the Water books, you will see the similarities between Sonja Blue and Louie Thorne almost instantly. I dressed Louie in a beat-up leather jacket and mirrored shades—just like Sonja Blue. I've made her nearly indestructible with an affinity for darkness, like Sonja Blue. And you may have even noticed that Louie's father calls her Lou-Blue. I can't get any more overt than that, people. I'm clearly fangirling here. And while it's true that Louie Thorne isn't a vampire, we can certainly agree she's blood-thirsty.

If I was pressed to name my favorite book of all time—an impossible task for bookworms—it might very well be the Sonja Blue series, particularly books one and two. But if I was forced to name my favorite *vampire* story of all time, it would be, without question, *Fledgling* by Octavia Butler.

I was so sad that Butler died before giving us more of that world. And I'm so desperate to know what happens to Shori and her tribe that I might break down and write myself a fanfiction one day, just so I can tell myself *something* and get the resolution I crave.

Another vampire series that influenced Louie Thorne's development is the Necroscope series by Brian Lumley. I was absolutely *horrified* by these vampires, and if you read any of the books, I think you'll see why. They are not beautiful or alluring in the sense we usually think of vampires today. Okay, there is *one* gorgeous vampire named Vavara who takes over a Greek monastery and she turns all the nuns into creatures who—well, I can't even say it. I'm still shocked by it all. But the title of that volume is *Necroscope: Defilers*, so I'm sure you can imagine.

My point is that Lumley's vampires are blood-guzzling aliens who desire only to enslave humanity. And the only thing stopping them from doing so is Harry Keogh, the hero. Harry's ability to move through space using what Lumley called the Möbius Continuum inspired Louie's ability to move through shadows. I'm sure Lumley's words planted the seeds for how I might describe such an ability to my own liking one day.

Other vampire works that I've found influential over the years include Anne Rice's The Vampire Chronicles, as mentioned, but also Laurell K. Hamilton's Anita Blake series. Anita Blake is a leather-clad hero who wields a gun against the bad guys, often referred to as the Executioner. Sound like someone we know? *La Strega*, perhaps? And both Louie and Anita would know something of having to team up with the very monster you're hunting before having a change of heart.

Anne Rice also sparked in me a fascination with the city of New Orleans—which has since become homebase for King, Piper, and all the rest—but what to say about Rice's vampires?

They changed much of what we know about vampire fiction because Rice humanized vampires. She gave them feelings, perspective, and the ability to love deeply. Much like Angel from *Buffy the Vampire Slayer* (yes, I watched every episode of both series), they had a soul. And most of the time that soul was tormenting them.

That was very different from the sort of vampires we saw in *Salem's Lot* by Stephen King, and its companion story *One for the Road*—vampires who, once turned, were never human again.

In fact, vampires do quite a bit of genre-hopping. They appear in mysteries and horror. They grace the pages of gritty punk tales and satire. Or sometimes they're sexy in contemporary paranormal romance or a good romantic comedy. In this collection alone you will find science fiction vampires and fairy tale vampires. Scary vampires and sexually frustrated vampires. And a young vampire in love. And there's even a vampire nurse. I also included a tale in the vein of Anne Rice, which is to say, historical fiction masquerading as vampire fiction.

It will be clear to you after reading this collection that I love vampires no matter the genre they present themselves to me in. It will also be clear that if you've ever read and loved one of my stories, you can thank my love of vampire fiction for that. The inspiration these creatures have given me creatively is all over the page, even when the vampires themselves are not.

While it's true that I will always love Sonja Blue and Shori best, I suppose I love the Anne Rice Vampire Chronicles for a more personal reason. Because one day, my mother gave me a special book—a brand-new copy of *The Vampire Armand*, which I still have on my shelves.

I share the story of this gift and how much it meant to me in *Who Killed My Mother?*, and I suppose all that can be added here is an emphasis on how touching it was to receive a twenty-five-dollar hardback at a time when we were really struggling financially.

By the time I'd received this gift, I'd already read every vampire book there was to read in our small county library—many more than once—and brand-new books took longer to be cataloged, so I was resigned to not knowing what would happen to my favorite vampires for many months to come.

And yet, my mother surprised me by handing over the book not long after its release.

God, it smelled amazing. I still remember that.

I also remember the smile on her face just before she closed the door behind her and left me to the task of devouring the book.

So it all comes back to my mother, I suppose—my love of vampires and all things that go bump in the night. And that's why I've dedicated this collection to her, because I know, if she had been alive to read it, she would have liked it very much.

THIRST

Her stomach spasmed, curving her spine into a sharp C. Her fingers clenched the rim of the toilet as if to pin the bathroom in place around her. Shaking and covered in sweat, she pushed away from the toilet. She raked one hand across her brow and her palm came away sticky. She crawled toward her cool sheets. Her rapid heartbeat matched her shallow breathing.

Somehow she made it back to her bed. As she fell against the pillow, the wristwatch on her left arm beeped four times in quick succession. She raised the watch, the luminescent face glowing green.

Eleven percent. Her dehydration level was too high.

The face blinked before turning itself off to conserve the power generated by her own body heat. If only her body was as adept at saving water.

She reached for the cup of lukewarm water beside her bed but found it empty. A single drop rolled around the bottom's rim. That was the last of it then. No water in the fridge. And she couldn't afford more. But even without the possibility of relief, her misery wasn't enough to keep her awake.

The weight of sleep pulled her down into feverish dreams again.

Freezing hands lifted her from the bed and her head fell back between her shoulder blades.

"Ellie?" a distant voice called, as if through a thick fog. "Eleanor?"

The watch beeped again and a hand snatched at her wrist, a hand so cold it felt like fire against her skin. She tried to open her eyes, to pull away, but the dark room spun.

She went limp in the tight grip. She didn't have the strength to fight back.

"Ellie, listen to me."

Go away, she wanted to say. But she couldn't make her mouth move. Couldn't get her swollen tongue to form the words: *Stop touching me. It hurts.*

"You need to drink this," the voice said. "Come on, open your mouth. Please."

Sebastian, she thought, finally recognizing the voice. *Sebastian, what the hell are you doing here?*

He shoved something metal into her mouth, a strange brace that scraped against her teeth, forcing her lips apart. A rough mesh lay over her tongue and cheeks. She tried to push it out with her tongue, but it didn't budge.

"Leave it in," he commanded. "It's a filter. You can't drink this unfiltered."

Still, she managed to spit the filter out before he pried her mouth open and shoved it in again, this time pinning it in place with his hand.

"You need this," he said patiently. "You've got to drink this or you'll die."

Drink what?

She wished she could explain that it was just a stomach

bug. Half the servers at work had come down with it. If he would just leave her alone to sleep, she would feel better.

But before she could form her argument, the viscous medicine spilled over her tongue and hit the back of her throat. Her stomach churned.

The taste was terrible, like iron.

She started to heave but Sebastian clamped his hand over her mouth.

"Swallow. *Swallow.*"

His hand was clasped so tightly to her lips that there was nowhere for it to go but down. The medicine that had hit his palm before she could swallow smeared against her lips and cheek. He lifted her shirt to wipe it away.

How long would this go on?

She felt as if she'd slipped into sleep a hundred times, only to be awakened at his insistence.

Every time her watch beeped, he forced her upright and shoved the filter into her mouth again.

Though he was gentler this time, fitting the filter into place without hurting her, the medicine did not taste better. It was still too rich and metallic on her tongue.

Her fever broke sometime in the night.

When her eyes finally fluttered open, she saw daylight reflected off the window's solar cells, filtering into the dark room like a honeycomb of light. The solar cells not only powered the building but they helped block out the heat and sunlight—important for keeping her apartment cool and minimizing water loss. She watched the sunbeams glitter on the dark panes for a moment before she could bring herself to sit up.

Sebastian sat beside her bed. He looked too clean, too fresh, in her creaky kitchen chair. She became very aware of her filth, that she could smell herself and the stench of sick all over her.

The chair groaned as he leaned forward to rest his fore-arms on his knees.

"How do you feel?" he asked.

"How did you get in?" Her voice cracked at the edges.

He held up a key. Her shoulders slumped. She'd neglected to ask for it back six months ago. It had occurred to her to change the locks, of course, but she was too broke to pay a locksmith. And she was not afraid of Sebastian stealing anything. What would he take? The mattress on the floor? The wobbly furniture amounting to only two kitchen chairs, a dented card table, and a dresser—perhaps the one sturdy piece of furniture in the whole place?

It was huge and industrious. He could hardly make off with it.

The idea of changing the locks to protect herself was as ridiculous as the idea of protecting her belongings. He'd never so much as yelled at her. Once, when a spider had entered through some unseen crack, Ellie had insisted he kill it. He'd only laughed at her hysteria as he caught the bug in his hands and placed it gently outside the window on the ledge.

"That's new." He was pointing at the curtains, the one change since he'd emptied his allotted dresser drawer and taken his toothbrush out of the plastic cup by the sink.

Since he'd left her.

"Amaya made them," Ellie replied, looking at the vibrant pink-and-green fabric hanging from the ceiling. Ellie guessed that perhaps her curtains had been a sari in another life, maybe even worn by Amaya herself.

He went to the window and ran a pale hand over the fabric. "A generous gift."

"I put out a fire in her apartment."

His eyebrows arched. "How did you manage that?"

"I used my rations." Ellie remembered Amaya's screams in

the corridor, the way the children had wailed, how even the orange tabby had run into the hall, ears pinned back, back arched.

"No wonder she was grateful," he said softly, and let the fabric slip from between his fingers.

"I told her she didn't have to give me anything, but she insisted," Ellie said.

Ellie had refused the woman's rations. Amaya and her two children shared a room no bigger than Ellie's. She doubted that Amaya's rations were any bigger than her own. She hadn't expected Amaya to show up at her door a week later, curtains and pins in hand. The two women stood on opposite sides of the window, balancing on Ellie's wobbly kitchen chairs to hang them.

Ellie had tried to improve the bare apartment in other ways after Sebastian left. Her one true extravagance was a single sunflower on top of the dresser. The inch of water at the bottom was worth more than a hundred curtains.

"I could have drunk that," Ellie said, eyes still fixed on the flower. "I completely forgot."

He sank into the chair beside her bed again. "How do you feel?"

He leaned forward to place a cool hand against her forehead. She pulled away from him, horrified by the idea that anyone would touch her while she was so filthy.

Her watch beeped, drawing her eyes down to the luminescent screen.

Four percent.

"How is that possible?" she asked, unable to hide her shock.

"Amy called me looking for you." His blond hair fell into his eyes as he leaned forward again to offer her a bowl of broth. "You missed two days of work."

"I'm so fired."

"No, I spoke to her," he assured her. "She's too short-staffed to lose you."

Ellie had never changed her emergency contact information. The fact that he was her contact after only eight months of dating was ludicrous. It was even more embarrassing when she considered how good it had felt writing his name in the blank, after so many years of not having a name to write down at all.

She looked at the bowl of broth now in her hands. "Where did you get the water for this?"

She took a sip. Fortunately, it tasted nothing like the horrid medicine she'd been force-fed during the night.

"I used your rations. And when that was gone, I used mine."

She almost spat out the broth. "It's only Tuesday!"

"It's Wednesday, and I'll get you more."

"I'll be delirious by Saturday." She lowered the broth, intending to put it on the bedside table, but he stopped her by placing his hand under the bowl and easing it toward her lips.

"Drink it."

"I need to save it," she said, and turned her face away. He couldn't shove it into her face any more without spilling it on her.

"I can get more."

"No, you can't. No one can just *get* more."

Then his own watch beeped, and she instinctively looked at the large dial.

"Point oh five percent." She met his dark eyes, but he gave away nothing. He only waited, broth hanging in the air between them.

She snatched his wrist and looked at the number again, unable to comprehend it. She'd never seen a number lower than two percent.

"How?" she asked.

"Like I said, I can get more. Please drink this."

She was too weak to fight him. And she wanted the broth. Her belly ached for it, having emptied its contents hours ago. Or was it days? Time felt fuzzy at its edges.

She took the bowl.

But as her awareness grew, so did her discomfort. There was no ignoring the fact that her body was covered in that sticky sweat that overtakes one in the throes of illness, a film born of bacteria grown beneath old, unwashed sheets.

And here was her ex, looking cool, clean, and better than she'd ever seen him. A little tired, maybe—from caring for her all night, no doubt—but his hair had been washed. His clothes smelled like detergent. His hands were freshly scrubbed, the nails gleaming.

She took another sip. It was *heaven.* "How do you have all this water? Does your new girlfriend work for Osmotics or something?"

As far as she could tell, water was tight for everyone in the zone. Pollution and leaky pipes kept slowing production. If people had the energy, she was sure they'd be rioting in the streets by now.

"I'm not seeing anyone," Sebastian said.

"So you're single again?" she asked.

"There was never anyone else. I told you that."

She harrumphed. A sound meant to illustrate her skepticism.

"You were certainly sneaking off to do something." She tipped her head back to get the last of the broth down her throat. "Don't tell me you weren't."

His dark eyes measured hers as if deciding whether or not he wanted to revisit this old argument. In that last month of their relationship, when she'd seen less and less of him, it felt like his mysterious comings and goings were all they'd talked about—or rather fought about.

"You didn't have to come just because Amy called. I'm not your problem."

She set the emptied bowl down.

"Do you want me to tell you I was worried?" He looked tired. The cool light coming through the old sari curtains made his face look paler than usual. But they were all pale. Osmotics employees could afford to risk sweat and exertion in the sunlight and therefore worked comfortable nine-to-five jobs.

Sunlight was a luxury.

The rest of the workforce began after the solar generators switched over into their reserve cells at sunset each day.

"Well, don't *lie*," she said.

"When have I ever lied to you?"

"You wouldn't tell me what you and Devon were doing."

"We were working," he said. "That wasn't a lie."

"Working on what? *Drugs?*" She tried to ignore her itchy hair. She was desperate for a shower. "Are you selling Dust now? Is that why you have enough money for extra water rations?"

Ellie saw the irony. The scarcer water became, the more Dust poured into the streets. It was a drug that could be made with chemicals, no water necessary. It was a stimulant welcomed by anyone desperate to overcome the sluggish fatigue plaguing their dehydrated bodies. Ellie hadn't used it herself—but she'd certainly considered it after pushing through some of her more brutal shifts at Lioncourt's.

Sebastian tilted his head. "Could you see me selling anything?"

She had to smile at that.

It was true—he couldn't sell a cup of water to a desiccated mummy on the street. His interactions with people had always been strained and awkward. Conversations, much like this one, always seemed to exhaust him.

"No, you don't have the skills, but you're smart. Maybe you invented a new drug and Devon sells it. He could sell someone their own pants."

"We're not making drugs, Ellie."

His watch beeped again, but he did not look at it. Since it had not been a full hour since the last beep, his percentage must have risen.

"Better go get some of your secret water stash," she said.

He turned toward the windows. "You need to get more sleep."

"My apologies, but I thought you were an engineer, not a doctor," she protested, but she was already lying back down. She felt immensely better, but her head had begun to throb.

She felt small as he looked down at her, most of her hidden in the heap of blankets.

"Can I come back and check on you?" he asked.

"Okay," she heard herself say, but immediately doubt leapt up within her. Why should she invite him back? He'd broken her heart. They'd lived together for two years, and it had taken her that long to realize she didn't know him at all. He said he loved her, but someone doesn't keep that many secrets from someone they love.

When Sebastian reached for the door handle with his right hand, the sleeve inched up, revealing a pale, bandaged wrist.

She wanted to ask him about it, how he had gotten hurt. But he was gone before she could.

ELLIE WOKE TO THE SOUND OF A LOW THRUM IN THE DISTANCE. Her eyes blinked open just as the last bit of sunlight dipped beneath the buildings. The world looked like it was on fire, aglow as it was with diffused orange light. She watched the solar cells grow bluer and bluer as the sunlight faded, as if the two were locked in battle.

The glowing cells prevailed until all the remaining orange was swallowed whole by the radiant, electric blue.

She'd often heard customers complain about how ugly these high-rises had been before a developer transformed them into energy towers, covering them top to bottom with solar cells. Women who could afford to have their hair washed daily often sat at Lioncourt's white-clothed tables and spoke of The Blue District as if they were even old enough to know a time before it, as if they knew firsthand the burden of seeing the dead and blackened buildings as they were before they were brought back to life.

Again the low thrum caught her attention, and she pulled herself from the tangle of bedding. The tower opposite her own was burning bright and the blue obscured her view. But if she looked to the east, she could see the fields outside the city, stretched long in the purple twilight. Small planes, like metallic dragons, swooped up into the low-hanging clouds. They were seeding the clouds with silver iodide and propane, trying to coax the rain to fall on the crops below.

She watched the planes rise into the clouds, disappear, and resurface in the twilight—again and again, until the twilight became a rich darkness.

Still she stood at the window, listening for the thrum of the planes, until it too was swallowed up by the sounds of the city, of all its dark creatures crawling out from under their rocks into the safety of another cool night.

Ellie forfeited one of her eight monthly shower tokens for the pleasure of washing her hair. She knew that a simple antibacterial wipe would not take care of the level of filth she'd acquired after days of vomiting and sweating all over herself. Even worse, she felt as if the grime on her skin was putrefying in the humid night.

Though the shower token allowed for three minutes of low-pressure water to pour from the spigot, she could turn it on and off with a red-handled control valve—drawing the pleasure out for as long as possible. She'd gotten very good at wetting herself in just seconds before turning off the valve and scrubbing down with a coarse bar of lemon-scented soap, including her hair. Then she'd rinse off the lather and finish by applying conditioner, sitting on the cool bench in the stall until she shivered. This always left her with a minute or more of water trapped in the timed valve before her precious token was spent. Or when she had only a token or two left, she'd let the extra water collect in a bucket between her legs, saving it for when the tokens were gone.

Now that she was clean, she lifted the red handle up, opening the valve wide.

For that minute and a half as the water poured freely down on her, life was perfect. There was no counting. There was no scarcity or panic. She let the water fall on her bare face, eyes and mouth pinched closed.

Only—

She wished she could drink the water. She wished she could open her mouth and gulp it down, turning the valve on and off to make sure she did not miss a drop. But shower water was not potable. Even if she collected it and boiled it, the chemicals used to sanitize it would make her sick. Once, in a very desperate moment, she *had* tried to boil it and drink it, but the diarrhea that followed had been awful.

An experience she hoped to never revisit, especially not with the last few nights so fresh in her mind.

Her hair was still drying as she dressed, locked up her apartment, and headed off to work.

She walked slowly and deliberately to prevent raising her heart rate. By now, it was instinct to preserve water through even the smallest of actions. She hadn't drunk all day, instead choosing to hoard the half gallon that Sebastian had left in her fridge, in a blue Hydra bottle.

A Hydra bottle.

In *her* apartment.

The bottle itself with its advanced circular design created for the sole purpose of minimizing evaporation cost more than all her utility bills combined. The fact that he had one at all and could so easily leave it with her only raised more questions about exactly what the hell he was up to.

She passed beneath the panel projectors illuminating the street, the posts evenly spaced and creating square spotlights on the road. She measured the darkness with her steps. Eight steps in light, six steps in shadow. Nine steps in light. Five in shadow. Eight—and she noticed that even though she'd neglected the itch in her throat all day, she felt good. Her moisture monitor only registered a one-percent increase in her dehydration levels. She kept raising the green dial to her face in disbelief.

A total deficiency of four percent was amazing.

A wild thought overtook her then. What if she ran? What if she bounded through the next ten or twenty steps? Her arms pumping and stagnant air pushing her hair back from her face—much like she had as a child, before her mother, coughing, would scream desperately after her to stop. It hurt to think of her mother, of how ignorant Ellie had been of their poverty. Of how much stress it must've caused the woman, unfortunate enough to bear a rambunctious child.

Ellie remembered tearing into the house at a gallop, then stopping in the dark hallway outside the bathroom door. She'd heard a small sound, a hiss. A quiet whimpering muffled by the door. Ellie threw the door wide and found her mother standing at the sink, sewing needle in hand. She did not look up at the girl as she pushed the needle through a raised blister, the little pustule bursting with water.

"Gross, what are you doing?" Ellie had asked. Now she was ashamed that she'd ever spoken to her mother that way. To the woman who had worked all night, every night, to earn the water they needed to survive. The woman who'd been nothing but ecstatic for Ellie when she'd received the news of her lottery visa, her chance to move to a more water-stable zone.

"I'm fine," her mother had replied with a weak smile. Her dark hair, darker even than Ellie's, was pulled up in a loose bun on the top of her head to reveal her elfin ears. She thought those ears were the most beautiful attribute that she'd inherited from her mother.

"Waste not, want not," her mother whispered, and lifted the blister to her lips. She sucked the pale flesh hard before a short, choked sound—a forced laugh—escaped her.

Ellie noticed the catch in her mother's voice. Embarrassment? Her mother didn't look up as she pulled a white bandage from an ancient and nearly empty kit and wrapped it around each of her fingers.

"See?" she said, turning toward Ellie and showing her the bandaged fingers. She wiggled them, giving the impression of four tiny caterpillars trying to wrench themselves free of their suffocating cocoons. "Good as new."

Mom, Ellie thought. *I'm sorry for being such an ungrateful little—*

A siren exploded in the night, tearing the memory in half. Ellie turned to see the flashing lights swirl off the dark buildings and fly past her, whipping themselves around another corner two blocks ahead. Before disappearing into the dark, Ellie glimpsed two faces through the tiny windows in the back doors. Paramedics moving around another person that she could not see.

She wondered who might be inside dying, and if they did die, who would find out later.

Ellie still remembered her mother's death clearly. It had been a Thursday night. She'd been at work, in her crisp white shirt and black apron. She'd been pouring some rich asshole a tall glass of water in the candlelight when Amy had bent to her ear, asking her to come back to the office for a moment. The look on Amy's face as she'd said the perfunctory words: "I'm sorry for your loss."

If Ellie died now, there would be no one to say those words to.

Not really.

"You survived!" Her boss pulled her through the office door and let it swing shut behind them. Ellie's eyes adjusted to the low lights, bringing Amy's round, freckled face into focus.

Lioncourt's Cafe was packed tonight.

"Well, say something. Did you vomit up your voice as well as your guts?" she asked, her hands on her wide hips.

"No," Ellie said. "Sorry."

Amy scratched the side of her head with one long fingernail, careful not to bother the tight ponytail jutting from the top. She was at least ten years older than anyone on her staff, and the daughter of an Osmotics executive. He'd given her the funds for this place. Amy didn't have to be here herself, having enough money to hire someone else to run her retro lounge, just as she'd hired someone else to pour the high-end cocktails and cook the food. But Amy liked getting her hands dirty—as she called it. She used a lot of catch phrases like "creating jobs" and "serving the community."

"Sorry," Ellie said again. "I'm really sorry I missed work."

"Yeah, yeah," Amy said, flipping her ponytail over her

shoulder. "Even if you weren't my best server, your boyfriend already explained you were on the brink of death."

"He isn't my boyfriend," Ellie said. Already her face was flushing.

"He sure as hell can be mine then. He is *so* handsome," she said, throwing a dry rag and towelette packet at Ellie, forcing her to jerk her hands up and catch them. "Wipe down these tables and I'll send out Sam with the fresh tablecloths."

"Sam?" Ellie asked, and tore the corner off a sealed towelette. "Where's Jaz?"

"Sick," Amy said with a derisive laugh. "One week I'm overstaffed with three girls folding towels and the next I'm sanitizing my own floor. Running a business is *wild*, I tell you."

Ellie heard it again, the pride in her voice, as if sanitizing a floor really made something of a person.

I've got some character-building activities for you, Ellie thought. *Try eating, sleeping, and shitting in a room no bigger than your office.*

But even as she thought this, her heart sank. She thought of Amaya and her children, more mouths living on even less than what Ellie had.

Technically Ellie had a second room—the bathroom— even if it had no door. And she had Amaya's nicest dress hanging from her windows. Then there was that ridiculous sunflower in its inch of water. God, why had she even bought that stupid thing?

'Cause the woman selling the flowers in the street had been so hopeful when they locked eyes that Ellie hadn't been able to tell her no.

"So needless to say," Amy said, unaware that Ellie's mind had wandered off, "I'm glad someone else is here to *actually* work. Do you feel well enough to pull extra tables tonight?"

"Yes, I can do it," Ellie said quickly. Even if she had blood coming out of her eyes, Ellie would have said yes. As unimpressive as it was, her apartment wasn't going to pay for itself. "I'm a little shaky but I'll make it."

"Shaky, huh? I would have never guessed. You look amazing," Amy said, heading toward the kitchen door. "I think this is the first time I've seen color in your cheeks."

It was almost dawn by the time Ellie exited the elevator onto the fifteenth floor of the Eastern Tower. As soon as the door to her apartment came into view, a small wave of sweet relief washed over her aching limbs. After days of being sick, ten hours on her feet had wiped her out.

A couple of rich housewives had insisted the band, Oceanic Mnemonics, keep playing, and Amy told Ellie to keep the drinks flowing. Ellie had not dared to complain. She was making good tips, the drunk housewives carelessly letting their money fly, and she needed to make a few extra bucks to cover what she'd lost while out sick.

It helped that the alcohol was just as expensive as water. Not just in its outright cost, of course, but in water loss. Ellie didn't know anyone who could afford the water loss on something as extravagant as a glass of wine.

Ellie's keys slapped against the wooden door as the deadbolt rolled twice to the left.

She saw the jug as soon as she crossed the threshold—the Hydra bottle, whose thin casing reflected the blue light of the solar cells outside, making the water inside luminescent.

She had not left the Hydra bottle on the counter.

To be certain, she went to the small white fridge beneath the southwest window and yanked open the door. Sure enough, the first Hydra bottle that Sebastian had left her still sat there, the exterior frosted with cold. She closed the door and turned to the second bottle, and considered the possibility that it really was magical. Possibly self-replicating technology.

Then she saw the note.

> *Don't be stubborn. Just drink it.*
> *—S*

She recognized the hurried scrawl. But why would he bring her more water? Now that she was better, he had no reason to contact her again. And when did he come? If he kept slipping in and out of her apartment uninvited, she would have to demand he return the key.

Ellie snapped off the lid of the Hydra bottle and lifted it to her lips. She knew she should be careful, not drink too much too quickly. But she gulped. Once, twice, three times, and then she quit counting. Her mouth worked furiously at the lip of the Hydra bottle, as if she hadn't had a drink in years. When the last drops hit the back of her throat, she turned the empty bottle up, craning her neck back, tongue lolling wildly around the rim for any trace of moisture.

With a loud, satisfying belch that gave her indescribable pleasure, she laughed and wiped her mouth with the back of her hand. Then, head cooling pleasantly, she turned the bottle in the light as if she might find a secret message scratched onto its surface.

No message, but she could see a fingerprint, much larger than hers, on the opposite rim, shimmering and alive. She placed her own over it until the whorls were indistinguishable.

ELLIE WAS ALMOST ASLEEP IN THE MOUND OF HER GROSS sheets when her moisture monitor beeped. The MoistMonX read two percent on its large green dial. That was a record for her. Anything below the People's Hydration Administration's recommended 10–12% max range was astonishing. Apart from Sebastian's miraculously low reading, Ellie had never even seen a rating so low. Granted, the upper classes who frequented Lioncourt's Cafe never wore monitors.

Two percent.

Two percent.

She kept thinking about it as she moved through her afternoon.

Often she slept right up to sunset, but now her energy levels were amazing.

She'd been able to change her bed sheets and replace them with her only spare set. Then she carried the grimy sheets down the four flights of steps to the shared laundry room in the basement of her apartment building, without having to stop and rest, as she usually did. Loading her comforter into the large industrial machine, she knew she would not be missing the sour smell of her own vomit or the musty old scent of sickness. She shoved her clothes in on top of the comforter and caught sight of the shirt she had been wearing the night she came home sick. It was a white dress shirt, the same style that all the girls at Lioncourt's Cafe wore. But this shirt had red splattered all along the front. She ran a questioning finger over the stain. Then she remembered coughing once or twice as Sebastian force-fed her the terrible medicine through the metal filter.

It looked like blood.

God, had she really been that sick? Vomiting up her own blood?

An unnerving feeling she couldn't quite articulate rang through her mind. She did not want to waste energy sorting through the bizarre fugue of nightmarish visions that had come to her at the height of her oblivion.

Instead, she threw the ruined shirt in the trash. No need

to waste one of her two precious monthly laundry tokens on a lost cause. It was cheaper to throw it away than to try to clean up the mess.

Dressed in a fresh white-collared shirt, Ellie rushed back to Lioncourt's Cafe. Her shift was long and exhausting. Not just physically difficult on her healing body but mentally as well. Pouring glass after glass of water for her spoiled customers always challenged her. Her thirst escalated, hour over hour, as she poured countless glasses of water she could not drink. And this torment was made worse by her entitled customers.

"Do you need me to count it out for you?" a woman asked with a sneer.

She sat poised on her seat, her posture perfect, clicking her crystalline nails impatiently on the white starched tablecloth.

Ellie looked down at the money in her hands, the silver coins blurring in and out of focus in the table's candlelight.

She could admit to herself that her brain was foggier today, her watch registering a dehydration level of nearly five percent.

"Give her a break. She isn't paid enough to deal with your bullshit, Gretchen," a man said. He sat across from the woman, one leg crossed over the other, holding his own glass of water. He'd barely drunk any of it. "Not everyone can afford college."

The insult stung.

Ellie had gone to college. But just like Sebastian and most of their classmates, a degree hadn't helped her get a job. It didn't matter that she was smart or that she'd done well in her classes. In a zone where so few jobs were available, connections mattered. And Ellie hadn't known anyone.

"Christ," the woman said, and shoved back her seat. "Keep the change, sweetie. Let it be something for you to practice with."

Laughing, her friends stood with her, and all of them made their way to the exit as a pack.

Amy came to stand beside Ellie. "What was that about?"

"I didn't count out her change quickly enough. Apparently," Ellie said. No point in lying. She knew Amy probably heard the conversation herself. She couldn't control the tears stinging the corner of her eyes. "I'm sorry."

The full water glasses on the table were carefully placed in the bus bin. Amy handed the bin to Ellie. If Amy noticed the tears, she didn't point them out.

"Go tell Mike to give you a half," Amy said. She nodded in the direction of the kitchen door with its porthole window. "Go on."

Ellie took the bin, careful to keep the bottom even so the water wouldn't slosh. She told Mike that Amy had approved a half glass of water for her, and Mike poured it dutifully. Ellie gulped it down in three meager swallows and handed the wet glass to Mike, who only grunted and put it in his pile, his dark hair hiding his face. He barely looked up from his dishes as he loaded them into the heater to be sanitized.

Ellie arranged the used water glasses, placing them on a prep table with the others collected during the night. At the end of their shift, all the closers would gather around and divvy it out, pouring the water collectively into a giant pitcher before redistributing it evenly amongst themselves.

Some nights they laughed, delirious with happiness to find they finally had what they'd worked for all evening, gulping water with cheerful faces.

But then there were nights like tonight, when they were silent, each mouth too tired to spare a laugh or a smile as they drank what they could.

On nights like tonight, it felt like nothing would change.

AN HOUR BEFORE DAWN, ELLIE HEADED HOME. SHE KEPT thinking about the woman who'd walked out on her rather than wait for her to count the change.

Where was she now? Ellie wondered.

Sleeping in a big bed in Palatial Paradise? Cream on her face? Glass of water by the bed? Maybe she was talking to a friend on the phone? A bored husband, clean-shaven, reading beside her?

Or better yet—Ellie mused—an empty bed, the husband sleeping somewhere else. Maybe she was just as lonely as Ellie was when not surrounded by her cackling friends.

A pang of guilt made Ellie want to retract that last thought.

When she'd thought Sebastian was cheating on her, she'd been crushed. Every time he'd taken off after some mysterious text, offering little to no explanation and returning hours later—or sometimes not at all—it had been gut-wrenching. It had pushed her toward an obsessive feeling that she'd never experienced in her life.

No, Ellie would not wish that feeling on anyone, not even a spoiled bitch.

She tried to shake these feelings as she turned the final corner before her apartment building. A burst of blue from the solar cells fell across her face. And just below that, in its shadows, the body of a man lay half in the light, half in the shadows.

Some drunk—or dehydrated—soul had fallen over, his one bare foot exposed to the night.

I shouldn't complain, Ellie thought with renewed conviction. *Getting my visa, moving to this zone, and getting a degree. Sure, I didn't get a great job, but I do have a job.*

That job, as horrible as it could be, kept her residency in the zone valid.

And residency was the only reason she could buy water rations at all.

She looked away from that vulnerable bare foot, the toes blue and cadaverous in the light.

Her birth zone, the dreadful place where she'd left her mother to die alone, *that* had been worse.

Ellie needed to remember that.

It could be worse. So much worse.

On the fifteenth floor, Sebastian stood outside her door. Stepping off the elevator and seeing him there was shock enough. But then the uncomfortable weight of self-consciousness settled over her, rolling her shoulders up closer to her ears, turning her gaze downward. As if she could will herself to be smaller, or better yet, invisible.

But there was no use. He was blocking her door.

"What are you doing here?" she asked. She tugged at her dirty apron and stopped herself from scratching self-consciously at a large condiment stain.

"I just came to check on you," he said. He shuffled his weight as if he were the nervous one. "Are you angry at me?"

"No," she said, but she could not quite keep the bite out of her voice. "But there's no need to talk out here where everyone can hear us."

By everyone, she meant the neighbors who could no doubt hear them through the paper-thin walls.

"Can you move, please?" she asked.

He did, and she was able to unlock the door. Though neither of them looked any more comfortable inside the little studio than they had in the cramped hall. She took off her work shoes, feeling the rush of relief that followed when one was allowed to press their entire foot flat on a floor. Then she pulled off the itchy stockings and grimy apron.

"So?" she prompted when he seemed unwilling to speak. "Are you just here to gawk at my shitty apartment and appreciate how far you've climbed?"

"What?" he said, his mouth parted. "I'm not *gawking*."

"Then why do you keep coming back?" she asked. "There's nothing here for you. Except for your water in the fridge. If you want that, just take it."

His brow furrowed. "Where is all this coming from? Why are you so mad at me?"

Before she could answer, her watch beeped, and they both looked at the bright green dial. Before she could pull away, he turned her wrist over gently in his hands, his skin so cool compared to hers.

When he saw the number he swore.

"Disappointed I'm not dead?" she asked. She saw the grime under her nails and winced before pulling herself free of his grip.

"Why is it climbing again?" He pressed a hand to her forehead. "Did you drink the water I left?"

"Why does it matter? I'm not your problem. Just leave."

Like everyone else who says they love me, she thought.

His face evened out. "We need to talk."

She snorted. "About what?"

He pressed his lips together and ran a hand through his hair. "Can you just come with me? Or maybe another night would be better. I thought your levels would be better, honestly."

"Go where?" She tried not to sound too eager.

The truth was anywhere else would be a welcome change. She couldn't be in this tiny room with him a minute longer. Every scuff on the wall and dent in the furniture set her teeth on edge.

"Please empty that Hydra bottle before we go."

"Go *where?*" She took a clean pair of clothes into the bathroom nook and changed. "Can you just not be Mr. Mysterious for once? I'm begging you."

"I'll tell you everything. Or rather, I'll show you." When she reappeared, he was holding the fullest of the two bottles out to her. "But please drink this first."

As she took the bottle, she saw the bandage on his wrist peeking out from beneath the cuff.

"What happened?"

He grimaced and pulled his sleeve down. "We can't begin this way. I'll explain everything at the lab."

"You have a lab? That's where we're going?" Her curiosity was piqued. And the water she drank cooled her face. Her thoughts were sharpening.

She offered him the empty bottle.

"Keep it," he said.

"I'm not a charity case," she said. But her earlier anger was fading fast. It was amazing what a drink of water did for her irritability.

"It's not charity. Everyone should have them," he said.

"They're too expensive."

"They shouldn't be," he said, his jaw clenching and unclenching. "The manufacturing costs are so insignificant now it's a crime that they overprice them the way they do."

She put the emptied bottle back on the counter. "So are we going or not?"

He gave a weak smile. "It's too late to turn back now."

At first, he walked far too fast for her to keep up. When the dizziness overtook her and her pace slowed to a crawl, he turned back for her.

"I'm sorry," he said, and looped his arm through hers. "I wasn't paying attention."

"You have longer legs."

"And you're dehydrated. I need to be more careful. Even if I gave you ten cups a day for weeks your levels would need more time to recover. You've been deprived for too long."

For my whole life, she thought, but she didn't say it. The image of her mother pouring the last of the monthly rations into a cup for her flashed in her mind.

But Ellie wouldn't dare complain about what she did or didn't have as a child. How could she?

They walked on but did not speak. As they walked through the city, the solar cells switched off, the blue light replaced by the growing yellow light of day.

The soft music seeping through open windows faded. The fragments of conversation wafting past them as Sebastian gently shouldered her down the avenue also died away as people settled into their beds for the day.

Ellie had just grown accustomed to the growing silence when they abruptly stopped at the back of a building.

Sebastian knocked loudly on the heavy metal door.

How can he be so strong? she thought. For her, every movement took a tremendous amount of exertion.

"Name?" a man called through the door as Ellie shifted her weight from one aching hip to the other.

"Nile."

"Nile?" she snorted. "Is that a password? Is this a secret clubhouse or something?"

"Be quiet," he said, his voice stern. The words hung there in the dark between them until the metal locks clanked back and the heavy door creaked, echoing in the dark alley.

Oh god, it is drugs, she thought. *Am I entering a drug den right now?*

"There's a step here." Sebastian helped her over the door's small lip. The darkness inside the hallway was so thick that she couldn't even see who had opened the door. When Sebastian pulled her forward suddenly, a surprised gasp escaped her.

"What's wrong?" he asked.

"I can't see anything."

He pulled her tighter. "I'll guide you."

"How can you see?" she asked. She was hyper-aware of the length of his body pressed against hers. And while the last bit of her pride wanted to push him away, refuse him, she didn't dare. She didn't want to be alone in this darkness, as complete as it was.

"Sebas—uh, *Nile*? How can you see?"

"I come here a lot."

"Where is *here*?" she said softly, feeling his hand brush the back of her neck.

"I'll explain soon," he said in a low voice. "For now, just trust me."

Finally light appeared at the end of a hallway, forming a thin line around the frame of a door. Sebastian released her in order to knock again.

"It's me," he called out.

Footfall approached. Then the light burst through. Ellie shut her eyes, opening and closing them slowly until they adjusted to the solar lamps burning inside the room.

"So you brought her," a man said. "You *idiot*."

Ellie knew this voice—Devon.

She didn't know much about the man standing opposite Sebastian except that they met at college a couple of years before Ellie and Sebastian started dating.

Devon had been offered a job after school, protected by his family's wealth and connections. Sebastian had taken a job at Lioncourt's Cafe with her. It had surprised her that they had stayed friends even as their circumstances had taken them in opposite directions.

Nothing much had changed.

Devon still had an amazing, clear complexion, nice clothes, and shiny shoes. But he wore a water monitor on his wrist, though its face was dark and unreadable.

"I hope you know what you are doing," Devon said, and opened the door wide enough for them to enter.

"She—"

"She almost died. Yes, I know," Devon said in a cold voice. Both of his brows shot up in annoyance. "That doesn't mean she'll like what you have to say."

"Uh, I'm right here," Ellie said.

"Yes, you are," Sebastian said, and gave Devon an unfriendly glare.

Devon forced a tight smile. "Hello, Eleanor. Nice to see you again. It's been a while." He took her hand and pulled her into the room. "Come into our humble abode."

"You live here?"

"*Nile* does. The man is a workaholic." Devon lowered his voice. "You told her not to use our real names here, right? I'm Amur, by the way, if anyone asks."

Neither Sebastian nor Ellie spoke.

Devon nodded. "Good. As long as we're all clear on that."

Sebastian pulled her away from Devon and eased her into a metal chair. Her eyes roved the room. Machines clicked on and off, giving the impression of a sleeping beast, breathing.

"What is all this?" she asked, a little embarrassed to admit her own ignorance.

"This is where I work when I'm not working," Devon replied. He leaned past her to punch a few buttons on the screen that flashed and blinked.

"I mean, what do you do here?"

Devon looked at Sebastian, who stood awkwardly in the center of the room.

"What *do* we do here?" Devon asked him with an amused expression, eyebrows still high.

"I'm going to tell her the truth," Sebastian said.

"Oh, well then," Devon replied. He had the sarcastic air of a man whose friend had just told him they were going to do something crazy. "Don't let me stop you."

"We're exploring alternative water sources," Sebastian said.

Devon laughed. "How sanitized your version of the truth is."

"Can you give us a minute?" Sebastian's irritation was turning his ears red. "This is hard enough without you chiding me."

Devon leaned forward. "But I'm desperate to know how you'll break it to her."

"Break what to me?" Ellie said, more than frustrated that they kept talking over her as if she weren't in the room.

"Please," Sebastian begged.

Devon's amusement faded. "All right, fine."

He grabbed something from one of the tables and clapped Sebastian on the shoulder.

"I'll just step out for a *drink* then. If this little talk of yours goes well, maybe the two of you can catch up to me later."

Devon grabbed his jacket off the back of the chair. He clicked his tongue. "And pour her a fucking drink before you start talking her ears off. She looks like she's crossed a desert."

Devon pulled the door closed and was gone.

"I'd forgotten how charming he was," Ellie murmured, but Sebastian made no reply.

She was still staring at the back of the metal door when Sebastian put a glass of water in her hand. Her stomach clenched. She turned it up and sucked it down without complaint. Her belly sloshed with the fluid. She couldn't remember the last time she'd had so much water.

"I'll give you more in a few minutes," he said. "I just don't want you to make yourself sick."

"I don't understand," she said, gesturing with her empty water glass. "You have a lab and enough water to keep a horse. And you're trying to solve the water problem? Right?"

"Yes," Sebastian said.

"None of that sounds bad. Except for the code names part. That's suspicious," she replied. Already her head felt better. The heat around her face was cooling. "So why are you acting like you've killed someone?"

He didn't say anything.

"*Have* you killed someone?"

"Yes," he said simply.

Maybe she was still too dehydrated to understand what he was saying.

"Like, on accident?"

"Not exactly." His eyes clamped on hers, studying her as if watching for any change in her expression. "Science is an imprecise art. There was some trial and error."

"Did they drink poisoned water or something?" she asked. "What, like, you tried to filter it and it didn't work?" Her stomach trembled with the memory of drinking her shower water.

"No," he said, and again that pained expression seized him. "Let me start from the beginning."

"Wait," she said. "Is that the worst of it? That you've killed people—in the name of scientific advancement?"

His face tightened again. "It's a little more complicated than that."

"Am I in danger?" she asked. She waved the glass at him. "Was this poisoned?"

"I'd never hurt you."

"Then I'll have that second glass of water, please," she said. She held the glass out, waiting.

He refilled it from a nearly full Hydra bottle and returned the container to the fridge.

"Is this water that you filtered using your fancy technology?" she asked, swirling the last of it in the bottom of the glass.

"No," he said. "It's Devon's."

"I should drink it all then," she replied. "He can afford all the water he wants. Do they even ration the rich?"

"He prefers to hunt for his water these days," Sebastian said.

"How does one *hunt* for water?"

"I'll show you," he said, and pulled her up to one of the long worktables.

The table illuminated under Sebastian's touch as if waking just for him. With a few furious taps the screen blinked on, giving off a low green light much like her water watch. Images and pictures filtered past the screen enlarging and disappearing as Sebastian sorted through his files, searching for something specific.

He pointed at an image. "Do you know what this is?"

"It looks like a bug," she said. And it did. Many legs and a round body.

"It's one of my watbots. Their goal is to make my cells, tissues, and organ systems as water-efficient as possible. They do that by entering my cells and manipulating their functionality."

"Clever. Or dangerous. Side effects?" she said.

"None. They work well."

Ellie didn't understand why anyone would want a bunch of bugs crawling around inside them, but she also didn't fully understand what he was telling her yet. "Is this what you were sneaking off to do all the time? Is this what we broke up over?"

"If you broke up with me because I couldn't tell you what I was doing, then yes. This is it."

"This?" She pointed at the bug on the screen. *This* was the secret? Nile the mad scientist creating swarms of bugbot thingies? "There wasn't another girl?"

"I told you there was never a girl."

She swore and poured herself another glass of water from Devon's stash.

"Easy with that," he said. "You'll make yourself sick."

"Don't worry about me, *Nile*," she said. "Tell me about these bugs."

His gaze narrowed on the screen. "When Devon came to me, he said he needed help with a bioengineering project. A project with two objectives. The first was to design biotechnology that could alter the human body's physiology enough to turn us into walking Hydra bottles."

She gulped down the glass. "And the second?"

"To create a filter that could filter water automatically from impure sources, in places where clean water wasn't available. I couldn't tell him no. There was so much money on the table. Real money. The kind of money that could change our lives and get us out of here."

Our. Ellie wasn't sure if he was talking about her or Devon.

"I couldn't tell you because he wanted the project done under the table with a signed non-disclosure agreement. He's bankrolling all of this. The building. All this equipment. The guards outside."

"If he's hellbent on secrecy then why am I hearing about it now?" she asked. "He planning to kill me?"

Sebastian turned off the screen. "He knows I'll quit if he does."

"Wait, are you saying he *wants* to kill me?"

"Don't worry about Devon," he said. "I can handle him."

As long as he needs you, she thought darkly.

Her watch beeped, flashing one percent on its face. "This is the best number I've ever had."

He grimaced again. "One percent is still dehydration."

"Yeah, but compared to the standard ten to twelve percent—"

He cut her off, his voice rising. "You *die* at fifteen percent. The idea that you can function at anything less than ten percent is insane."

"So the government lies about what's safe," she said with a shrug. "That's hardly news."

He didn't reply, and she couldn't help but feel like she had said something wrong.

"What number should it be?" she asked.

"Zero," he said. "Maybe one percent after a vigorous cardio session or some sort of serious exertion."

"So how did someone die? Did your bots go crazy and eat people's insides or something?"

That earned her a small smile. "No. The bots are harmless. It's the—filter—that's problematic."

"The filter doesn't work?"

"It does. Now." Sebastian turned away from the screen. "The bots are just supplemental technology. They maintain optimal functionality and help my body conserve water. With the bots, essentially I can do more with less—but I still need a water source. The human body needs water."

"I'm still waiting for you to get to the point," she said. "How did the filter kill people? And how many people are we talking about here?"

She'd studied science too. She knew that every invention, medication, and advancement had come at the expense of life

—human or animal. But his reluctance to tell her what was going on unnerved her.

After an exaggerated exhale, he led her over to the next table.

On it lay several chunks of metal, which at first glance, Ellie assumed were the filters in question. Some were bigger than others, but most had a similar look—a flat mesh backing and a curved rim. Sebastian lifted one of the clunky-looking contraptions from the table, and again the surface blinked awake.

"This is one of my first prototypes," he said. He opened his mouth and slipped the filter inside. The contraption fit over his teeth. His lips stretched over the metal. When he opened his mouth, the wire mesh expanded, covering the tongue and cheek walls like a protective barrier from any fluid that might pass the lips.

He spat the metal guard back into his hands. "The mesh works as a filtration system, pasteurizing and sterilizing the water source as it passes through the mesh—before it is ingested."

"That's cool," she said. She picked up another guard and turned it over in her hands. This one was smaller and sleeker, with a tighter mesh. "I could probably drink my shower water with this."

"This is the newest design," he said, grabbing the smallest of the mouthguards from the table. The exterior of the guard was almost invisible, catching and illuminating the light from surrounding monitors. When Sebastian slipped it into his mouth it disappeared completely. His lips did not bulge or struggle to conceal the metal rim. It wasn't until he smiled at her that she saw the fangs, which the first few prototypes did not have.

Sharp canines jutted from his upper teeth, and there were two smaller fangs along the bottom.

"What the hell do you need *fangs* for?" she asked, laughing. "Is the water going to put up a fight?"

Sebastian spat the filter out and placed it back on the table.

It was several minutes before he finally met her gaze. "Blood plasma is composed mostly of water. If you were to drain a person of all their plasma, you would ingest roughly eight to nine cups of water—the standard daily amount to keep a body fully hydrated."

She turned the guard over in her hands, pressing the tip of her finger to the pointy end of one of the fangs, watching her flesh dent around it. "You bit people with this?"

"Yes."

"You *drank* their blood?"

"Yes."

"Like a vampire?"

He grimaced and ran his fingers through his hair. "Yes."

"Like a *fucking* vampire?"

"*Yes.*"

"What did you do? Just prowl the night and attack someone on the street?" she asked.

"It is best to target someone well hydrated, so members of the wealthier classes are the best targets."

"Oh my god," she said. "You're telling me that you've been creeping around at night, jumping rich bitches and sucking them dry like some kind of vampire Robin Hood?"

"Ellie," he said.

"How many people have you bitten?"

"In the beginning, before I figured out how to control it—"

"How *many?*"

"—before I figured out how to include a heating element in the incisors themselves—"

"Seba—*Nile*—"

"—that would cauterize tissue and stop the bleeding—"

"Just tell me how many people you killed!"

"Eighteen," he said.

"Eighteen people bled to death because you bit them?" she asked. "Because you *bit* them, drank their blood, but then couldn't stop the bleeding."

"Devon—"

Devon, Ellie thought, realizing that the small contraption he'd grabbed from the table and put into his pocket had been one of these. *I'll step out for a drink.*

"Before I created a prototype that could cauterize the wound and allow me to drink from multiple people instead of a single source," he said. "Yes, I killed eighteen people."

She gripped the edge of the table.

"In comparison to other scientific failures, eighteen is a phenomenally low number," he said.

"Is that how you sleep at night?" she asked. "By convincing yourself that you're the next bloodsucking Tesla?"

"Ellie," he said.

But she wasn't listening. She'd let the mouth guard fall from her fingers and clank onto the tabletop.

"And here I was worried you were screwing someone," she said.

"If you want to go to the police," he began, "I understand, and I am prepared to face the consequences of my actions."

"How noble!"

"You were dying," he said. "If I'd had any other way to save you I would have done that instead."

It was as if he'd slapped her. She stood there stunned, blinking.

Sebastian didn't stop there. "I thought if you drank from me first, you would ingest enough bots to help the conversion along."

"It wasn't medicine," she whispered. It had been the metal filter he'd shoved into her mouth. The *medicine* had tasted like blood because it *was* blood.

"But you have all those Hydra bottles," Ellie said. "Couldn't you have made me some tea?"

"You were *dying*," he said. He emphasized every syllable as if to help her understand. "I had to get the bots inside you so they could help. I would have preferred to inject you with the bots, but I couldn't get you to the lab in the condition you were in. I'm sorry. I did the best I could."

She turned his hand over, looking at the white bandage. Touching the rough fabric, she imagined him lifting his wrist to his mouth, tearing it open, and then forcing the bite guard into her mouth. She had *drunk* him.

She had drunk *him*.

"I still want to give you an injection of the bots, if you'll let me. I know you hate needles but—"

"No, I need to go home," she said, pulling away. The room spun around her and she reached out and grabbed a table. "Get me out of here."

He'd insisted on seeing her home. They walked next to each other in silence, listening to the light rain hit the bottoms of pails placed on open windowsills and balconies. It was too acidic to drink as it was, but purification tablets were a hell of a lot cheaper than water itself, even if it did leave a funny aftertaste on the tongue.

As they walked, she couldn't look at him. At the door to her building, he stopped her on the steps. "Ellie, please."

"Why did you tell me?" she asked as she fell against the door and looked him dead in the eye. "What did you think would happen? Did you want me to turn you in?"

Because she thought maybe he did.

"Did you think I would start hunting in Paradise with you?"

His head fell forward.

"I told you because I missed you," he said softly. He looked up at her through his long lashes. "I didn't want you to keep thinking there was someone else."

"But there *is* someone else," she said. She'd spoken softly too. Her hand came up to push his bangs away. "There's Nile. This shady guy who goes around biting people in the dead of night and doing bizarre experiments in his dark lab with his creepy friend."

"I'm almost finished," Sebastian said, taking her hand. He pressed her warm palm to his cool face. "Once I sell the tech to the investor, then I can take the money I've saved and we can—"

"We can *what?*" she asked. "What can we do? Get better jobs? A better apartment? Go back to school? Hell, get visas for another zone? One of the really posh ones? One of the center zones? Zone 8, maybe? Hell, maybe even Zone 4? You're delusional."

She hadn't meant to sound so cruel. But it sounded like Devon had promised him the moon in exchange for his help. And Sebastian had been foolish enough to believe him.

"We can't just do anything we want, Sebastian," she said. "We aren't that kind of people."

Or at least I'm not.

She pulled herself free of him and entered the apartment building, leaving him on the steps in the light rain.

And when she fell into her bed, exhausted, she could no longer hold back the tears.

She'd cried a lot over the years. She wasn't immune to disappointment. But this was the first time in as long as she could remember that tears actually came.

They wet her cheeks, her lips. She licked them, marveling

at their saltiness, sucking every drop from her fingers, knowing that sleep wouldn't find her for a long time.

Twenty minutes after the sun had dipped below the horizon, Ellie woke to the bright blue glow of the Eastern Tower's solar cells.

Sebastian's confession hadn't changed much. Even after a long day of fitful dreams, she knew no *real* action could be taken. The idea of prowling the night with him was just as ridiculous as turning him in.

My boyfriend—ex-boyfriend—has killed eighteen people, she imagined herself saying. *He bit them. They bled to death.*

They would lock her up and test her for Dust—and that was the best-case scenario. If they took her seriously, he could be punished, possibly exiled.

He could drain all the rich people he wanted and she could still never wish exile on him.

She knew what life was like outside of the secure zones. In the truly poor zones—like the one she'd grown up in with her mother before she'd been offered a student visa and a place at the zone's university—terrible things happened. Not just murder. People were willing to do far worse when it came to survival.

"No," she said aloud. Even if she disagreed with his approach, he had saved her life. And he was trying to solve a problem that desperately needed solving.

As far as she was concerned, he was Youssef Firas.

Her history instructor, Dr. Jacqueline Duffield, had painted Firas as a Gandhi incarnation. Youssef had been a poor Egyptian trying to save his village from the worst drought the world had ever seen. By the time he was twenty-four, the Nile had flooded, wiping out all the coastal villages and forcing people to move further into the desert. Then the river began to evaporate, disappearing quicker than relocation efforts could be managed, and what water remained was too polluted for consumption.

Some families had been able to move to regions where water was more plentiful, but not Youssef and his family. They hadn't had the means.

It was exactly for this reason, *because* they couldn't escape, that Youssef designed the first Hydra bottle. He'd needed a bottle capable of storing water in scorching temperatures without any loss. He taught himself how to use the equipment and technology left behind by the occupiers who'd fled the area and saved his family from certain death.

Until one day, a surveyor came to take samples of the dwindling Nile as part of his research. Youssef made the mistake of giving the man one of his bottles.

The man—Franklin Lloydson—slapped a patent on the bottle's design and became richer than Youssef ever was. He and his family died in poverty, unaware of the difference his design had made on the rest of the world.

A cool glass of water warmed in Ellie's hands as she sat by the big windows in the glow of the solar cells, listening to the first sounds of the city waking after dark.

Sipping this water, she thought about the dangers that awaited inventors and creators of all kinds. How vulnerable they were.

How easy it would be for the right person to come along and steal everything.

A ROUGH KNOCK ON HER APARTMENT DOOR JERKED ELLIE awake.

Sebastian.

She searched frantically for a pair of pants, anything

decent to put on, and a hair tie too—something to pull her hair into a flattering knot on her head.

But when the knock came again, the voice through the door was not Sebastian's. "Awake, darling?"

She hesitated, pants stuck on her thighs. "Devon?"

"The one and only, sweetheart. Are you decent? Even if you are not, please let me in. We need to talk."

Of course we do.

She got her pants on, a t-shirt and a thin sweater—but she could not find a hair tie. Instead, she had to settle for finger-combing her wild mane into place.

The moment the door unlocked Devon bounded into the room. The smell of him was overpoweringly sweet. A mix of cologne and soap and a hint of booze.

"Am I interrupting something?" he asked.

"No."

"Have you got work this evening?"

"No."

"Good. I want to take you out. There's something I want you to see."

"See what?" Her eyes followed Devon's gaze. He'd spotted the Hydra bottle on the counter and lifted it. "You can take it if it's—"

"Don't fret, darling," he said. "We have crates of these in the lab. I was just surprised to see it. Though I shouldn't be. Of course Nile is foolish enough to walk around the city with one of these. He's lucky he didn't get killed for it."

"Does Sebastian know you're here?" She hated the sound of fear in her voice.

"Of course not," Devon said with a devilish grin. Then he dropped his voice lower, a tone that could be mistaken for a purr. "And he never has to know, if that's how you'd like it."

When she felt his breath hot on her face she darted away,

bumping ungracefully against the wall, scurrying toward the windows.

"Relax," Devon said, laughing. "I'm insatiable but I'm no idiot. If I harmed a hair on your pretty head Sebastian would fall apart on me, and then where would I be? Those maxillaries aren't going to design themselves. And while he's come a long way, the design isn't perfect. I would know. I test it more than anyone."

She said nothing, her heart beating wildly in her chest. As if sensing her horror, he let his gaze slide away. It swept the darkening room and settled on the sunflower on top of her dresser.

"From a Lioncourt place setting, no doubt," he said. "How many little perks must you get at such a place, Eleanor. You're luckier than most."

Ellie hadn't realized the water was gone and that the flower had begun to dry up, the edge of the bright petals starting to curl. Stopping in front of it, he touched one delicate petal with a finger. Then he went to her fridge and yanked the door open.

He began pouring water over the stem of the dying sunflower, swirling it in the bottom of the glass. When she realized how much he was pouring in, a small sound of horror escaped her lips.

"Don't worry," he said. "We will save your little daisy here."

"Sunflower."

"*Sunflower.*"

"Why are you here?"

"Because Sebastian insists on bringing you into the fold," he said. "And if you haven't noticed, what's good for Sebastian is good for me. I like a happy tinkerer."

"Will it be just the two of us going—wherever we're going?"

"Afraid so. Nile is quite busy tonight. So put on your best walking shoes, and wear something comfortable. All black, preferably. The idea is to *not* be seen."

Am I really doing this? Can I trust him?

She was still wondering this as she exchanged her clothes for darker ones and pulled on her shoes.

When she came out of the bathroom nook, he looked her over and nodded his approval. Then he extended the Hydra bottle toward her.

"Drink it," he said.

"But—"

"We both know he'll bring you more," he said. "And I can't have you all weak and pathetic tonight. I'd rather not carry you even if the situation calls for it."

She accepted the bottle and drank the water down, guzzling it until the last drops wet her lips. Then she said, "Tell me where we're going."

"Sebastian told you his side of the story," he said, placing the emptied bottle on the counter and opening her apartment door. "Now I want you to hear mine."

She watched him carefully, weighing his voice and posture, trying to detect any deceit. She couldn't. So she tied her apartment key into her shoelaces and followed him out into the night.

For a long time, they walked north and west through the most deserted parts of town. Even with the water she'd drunk and Devon's gentle pace, she became winded. They were far enough away from the city center that she didn't recognize any of these buildings or streets.

The uncertainty around their destination only made the journey feel even longer.

"Are you sure you aren't bringing me out here to kill me?"

She gripped her right hip where a stitch throbbed. "There sure as hell wouldn't be any witnesses. There's no one here."

She wasn't exaggerating. The buildings were dark and deserted. No one had even bothered to install solar cells in this part of the city. The few remaining unbroken windows reflected only moonlight, giving the impression of huge insectile eyes looking down on their fragile bodies.

"Hurry up." Devon grabbed ahold of Ellie and hurried her along the back of the dark buildings smelling of earth and concrete.

He didn't stop pulling her until they reached a large fence. Ellie could hear the electricity thrumming in the wires, and she smelled it too. Worse, something living had collided with the fence recently and had not lived to tell the tale. Its charred body was small and unrecognizable, but Ellie guessed it must have been some sort of bird. Perhaps a sparrow, like the ones that nested in the solar cells of the Eastern Tower.

"Up and over then," he said.

Fear washed over her. "What?"

He rolled his eyes. "You've no sense of humor, Eleanor."

"But—"

"*Here.*" He yanked a wad of fabric out of his inside coat pocket and handed it to her. "Put these gloves on and put these on over your clothes."

She was certain that the suit wouldn't fit. The thin fabric couldn't have been bigger than her thigh. She stared down at the limp material in her hands, not attempting to hide her skepticism.

Devon smirked. "It gets bigger. *See.*"

He pulled on his own suit, stretching it long over one leg, then the other. He was right—it did get bigger, covering him from head to toe, with the exception of the gloves, which had to be pulled on last.

He grabbed ahold of the fence, and she expected to see him convulse or scream but nothing happened. No smell of burning flesh filled the air. Instead he said, "Just don't whip your hair around, all right? I hate the smell of burnt hair."

Devon had already climbed one side of the fence before realizing that Ellie wasn't on his heels. He scowled down at her from his perch. "This area is patrolled, and if we are caught, we will each get a complimentary bullet to the head. So, if you don't *mind*, dearest, can you move your pretty little ass?"

Ellie reached out and placed a finger on the fence, testing it. After all, just because Devon was wearing some kind of anti-electricity suit, it didn't mean that he'd given her the same thing. The fact that she still doubted his intentions was probably a sign that she shouldn't have come out with him in the first place. But here she was.

And she had a feeling he wasn't lying about the bullet to the brain.

She grabbed the fence. And just as quickly let go. Nothing happened. Then she grabbed it again, holding it a little longer. When it became apparent it wouldn't shock her, she scrambled to catch up to Devon, who was already hopping down on the other side.

When she hit the ground and followed Devon out into the darkness, she found herself in a field, black and barren. And when she knelt to touch the dirt, it cracked and disintegrated in her gloved hand.

"I don't understand. Where are we?" she asked.

"Don't you recognize it?"

She searched the landscape for anything recognizable. The silence was deep and haunting.

Nothing. She didn't hear anything, nor did she feel any air on her skin or smell anything—except for the electric fence.

The dark expanse stretched before them like a great sea. Endless and untraversable.

"This is *the* field," he told her. "The planting fields."

"No," she said. "Where are the city crops? Where are the planes that seed the clouds?"

As if fulfilling her request, the sky cracked open. A jagged shot of lightning split open the sky, an explosion of white light coming alive above them. In this light she could see the land, looking far worse than she imagined. A field of death. Then the dark clouds were rushing toward them with a furious wind blasting across their faces. The gust knocked Ellie back against the fence, but thankfully, she caught herself with a gloved hand.

"We need to move!" Devon shouted over the thunder. Laughing wildly, he shoved against her bottom, forcing her up the fence.

"I don't understand," she said, but another crack of thunder swallowed her words. Hanging from the fence, she turned her face up to the sky and saw the corpuscular underbelly of a cloud above her. Then, as if someone had cut that underbelly, the cloud split and the rain fell.

"Shit," Devon said. "Move, move!"

She resumed her climb but the wires burned. She cried out in pain.

"Stop pushing me," she yelled. "The suit isn't working."

"It's the rain," Devon yelled over the next crack of thunder. "Hurry up and get to the other side."

Despite the pain, she did as she was told. She climbed the fence quickly, all but falling down the other side. A heartbeat later, Devon landed beside her, his knees bending to absorb the impact of his jump.

Devon tore off the suit and pulled something out of his pocket. He ripped open the packet with his teeth. "Where does it hurt?"

Ellie motioned toward her face and her hair, which were wet with the rain. Devon dumped white powder from the packet onto her skin, then onto her hair, and rubbed it in softly. A few more breaths and the pain disappeared.

"What is that?" she asked. Relief, clear and fresh as any cool drink, washed over her.

"It's a neutralizer," he said. "To counteract the acid in the rain."

"Acid in the rain?" She reached up to touch her face and felt the gritty powder rubbing under her fingers, irritating her raw flesh.

"Didn't you notice how dead that land was?"

"But the cloud-seeding," she heard herself say. "It's working, and we have good crops and—"

"We have *nothing*," Devon spat. "We couldn't grow a damn thing in that field if our lives depended on it, and they *do* depend on it. People are starting to catch on. This zone is falling apart and the people in power know it. But what are they doing? Nothing. They're making their escape plans and lining their pockets as much as they can before this whole place tanks. The zone is going to burn. The only question is who will have the balls to set the blaze."

"But when it rains—" Ellie began.

"The city center has a sky filter. A relic from a far more prosperous time," he said. "Have you never wondered why it only trickles into your little buckets? Have you even considered why we can drink water from filtered rain but not from our own pipes? Control, Eleanor. It doesn't matter how little the people have. It's all about who controls it."

Ellie watched the rain come down hard on the field, pounding as if to beat the land awake, while only a few droplets touched her face.

"We need to go," Devon said. "It's late. It isn't safe to linger here."

"They're going to abandon us? That's what they're planning to do?" Because she'd lived in such a zone before.

"Go, Ellie," her mother had said. "Go and don't look back."

"No, no, no. They can't do that," she said. This zone was supposed to be different. This *life* was supposed to be *better*. She'd left her own mother for that promise.

She'd worked so hard to build a life here. To survive her. To make her mother's sacrifice worth it.

Was she really about to lose it all?

Devon peeled himself out of the suit. "To save their own asses? Of course they can. That's all the wealthy ever care about. Themselves. All the rich want is to make themselves richer. Mark my words, Eleanor. It's us or them."

DEVON DRAGGED HER THROUGH THE CITY. SHE WAS DELIRIOUS with exhaustion, her body more thoroughly exerted now than it had been in years. It felt like an eternity before the blue glow of her tower's solar cells sprung into view.

She was weak with relief when she pushed open her apartment door with only thoughts of falling into her bed and sleeping the rest of the night and day away.

Or she *would* have been, if Sebastian hadn't been in her apartment, sitting in the blue light of the Eastern Tower.

He leapt up when he saw them.

"Ellie?" He rushed forward. He grabbed her chin and turned it this way and that, inspecting the burns. "What the hell did you do?"

"Unless I've turned venomous without my knowing, I didn't do that." Devon dug into his pockets for more sachets. He sorted through them, reading the labels as he shuffled them like playing cards. "Here. Wash her face with this one and then apply this ointment. There wasn't much exposure. She'll heal."

Devon was gone before Ellie could stop him. And Sebastian was too busy trying to get her to sit down on the edge of her bed and take off her wet clothes.

"Wait." She felt dizzy.

"We need to clean you up," he said.

"With what?" She held his hands. "Devon made me drink the last of the water."

"I brought more," he said. "Two Hydra bottles full. And I've got these. You can wash that stuff off your face."

He pulled a handful of shower tokens out of his pocket.

My god.

There must have been twenty or thirty tokens lying in the palm of her hand. She'd never seen so many all at once. It was a fortune.

Before she could process her surprise, he grabbed a Hydra bottle and offered it to her.

She had to place the coins on the dresser by the sunflower before she could accept the bottle.

"You have to stop walking around with these," she said, and took a long, desperate drink. She was so thirsty she drank half a bottle's worth in one go. "You're being stupid. Careless."

She wasn't sure if she was talking to him or herself.

Both.

He reached up and pulled her shirt off. His eyes slid over her breasts for the briefest of moments before returning to her face. Then, looking away, his face spectral blue, he focused his attention on her hands. He turned each of them over in his. "I think your face got the worst of it."

"My face?" she asked.

"As beautiful as ever," he said, with a smile that made her stomach drop. "But very angry at the moment. But the redness will go away."

Without thinking, she wrapped her arms around his neck.

He relaxed against her. "I'm sorry. I'm an idiot."

"For what?"

"I should have known Devon would try something. Telling you has made him nervous. I think he only caved and agreed to let me because he knew I missed you so much and it was affecting the work. I swear, Ellie, I only said yes to this project because I saw its potential. I thought it might be the only thing that could save us and—"

She pulled him into a kiss. His back stiffened under her hands, before relaxing again. She pulled back and licked the thin, sticky sheen now coating her own mouth.

"You've been—" The final word eluded her. *Prowling? Hunting?* "You bit someone."

He looked away and pulled something from his pocket.

He placed the guard in her hand. "I had to test the final prototype before Devon pitched it to the investors."

As if from a great distance, she heard herself say, "And how did it go? The testing."

"It's good," he said. And she could see that he was holding himself back. He still watched her carefully, as if he believed too much enthusiasm would turn her off. "It cauterizes instantly and doesn't burn the back of my lips anymore. The bite itself is also cleaner—it only leaves two small holes in the skin. The tighter design creates a suction that limits blood loss, and the plasma is being filtered better. It isn't quite so thick and goopy as it was in the earlier prototypes. It's going down much easier now. The most important part, of course, is that no one died."

She nodded because she didn't know what to say.

"And I've improved the bots," he said. "Devon thinks we can sell those to multiple investors for different applications. More investors means more money. And—"

Her water watch beeped. Their eyes slid to the face reflexively.

"I really wish you'd let me give you an injection. The bots will help your body conserve water better. Keep you hydrated. Especially if you get sick again. Is there anything else I can say to convince you?"

She shrugged. "What's the difference between getting a vaccine and letting your ex inject you with tiny robots?"

"Is that a trick question?"

But she wasn't kidding. She pressed her index finger to the tiny metallic fang until an expanding bead of red bloomed there on the tip of her finger.

"There is no difference," she said. Something inside her relaxed. Her mind had been spinning ever since Devon showed her that endless stretch of dead land. It was as if the captain had pulled her aside and confided that their ship was going down.

A ship that had once held all her dreams.

And whose fault was that? She'd been the one stupid enough to believe she was destined for a better harbor, a new world—for any future except a cold grave on the ocean floor, forgotten.

"We can even make an impression of your teeth if you want. In case—I mean, it would be nice to have an impression of a female mouth either way. Yours is much smaller than mine."

"Sure," she said, unable to free herself from the dark thoughts pulling her down.

He squeezed her hands. "Are you okay? Devon didn't do anything, did he? Or say—"

"He just took me to the fields," she said. "I saw the crops. Or what should've been crops. That's where we got caught in the rain that burned my face."

The fact that he looked relieved bothered her. It implied

there were worse places he could have taken her. Maybe places with even darker truths.

"I want to shower," she said. "And sleep."

He released her. "Would you mind if I stayed? It doesn't have to be all night, but—"

She pulled him toward the bathroom. "Let's shower and go to bed."

They used four shower tokens—what an extravagance— to wash their skin and hair. Her flesh felt raw in the water, but the coolness numbed the pain.

Clean, they fell into bed just before the sun rose, twined in each other's arms.

"I missed this," he whispered into her hair.

"You were right though," she said.

"About what?"

"I hate needles," she said. "Can you just surprise me?"

He laughed. "Surprise you?"

"Yeah. Give me the shot when I'm not expecting it. Don't tell me you don't have practice sneaking up on people with all this *water-hunting* you've been doing."

He snorted. "Fair enough. I'll surprise you."

"Good," she said, burrowing deeper into his embrace. The truth was, she'd missed this too. She'd missed it even more than she'd allowed herself to believe.

She woke late in the afternoon to a sharp pricking sensation in the side of her neck.

When she opened her eyes, she found Sebastian leaning over her holding a syringe. "Surprise."

"Was that it? I thought you'd wait a few days," she said, rubbing the sting.

"I know." He put the syringe on the table and climbed back into bed with her. He bent over her and kissed her neck, his lips feather soft. "That's what made it a surprise."

. . .

Most of the next night passed like a dream. She moved from one moment to the next with little connection to her body. She was pouring water, wiping down a table, listening to Amy. Each moment passed on autopilot, her mind continuing to return again and again to the dark fields.

Until the girl came. The noise at the door drew her eye toward the large glass window. There she stood in the archway, looking small and breakable. She was dirty, only the way someone who slept outdoors could be. It made Ellie remember the man who'd been outside her apartment the other night. She'd thought he'd been a drunk—but now she wondered if maybe he'd been homeless too.

There wasn't supposed to *be* any homelessness in this zone. Visa regulation and tight resource management were supposed to ensure that everyone had enough.

How could she have been so blind?

Now that Devon had planted that seed in her mind, she saw the signs of decay everywhere.

In the supplies that Amy lamented she couldn't get. In the fraying strands at the end of elegant dresses. In her own exhaustion and dehydration.

In this little girl's sad face, in the dirt under her nails.

"Can I have a drink of water, please?" the little girl asked. She stood just inside the restaurant door, her eyes sweeping the adults in the room.

"Get her out of here!" someone shrieked. It was the blond woman Ellie had been avoiding all night. She'd come back with the same group of friends, and to Ellie's relief, Amy had given the table to Jaz instead.

But now, hearing her voice and seeing her outrage at the child made her blood boil.

Amy gently pushed the little girl outside onto the sidewalk and shut the door in her face. But the little girl did not move away immediately. She watched the people through the glass, her eyes glazed with dehydration.

Any of them. Ellie's face burned. *Any of them could give her water.*

How many water glasses stood on the tables untouched, half full and forgotten?

Any one of them could give the girl the water she was begging for.

"She can't be in here!" Amy hissed as she pressed a dry cloth into Ellie's hands.

"Yeah," the blonde said. "Get the little beast out of here."

"She's just a kid," Ellie said, and nodded at the blond bitch. "*You're* the monster."

The blonde scoffed, touching her throat. "Someone has a mouth on them tonight."

The image of her own mother, fingers blistered, giving Ellie the last of their water. Those raw fingers turning the bottle up to coax out the last drops for her child.

"More, Mommy," she'd whined. "More."

It hurt, understanding more now than she ever could as a child—how hard it must have been to give her the water at all, knowing the woman must have worked no less than twelve hours that day, sucking at her own blisters for fear of water loss, saddled with an ungrateful child whining for *more.*

"Are you going to do something about your employee, Amy? She's fucking rude. I don't know why I even bother coming to this shit hole anymore."

Amy took Ellie's wrist and pulled her to the back of the restaurant. Ellie saw the blond woman snort, amused to see Ellie dragged off like a disobedient child.

That's why she comes, she thought. *This is fun for her. To see suffering, to—*

"What is *wrong* with you tonight?" Amy hissed. "Do you want me to lose all my customers?"

"Why didn't anyone help? She was just a thirsty kid," Ellie said. "There's at least eighty people in that dining room and not *one* of them gave that kid a drink of water. I meant what I said. They're monsters."

"I'm not a monster!" Amy said. "Those are my people."

My people.

Ellie laughed, bitterly.

Something cold was thrust into her hand. Amy had given her a glass of water. Ellie looked down at the shimmering surface as if she'd never seen it before.

"Well go on!" Amy said, and jabbed a finger over her shoulder at the back door. "Give it to her, but bring back my glass!"

Ellie rushed into the night to find the child but feared the worst. The girl could have already left, moving on to try her luck at another restaurant or store. She could trip and break the glass or spill the water. Someone could snatch it from her before she ever found them.

Relief washed over Ellie when she spotted the girl and her mother, crouched on the corner, not far from where Amy had turned them away. The girl was whimpering softly into her mother's shredded shirt, and the woman crooned something in a gentle tone. Ellie rushed toward them.

The mother yanked the girl up and started to hurry away as if sensing danger.

"No, wait!" Ellie said. She slowed her pace so that she wouldn't keep on frightening them. She lifted the glass, hoping it would catch the light and they would realize she was here to help, not hurt them. The mother hesitated but didn't move closer.

"It's for you," Ellie said. "You don't have to pay or anything. It's free. It's a gift."

Ellie held the glass out for the woman, begging her to take it. But the mother peeled the child away from her and pushed her toward the glass in Ellie's hand. Ellie involuntarily pulled the glass away from the child. She'd been offering it to the mother. She wanted the mother to take it.

Now that she saw the mother, she found she couldn't even look at the child.

"Take it. Please," Ellie begged.

The mother reached out and accepted the glass. After taking only the smallest of sips, perhaps only wetting her lips with it, she pressed the rim of the glass to her child's mouth. She watched as the child greedily gulped it down and smiled up at her mother.

Only then did the mother press the empty glass back into Ellie's hands.

WHEN DEVON ARRIVED IN HER APARTMENT JUST BEFORE DAWN, Ellie had been expecting him. She let him lead her into the darkest parts of town, to see the decaying buildings, the cracked concrete and dark doorways, in a way she had never seen before. But they also went to Paradise, saw the lawns turning brown, the flaking iron fences. To the high-end stores with their empty shelves.

Like a Dust addict, she was both horrified by all the decay she saw and desperate for more.

He showed her the electrical system that piped birdsong into the city to give the impression the population was healthier than it was. Past the security wire blocking off the reservoir. He pointed out the faint mark of where the water level *should* be, about thirty meters higher than where the water actually reached.

"A year at best," he said. "Then we'll be totally out. It's why

I keep pushing Nile to work faster. We're running out of time."

A year.

A year at best. Until the zone tore itself apart.

THEIR LIVES FELL INTO A RHYTHM. ELLIE STOPPED GOING TO work. The fact that Amy hadn't even called to ask where she was or beg her to come back told Ellie everything she needed to know. Amy needed people who could maintain the façade of wealth she'd so diligently crafted. Ellie couldn't do that anymore—not for Amy or anyone.

Falling into bed with Sebastian at dawn also became a habit. She pulled as hungrily on his belt and pants as she ever had at the lip of a Hydra bottle. She marveled at how much better the sex was now that she wasn't half delirious with dehydration. Now that she was staring down her own death. She was no longer trying to conserve her strength and moisture. She felt strong, her palms pressing down onto Sebastian's chest as she hooked her hips to his. She welcomed the oblivion he offered.

It couldn't come soon enough.

Her nights were often spent with Devon. Together they canvassed the city for signs of ruin as if they were doing a postmortem on a rotting corpse. While she fought off her nihilism, she listened to him pontificate about how the wealthy were to blame, and that the only way we were going to solve *our* problems was by taking back what belonged to the people.

The people.

It amused her that Devon, probably the richest person she'd ever met, considered himself part of *the people*.

Sebastian never asked what they did, even when it was close to dawn on some of the nights they returned. If Sebastian was jealous, it never showed. He'd thrown himself into his work harder than ever, seemingly focused on deadlines that Ellie only heard about in passing.

At night when they were in bed together, he told her that he was doing it for them. For their future together.

When he looked at her like that, his eyes so bright and hopeful, it took everything Ellie had in her not to say, *What future?*

A week after Sebastian took a mold of her teeth, he pressed something cool into her hands. It was so small compared to the guards he and Devon wore.

The tiny crescent moon of metal lay in her pale palm. She parted the upper and lower teeth with her fingers to see the four sharp canines—two above and two below—jutting from the bridge. A tight mesh expanded between them.

"Do you like it?" he asked expectantly.

"It's cute." And it was. He showed her how to slip it over her teeth. Offered his wrist for her to bite, which she refused.

"You don't have to use it," Sebastian said, trying to read the look on her face. "I just thought you might want one. In case we were ever in an emergency."

We are in an emergency, she thought.

"Could I kill someone with this?" she asked, meeting his eyes. She turned the device over in her hands, marveling at its sleekness. It was practically *dainty* compared to his.

"No," he said. "Well, I mean you *could*. But you don't *have* to. This is the latest model, like mine. You can cauterize as quickly as you like before any real damage has been done."

"Do you want to go out and try it?" she asked him. "Just you and me, a couple of water vampires prowling the night."

He laughed. "I can't. I still have a lot of work to do tonight."

He sank back into his chair, turning toward the large screen.

Ellie turned the filter over and over in her hands, tracing each of the sharp canines in turn.

"Nile," she said.

"Mmm?"

"Your earlier prototypes didn't have canines. Was it your idea to treat blood like a water source?" she asked.

"No, that was Dev—Amur," he said. "He thought we might be able to attract military investors if there was a combat element to the filters. There's a lot of money in military investments."

"I'm sure," she said.

How different your visions, she thought. *Yours and Devon's.*

A feeling of unease settled over her.

"I'll leave you to it then," she said. She bent and picked up her bag, signaling her departure.

"You don't have to go," he said, rising from his chair.

"We both know I should. If I stay I'll only distract you."

He couldn't deny it. "I'll see you later then? I sleep better with you."

She came up onto her toes and kissed him. "Of course. But I won't wait up for you."

She slipped the fanged filter into her pocket and pulled open the lab door. After walking down the dark hallways and out into the night, she had planned only to go home, take a shower, fall into bed, and sleep. Maybe do a bit of light reading, a luxury she hadn't been able to indulge in when she was too dehydrated to focus on the words seemingly crawling across the page.

She'd only made it three blocks when she picked up a trace of Devon's voice. She walked slower, hoping to mask her footfall.

She spotted him down an alley. She was about to call out a hello when she realized he had a phone to his ear.

"I'm telling you, it's worth a *hundred* times what he quoted you. And think of our cut if we split it two ways instead of three."

Ellie pressed herself against the side of the brick building.

"That's not going to happen. And if it did, I can handle it. I've been at the helm of every step in this process. We don't need him. Honestly, we *don't*. He's a liability. An idiot idealist. We both know it'll be riskier to keep him than cut him loose."

Devon turned then and saw her.

Ellie didn't scream. She didn't run. She smiled.

She even managed a little wave.

Devon pressed the side of his ear and the blue light of his call ended.

"Ellie," he said.

"Sorry if I interrupted," she said, keeping her smile bright.

"You didn't," he said, his own smile wolfish. He still had his filter in, his canines flashing.

Ellie had a moment to wonder if he would bite her. Instead, he only pushed a strand of hair out of her face.

"Is our man working hard?" he asked.

"He is. I'm headed home so he can concentrate. What about you?"

"I have a few things to take care of tonight," he said. "But I can walk you back if you like."

She shrugged even though her mind was screaming, *No. Don't let him. He can't be trusted.*

"Don't bother," she said. "I'll be fine."

And with that she turned away, using every ounce of her will to walk as if she didn't have a care in the world. As if she didn't want to take off running, either to her apartment or back to Sebastian.

Anywhere as long as she was away from the fiend at her back.

· · ·

ELLIE WOKE TO SEBASTIAN SHAKING HER. SHE WAS CONFUSED by the time and thought perhaps she'd overslept. Orange light spilled through the apartment windows.

"Ellie, get up! El!" Sebastian shook her again. When that didn't get the response he wanted, he pulled her from the tangle of sheets and forced a coat around her shoulders. He was looking for something on the floor when he bumped the dresser and the dried sunflower fell. The vase shattered.

"What's happening?" she asked.

"Where are your shoes?" He threw the comforter up into the air, finding one sneaker then the other. He grabbed her bag off the kitchen counter and began to yank open her drawers and put her clothes into it. After he'd stuffed half her belongings into the bag, he shoved the fullest of the two Hydra bottles on top. It wasn't until the pack was over his shoulder that he reached for her.

She was certainly awake now, adrenaline electrifying the blood in her veins.

"Sebastian, what the hell is happening?" she asked again.

"Devon is burning down the city."

Of course he is.

Ellie laughed. It was an involuntary convulsion. A tight sound in the back of her throat. But then she saw the fire. Where the towers should have burned bright blue, instead she saw red-orange flame. Now she understood why she was confused by the time. It was the light—the light was all wrong.

She knew the laugh was also born of relief. Because if Devon was burning down the city, then he wasn't here, stabbing his best friend in the back.

Sebastian picked up his own bag full of his overnight things. "We have to go. I've got our money and our visas. We just need to get to the station."

"Visas! How the hell did you get visas?"

"There's a guy in Zone 2 who helps people like us. He found out about my bots and wants to help. He's forged us papers so we can have residency there. And I have enough money to get us started. We have a chance at a new life but only if we leave now. *Right* now, before the last train leaves or someone burns down the station."

That got Ellie moving.

They ran down the halls, the stairs, then burst through the lobby door just as the thunderous roar of helicopters passed overhead.

The helicopters were dumping mounds of sand onto the fire, hoping to bury the flames. It wasn't working. Swirls of granules floated in the air, clinging to their hair, clothes, getting into their eyes.

Sebastian's grip on her arm tightened and she turned to see what he was staring at. A mob of people walked side by side down the boulevard, clotting the street shoulder to shoulder. All kinds of people, well dressed and poor, marched toward the government buildings on the far eastern hill. She saw them opening and closing their mouths awkwardly and realized they had bite filters, poorly fitted but functional. Would-be warriors, desperate to break in their new teeth. And in front of the mob was Devon, wild and menacing. When he saw Ellie, his grin split open his face.

Devon left the front of the pack and came to stand before them.

"What have you done?" Sebastian cried. "This isn't what we agreed to!"

"This place was coming down and you know it. Don't chicken out now! You made a revolution possible! In the history books, you'll be the great man who freed the people! You'll die a hero!"

In the history books. You'll die a hero.

That's when Ellie knew this was the night he intended to

betray Sebastian. Just another rich guy swooping in to steal the Hydra bottle and make himself even richer. Except this wasn't a Hydra bottle Devon wanted to steal the credit for but the fangs, the bots, the so-called revolution.

Why else would he speak of death and history?

"You know I'm right." Devon reached out for her. "Join us."

The crowd moved past them, still marching on Paradise. Devon pressed himself against Ellie's body, shamelessly. He didn't seem to care that Sebastian or anyone else could see them clearly in the bright fire.

"I know you want this. I knew it the moment I saw you in the field, the look of fury on your face when you learned the truth of how you'd been lied to. Those nights when I took you out and showed you what the world didn't want you to see. I have so much more I want to show you, Ellie."

She reached out and wrapped her hands around Devon's neck. Relief flooded his face, even as doubt and confusion overtook Sebastian's.

Trust me, she mouthed, hoping he could see her lips despite the darkness and the dancing firelight.

As close as she was, Devon didn't see her slip the bite guard into her mouth.

The kiss she placed at his throat wasn't a kiss at all.

She bit him.

Hard.

Devon tried to pull back, but she held tight.

Sebastian began issuing frantic instructions about how to cauterize the wound, and how to stop the bleeding.

But Ellie didn't plan to stop. She wanted to remain latched, letting the metallic taste of his blood wash over her tongue and hit the back of her throat, still warm.

Devon tried to pull her off him. He grabbed on to her hair and tried to yank it back, but Sebastian intervened, holding his hands behind him. Ellie came up onto her toes, trying to maintain the connection. Devon snapped and snarled at Ellie's shoulder, trying to latch on to her with his own fangs, but Sebastian was working against him.

He thinks he's protecting me. Ellie wanted to laugh. *When I'm the one saving him.*

Finally, she released him, and Devon fell to the street. His chest heaved with short pants of breath as if he couldn't get enough air into his lungs.

He would die here with the world burning around him.

Good, she thought. *That's how it should be.*

Sebastian slipped on his own fangs and Ellie knew he meant to bite Devon in the same place she had, to cauterize the wound she'd torn in his throat.

She stopped him, pulling him back.

"He's not your friend," she said simply. "He's definitely not worth saving."

Devon covered his wound with a hand, but blood still poured through his fingers. His gaze was fixed on Ellie.

"Why?" he sputtered, red blood wetting his lips. "Tell me *why.*"

She knelt, looking into his glassy, unfocused eyes. "Like you said. It's us or them."

BLOOD & CASTLES

for Chris De Francisci with thanks

Kal Haven put down the phone and looked out his portside window. Stars stretched endlessly in every direction. A fathomless sea of eternity. And yet—
Very advanced, the doctor had said. *Not much time.*

Kal considered the roster in front of him, the list of able-bodied men and women waiting for their next assignment. His eyes flicked to the age column.

26

32

46

44

21

31

36

He had twenty years on the oldest of them. And yet—
Very advanced. You should prepare.

The small chamber of his onboard office waited, the

ringing silence absolute. Lights blinked along the wall, measuring the room's pressure and oxygen levels.

You should prepare.

Prepare for what exactly?

He'd prepared for everything a man could possibly prepare for. In the event a space rock tore through the exterior wall of this office, for example, he knew how to strap himself into the chair bolted to the floor. How to commence the sequence that would seal the hole and repressurize the room.

If one of his crew got sick or injured with no doctor onboard—he'd prepared for that, too. For fuel shortages and food shortages. For in-fighting and mutiny. For loss of communication or navigation systems. For weeks without work or low to nonexistent supplies. For getting lost in space. For homesickness, his or another's.

He'd prepared for *everything* that could possibly ever happen in a man's life.

Everything except for his own mortality.

He wasn't sure how long he sat there like that, staring off into the room with only a vague awareness of the hum in his mind. But when the phone rang again, he jumped in his seat, jerking to the present.

He considered not answering it. He'd had enough bad news for one day.

But then he recognized the name.

"Haven, speaking."

"I have a job on Earth if you want it. Some rich fuck from the eighth quadrant wants Dracula's Castle. His *whole* fucking castle, taken apart and flown to his estate on Prion."

Bright went straight to business as always. He never said hello. It wasn't his style.

"Sounds backbreaking," Kal said. His voice sounded

strange in his ear. Like someone else had borrowed it, stretched it over their own.

"Not really. I've had *four* crews down there already. Four. They've got most of the damn thing packed up and ready for lift."

"Then why are you calling me?"

"Because people keep getting spooked and running off on me. They claim the place is haunted."

"Is it?" Kal asked, mildly curious. There were devices for that sort of thing now, handheld machines that could detect unseen disturbances in their reality. Ghosts couldn't hurt a person. They were little more than the residue of life, an echo in a dark, endless chamber.

But it seemed science had never been able to reason away the power of superstition.

Will I be a ghost? he mused.

Bright continued, unaware of Kal's wandering mind. "I've swept an EWD over the place several times and there's nothing. But there've been accidents. Nothing major, but between you and me, I just want the job to be over. I'll pay you three times your price if you just come down here and end this nightmare for me."

Kal was very aware that Bright hadn't called him first because his price was already one of the highest in the market. It wasn't only that Kal refused to accept less than what he was worth, what his retrieval crew was worth, but because his ship and crew were large. Hundreds of men and women counted on him for their livelihoods.

But having a large, coordinated crew meant they were faster and more efficient than anyone, and they delivered what they promised in the best condition, or no money changed hands.

That was the Haven promise.

The fact Bright was willing to triple the standard rate just to finish a nearly complete job would've astounded him, had his mind not already been laid to waste that morning by that one five-minute phone call.

He'd been expecting an infection—kidney or gallbladder. Maybe even something persistent like an autoimmune disease.

He hadn't expected a death sentence.

"I'm begging you," Bright said, and Kal noted how tired he sounded. "Just please wrap this up for me. I want to get the hell off this rock."

Kal's eyes fixed on the stars again, that wide, endless expanse. "Give me five hours."

Kal's vessel, the *Imperator*, passed through Earth's haze and into the lower atmosphere. As he navigated the congested skies, he heard members of his crew chatting excitedly behind him. For some, this was their first excursion to the planet—or what remained of it.

Even if they'd been born off world, they would have heard the stories about the deterioration of humanity's first home. How pollution and capitalism had caused the gradual extinction of millions of species.

And how, in the Earth's grim final hour, a long-sought mathematical calculation had made it possible to move humanity into the skies, toward possible new home worlds in a fraction of the time required before.

Because humans now inhabited twenty-three planets, Earth was little more than a fairy tale. An abandoned garden of Eden from whence they all came.

To Kal, it was little more than a trash heap. Maybe once upon a time it was full of beauty and splendor, but most of its treasures had been sold piecemeal to the highest bidders, the artifacts of humanity's reign on Earth now spread across the universe.

There was still a very small human population on Earth. Analysts put that figure just north of two or three hundred, maybe four hundred souls in all. But even that number was dwindling.

It seemed every time a crew like Haven's landed on Earth, any humans in the vicinity begged for a ride off planet. They were tired of struggling in a world that no longer favored their survival.

Kal noted the lush green overgrowth and herd animals wandering over the lands as they flew across Africa toward Romania.

If anyone was left in Romania, Kal knew they'd be squatting in the corpse of Bucharest. For this reason, it was unlikely they would see anyone but themselves in Transylvania except perhaps a few off-worlders from the last crew.

He was right. Only Bright's ship was parked on the mountainside beside the castle.

The pine forests surrounding the mountain stood guard, swaying in a light breeze. He'd heard that there were millions of people in Transylvania itself, once upon a time. But where or how they'd lived no one could be sure. No housing structures remained.

Metal shipping crates crowded the plateau surrounding Bright's ship. Kal squeezed his vessel into what little room remained, not wanting to make his crew hike far up the mountain. It was likely Bright had cleared these trees and made the parking space himself—best make use of it.

When he opened the door, letting in the soft evening light, the crew filed past him, chattering excitedly as they stepped off the ship onto solid land.

Dust rolled across the hills, and Kal pulled a visor down over his face to block the sun, wind, and debris assailing his eyes. Using the com system built into their suits, he advised his crew to do the same.

He spotted Bright immediately.

The gray-haired man hobbled toward him, swinging his mechanical leg forward with a pronounced gait, his hand extending. The castle rose stoically behind him.

"You're early. Bless you."

Kal shook the outstretched hand. "You sounded desperate."

"I am."

Kal gestured at the ship. "Where's the rest of your crew?"

"Everyone took off except for me."

"Why?" Kal turned his gaze skyward to watch a small flock of blackbirds swing by.

"There was another accident. Not an hour after I hung up with you. I told my second to take the main ship out to lower orbit. I'll bring this med vac tank up to meet it once I get you settled in."

Kal ran a hand over the dusty visor. Now that he was looking for it, he saw the red medical brand on the right side of the remaining vessel.

You're not paying attention, he chided himself. *Get your head out of your ass and into the game.*

"You want to tell me what's going on?" Kal asked. "How do people keep getting hurt?"

Bright ran a hand through his hair, knocking the dust off into the wind. "One fell down a well. Another broke her neck on a stone staircase. A third had a balcony collapse beneath him and splattered his brains all over the rocks below. I tell you, Haven, you know I'm not a superstitious guy, but this place has me believing in curses."

Kal surveyed the land. Perhaps they were on a fault line and light tremors were making the place unstable. Maybe the whole damn thing was a volcano ready to blow or a sinkhole on the verge of opening up and swallowing the mountain.

"What is this, red rock?" he asked, dragging his toe through the dirt.

"It's not rock, it's tile. From the roofs. This whole town had red tile on the roofs. Hundreds of years ago."

Kal gazed out across the landscape, gray, barren. "There's no town."

"Lost to the sands of time, I'm afraid."

Like me, Kal thought. *Soon.*

You need to prepare.

"Look, I've got three of the outer walls packed up." Bright pointed at the steel shipping crates, stacked higher than the pines surrounding them. "And I've got all the interior packed away. You just need to take down the remaining staircase, the fourth outer wall, and the real problem."

"What's the real problem?"

Bright waved, beckoning Kal to follow him up the slope toward what remained of the castle. The dirt shifted under his boots as they made their ascent. The wind whistled past his ears. He could feel his pounding heart in his temples.

Here the dirt, pine needles, and crushed red tile gave way to stone. Perhaps the remnants of a courtyard.

"You'll have to pull all this up as well," Bright said. "The rich bastard wants every stone. Said he's going to rebuild it. I hear he's got the bone cathedral of Kutná Hora too. Weird tastes, this guy."

"We all have our hobbies," Kal said, resisting the urge to lift his visor and scratch his nose.

He knew his skin was sallow, pale. He didn't want to give Bright any reason to believe he couldn't do the job.

"What do you know about hobbies?" Bright snorted, his jagged nails scratching at the scar on his cheek. "You're like me. All you do is work."

And what will I have to show for that? he wondered. *Nothing.*

A sharp pain ran up the right side of his back, winding him.

You'll feel mostly fine for a little while longer, the doctor had said. *But the bad days will start to outnumber the good ones quickly.*

Bright stopped abruptly, his boots scraping to a stop. "This has been my worst nightmare."

Kal looked down into the hole, glad the visor hid his grimace.

He tried to make out the rough outline of steps disappearing into the darkness below. "What is it?"

"The stairs lead to a passage and there are four rooms on each side. We've cleaned those out already, and you're welcome. They were torture chambers. Literal torture chambers. Manacles and knives. Golden cups that looked bloodstained to me. And skeletons. *A lot* of fucking skeletons. I don't know what went on down there, but I'm sure the visitors didn't leave five-star reviews. At the end of the passage, there's a locked door. Every time we try to open it, something happens. Someone gets hurt or loses their mind. I've tried everything I can think of, but it won't budge. I even tried to tear down the fourth wall, which connects to it on the one side, but that didn't end well either."

"You tried a bomb?"

"Ha *ha.* No. The rich bastard wants all the pieces intact, I told you. But yeah, apart from blowing it up, I've tried everything. Listen, please don't blow it up."

With the pain gone, Kal lifted his visor and peered into the dark, something turning over in his stomach.

Just a little nausea, he told himself. *You're fine. Carry on.*

"You okay?" Bright asked, a frown spreading across his face. "You look a little pasty."

"It's just the lighting here. Let's take a look." Kal forced his foot off solid ground and onto the first stone step.

At the bottom of the stairs there was only darkness, absolute. He turned on his visor's headlamp, its beam shooting forth into the dark. The stone continued in an uneven, sloping passageway. And at the end, the door, or at least, the suggestion of a door.

Kal looked up at him from below. "You coming or not?"

"Shit, yeah. Okay." Bright exhaled and began his descent.

At the bottom his light joined Kal's, brightening the passage considerably.

They passed each doorway and Kal couldn't help but look inside, surveying the interiors. But there was nothing left. No chains or bloodstained cups as Bright had described. All that was left was the hardpacked dirt floors, walls, and crumbling ceilings with tree roots and cobwebs hanging down.

But there was an ominous feeling, looking into those windowless rooms. As if Kal needed only squint harder to know what terrors had happened within those walls.

"It's not so bad now, without the chains and doors. Still creepy though."

"And you swept this with the EWD and found nothing?" Kal wasn't sure why he was whispering.

But Bright was whispering too. "Nada. It's just dark as hell down here. For all we know, we *are* in hell." He pointed up at the sliver of sky behind them and then at the door at the end of the hallway. "Earth. Hell."

Kal swung his light toward the door.

"That's the problem," Bright said, his finger still pointing.

Kal started toward it, his hand already lifting to take the handle. Bright trailed behind.

"If it just opens for you, I swear to God—"

The handle rattled but didn't give. It was warm in Kal's

grip, and he turned it again, rattling it more as if this might shake it loose.

"Why didn't I think of that?" Bright asked, but his voice was relieved. "Just shake the handle until it opens."

"Have you tried to saw off the handle or melt it off?"

"Yeah, it's welded together somehow. I put two thousand degrees on it, and it didn't give. It's made of tantalum or something."

This close, Kal realized the door was red, not black, and it had a window. An arched pane of stained glass sat level with his nose. But if he looked close enough, he saw the metal bars dividing the glass into quadrants. Even if the glass was shattered and art lost, it wouldn't open the door.

He stooped and tried to peer through. He saw nothing but the color of the glass, reds and golds, twisting in his vision.

A shadow moved.

He pulled back, looking through the window, trying to make sure it wasn't a trick of his lashes or their shifting beams.

But he thought he saw it again, something moving behind the glass.

A figure.

Then the handle in his hand turned, softly, but enough that he felt its warm edge press harder into his palm.

"If I didn't know better, I'd say there was something braced against the other side," Bright said, unaware that Kal's pulse had leapt into his throat and was choking him.

Kal let go and stepped back, waiting to see if the door would open now.

But it didn't.

Nothing happened, and he was beginning to think he'd imagined it all.

Bright's stomach rumbled and Kal jumped.

Bright didn't even notice. "I'm hungry. Let's get out of here."

He threw a look over his shoulder at the waiting stairway. At salvation.

"Seriously. Let's have dinner. My treat."

Kal needed no convincing. At the base of the stairs, he looked back, expecting to see a monster pursuing them, but there was nothing but the closed door.

In the light, Kal closed his visor and took a deep breath.

"I've got venison and lamb on the ship, and more salt potatoes than you can possibly eat. Let's crack open a beer and—"

"What does it say about our friendship that the first person you call here is me? You hoping I die or something?"

Because careful about what you wish for.

Bright shook his head and laughed. "No, you devil. I called you because you're the luckiest bastard I know."

"I'm not lucky," Kal said, his voice tight.

Bright misinterpreted this. "You have the training for difficult jobs, sure. I didn't mean you aren't qualified. If anyone can get through an unbreakable door, it's you. But it's more than that. Every time some horrible bullshit should kill you, somehow you come out ahead. Remember the cougars in New Rome? Or the Yrezin invaders on Ragna? Or the—"

"Okay, I get it." Kal couldn't bear to hear any more. It was taking all his concentration just to breathe, just to blink, as his mind remained fixed on that red door, on the red-and-gold glass, and the shifting shadows it concealed.

The feeling of the knob turning ever so slightly in his hand—had he imagined it? That breathing that had seemed to fill his mind? Was that only his panic, or was something really, truly in there?

He looked up at the trees, watched them sway in the wind, and collected himself.

Had it been his own streak of unbroken luck that had given him this false sense of security? Had he formed the erroneous belief that he would always come out ahead? That maybe he would escape even what no one in the history of mankind had yet escaped?

"I'm not invincible," Kal said quietly. *And everyone's luck runs out.*

"Don't go getting modest on me," Bright said, and clapped his shoulder. "I need you in full force here. Tell me you're going to solve this for me and I'll transfer the money now. Right this minute. Then I'll feed you the best meal of your life. And go the fuck home."

He thought of the dark, of the way it breathed in his mind. Of the figure. Of the handle turning in his hand.

Don't, his mind begged. *Don't say yes.*

"I'll do it."

WHILE KAL AND BRIGHT HAD DINNER IN EARTH'S ORBIT, KAL'S team prepared the ship. He thought it would do all of their bodies good to spend a night in gravity. To let their bones settle, as folk used to say.

And it was nice to return to the surface in the soft, warm night with a full stomach and find his quarters ready for him.

He washed and slipped into bed, his mind reviewing the final report from his second-in-command.

While he'd caught up with his old friend, his second, Alia, had given everyone their assignments for the following day. The tasks of breaking down the last exterior wall, tearing up the remaining staircase, and moving the already packed crates onto the ship were divided amongst them.

She estimated they could do it all in two days. Tops. Without compromising the quality of their work.

Especially since they had all the excavation equipment

from their last job still on board. It would require little heavy lifting from the team themselves.

Everything felt settled and he liked that feeling, holding on to it as he lay down to sleep in his bunk and closed his eyes.

He woke, skin on fire.

His stomach twisted as if full of acid, his heart hammering in his throat. He made it to the sink and splashed cold water on his face. He dry-heaved twice, but nothing came up. He wasn't sure if he was grateful for this or disappointed. Maybe purging would've provided relief.

It wasn't the dinner, he knew. Bright would've never served him bad food.

He looked into the mirror and saw the deep circles beneath his eyes. The sunken whites and trembling lips.

Soon the bad days will outnumber the good.

"Just let me finish this job," he whispered to his wide-eyed reflection, to the waxy sweat on his brow. "Then I can give everyone a couple of weeks off with pay and figure this out."

Maybe he could find placements for everyone on crews he knew and trusted. Crews like Bright's. Maybe Ajax and Tomlin's too.

"Just give me time to do what's right."

Who are you bargaining with? a little voice asked.

It was soft, childlike, and quite different from the usual menagerie of imaginary consultants occupying Kal's mind.

I don't know, he told it. *God, maybe.*

If he was ever going to start believing in God, now seemed like a good time.

Dabbing a wet cloth to his face, Kal returned to bed, sitting on its edge, his feet flat on the floor. He took several slow breaths. He was about to lie down and close his eyes when something outside caught his eye.

He crossed to the window. It offered a view of the castle's ledge, just a ridge of crumbling stone against the starry sky.

A white specter stood there in the moonlight. A dress or gown billowed in the wind.

A woman? He squinted, pressing his face against the glass, trying to see better.

A shadow darted past.

Then another.

Frantic voices trailed after them. Those were his men yelling.

Grabbing his shoes, he followed suit.

When he stepped out into the night, feeling the cool mountain air hit his feverish skin, he called out, "What's going on here?"

"Sorry to wake you, sir," Alia said, a gun in her right hand. Her silvery hair looked white in the moonlight.

Kal had no interest in correcting her. How could he explain that it was his sickness that woke him and a ghost that had kept him up?

"Reneas isn't in his quarters and we can't find him aboard the ship. His bunkmate says he left their room twenty minutes ago. We think he's sleepwalking."

"Where's the bunkmate?"

"Here, sir." A boy of no more than eighteen stepped up, his shoulders rolled forward. "Tobias, sir."

"Has he sleepwalked before?"

"No, but he talks in his sleep all the time. And he was talking this time, too. When he got up, I mean. Sir."

Kal's gaze slid to the ridge again, expecting to see the white specter there, waiting. Watching.

But there was only the moonlit stone and silent pines.

"Alia, do you have the locator in Reneas's suit turned on?"

"I do, sir."

"Then let's go find him."

After an hour of crashing through the pine forest, calling his name, they found him in a tangled patch of brambles. His arms and legs were scratched and bleeding.

Halfway to the ship, he seemed to come to his senses, his eyes focusing at last.

"What the hell happened?" he asked as the medic sat him down in the light of the medical room and set about the task of wiping the blood from his wounds.

"You were sleepwalking. You didn't list that condition in your record." Kal sounded angry even to himself.

"I-I'm sorry, sir. I haven't sleepwalked since I was a kid," he said, his eyes wide with surprise. "I thought it was something I'd grown out of, sir."

The medic looked up and caught Kal's eyes. He nodded ever so slightly toward a mark on Reneas's shoulder.

Kal came around and swore.

There was a wound where the shoulder and neck met. It was ragged and clumsy.

"Does that hurt?" Kal asked. "Because it sure as hell looks like it hurts."

It most certainly was not caused by brambles or stumbling blindly through the woods. Seeing the wound made Kal's skin crawl. Something had bitten the hell out of him.

"What is it?" Reneas asked, craning his neck. "What are you looking at?"

"Face forward," the medic begged as more blood gushed down his back. "I need you to hold your head still. When you turn your neck like that you open the wound up."

Reneas's wide, frightened eyes remained fixed on Kal's, but he wasn't registering any pain from the wound.

Interesting.

"It's all right," Kal said. He placed a hand on the kid's uninjured shoulder as the medic pulled a suture pack from his drawer. "You're going to be just fine."

. . .

KAL LET HIS CREW HAVE A LATE START, HOPING THEY'D USE
their time to catch up on the sleep lost in the night. Reneas was
resting in the medic's suite, sedated to help manage the pain.

Kal thought the day might pass uneventfully, as they
made it all the way through lunch and a siesta before
anything changed. The top half of the fourth wall came down
as well as one of the staircases before the next incident.

It was when the first team went down to inspect the door,
with the idea that they might dig through the wall of the
adjacent room and come to the inner chamber that way.

That's when the screaming started.

First one, then all five of the excavators fled the chamber
with their hands over their heads.

"What?" Kal demanded, lifting his visor. "What
happened?"

"Bats!" they cried.

Kal had seen none, but all five of the crew members had
been convinced that bats had flown—somehow—through the
ceiling and into their hair, chasing them through the dark.

Kal sent a second team, but again, they emerged screaming, this time crying about spiders the size of their fists,
assailing their ears and biting them under their clothes.

Kal asked several of the men to lift their shirts and they
obliged, but there were no marks. No evidence of the attack.

A third team said the floors were covered in snakes and
the fourth team complained that the walls in the passageway
were bleeding.

This, Kal decided, was something to see for himself.

But in the dark, there was nothing but his own nervous
breathing. His hands pressed against the door.

You don't see what they see, a voice breathed.

"Please," he whispered, his hand wrapping around the handle again. "Don't make this harder than it has to be."

I don't have the patience or the time, he thought.

Again the voice came. That dark breathing in his mind. *What is it that you desire?*

Was this a ghost talking to him? Some spirit of the castle itself?

If so, fine. Kal could play that game.

"I want you to open this door," he whispered, making damn sure no one outside could hear him. "They won't stop until they take this place apart. It might as well be me that takes you."

You? the voice breathed.

The handle twisted in his grip and the door sighed inward. It pulled so fast that he was yanked forward into the room. His knees hit the dirt and pain shot up through his body.

He thought he might choke on his heart, on the fear saturating his heavy limbs.

He waited for the monstrous beast that would fall on him. Something capable of tearing open his throat the way it had nearly done the kid's.

Despite his pounding heart and panicky breath, no monster came.

Nor were there bats, or spiders. No walls oozing blood.

This room had the tree roots and cobwebs like the others, but it was empty save one thing: a stone sarcophagus in the center.

His eyes searched the shadowed corners and ceiling for something to drop on him. But there was only the sarcophagus, sealed with a stone lid six inches thick.

You, the voice breathed again. *You may take me.*

Then the earth began to shake, rumbling around him. He

was sure what remained of the castle would now come down on him.

He covered his head.

This is it, he thought. *Now I die.*

And he couldn't decide if this was better—being buried alive on a job—or worse than being consumed by his own body.

The outer wall gave, sending a wave of dust and dirt into the room. Cold mountain air crashed inside and light spilled across the dirt floor.

But he was not crushed.

He stared through the new hole in the wall framing the Carpathian Mountains.

Alia lifted her visor from her face, peering into the room with a deep frown. Others in work gloves and leathers crowded the hole, looking in on him.

"The fourth wall is down, sir," Alia said.

"Yes," he said, his hand gripping the cold lid of the sarcophagus. He used it to pull himself to standing. "I can see that."

They were able to lift the sarcophagus to the surface, but they needed a triple crane to get it onto the ship due to its immense weight. He called up Bright, who said he could loan him one in the morning if they didn't mind delaying the job one more day.

He did, but there was no backing out now.

Meanwhile his crew used their final hours of daylight to crate the last of the castle and load it into the cargo freighter.

When they retired to the ship for dinner and showers, Kal remained with the sarcophagus, watching the wind blow dust off its stone surface as he drank a beer. The stone turned from gray-blue, to orange, to purple in the twilight.

Did I imagine it? he wondered. *The voice. The ghost.*

He asked these questions until drowsiness pressed against his mind and he carried himself to bed.

The scream was jarring.

It ricocheted electric along his skin.

He bolted upright in bed, his hand going to the gun beside him.

He checked the medic bay first, thinking perhaps it was Reneas who'd cried out. But the scene that greeted him stopped his heart cold.

Reneas was dead—his eyes rolled up in the back of his head and throat torn open. Blood stained the sheets and his hand held a fistful of long black hair.

The medic too was bloodless, his throat a ragged impression of a neck.

In a daze, Kal stumbled through the ship and out into the night.

The sarcophagus was open to the sky above. On its edge sat the ghostly specter he saw before. No, not a specter. A woman. With long black hair nearly to her knees.

She dropped from the edge of the sarcophagus into a crouch. Before he could reach her, she sprang up and ran into the forest.

"Hey!" he called. "Hey, where are you going?"

He chased her into the forest. Through the trees into the thickening dark, she ran. When his chest began to burn and his breath gave out, she slowed. She stopped, as if knowing he couldn't follow her any farther.

When he collapsed against a pine tree, all the strength leaving him, she stepped into the moonlight.

By the sarcophagus, she'd looked like a girl, no more than fifteen or sixteen years old. But here, in the moonlight, she was no child. Her mouth and gown were soaked with blood. Her teeth were sharp and gleaming.

"Was that your plan?" he wheezed. "Lead me out here and eat me?"

"No."

The voice was the same as the one that had been in his mind before. Soft, girlish. But now it was as real as the pain piercing his chest.

He had to sit down or fall down. He chose the former.

Through gritted teeth, he hissed, "What are you?"

"Earth is dying," she said.

"No shit. Where've you been?"

"Sleeping."

He tried to steady his breath.

I'm going to puke.

Why in God's name had he followed her out here?

"I needed to see if there was still strength in you," she said. "There is. That's good. It will not work if you aren't strong."

"*What* the hell are you?" he demanded. "Why would you—"

His mind was filled with Reneas's torn neck and the gore spread along the floor.

"—W-why?"

"I need the blood," the creature said.

"Not from my crew. They're my responsibility. Take mine."

He sounded weak. Exhausted. He hated it.

She tilted her head. "You want to die."

"No. But I'm already dying."

"I know." She said it so plainly, as if remarking on the stars in the sky. "But you won't if you help me."

Kal couldn't imagine a world in which he could help this creature—this thing.

She squatted down in front of him, searching his face. "I've slept for too long. I see that now. I can tell by—by the smell of this place that there will not be enough food for me here. And your—"

She gestured at his ship in the distance.

"My ship," he said.

"It takes you to others, doesn't it? You can take me into the stars. You can explain this new time to me."

He thought of the hundreds of souls sleeping on the *Imperator*. His life might be over, but they had time. They *deserved* to have their time. He wasn't going to bring her onto a ship with them if she couldn't control herself. But if he refused, he understood she would kill them all anyway.

Maybe she would slaughter them outright or maybe she would stow away and eat them one by one as they headed home.

He licked his parched lips. His pain blurred his vision. "If I help you, if I teach you, you have to promise not to hurt any more of my people. That's the deal."

"I will make you like me, and you will show me how to live in this time. That is the *deal*."

"And you will not hurt them. Not *one* more of them. Can you survive on my blood alone for a few days?"

She spoke directly into his mind again. *I can survive until we get to Prion, yes.*

Prion. So she'd been listening to them. For how long?

"But will you control yourself?" he asked. He wanted to hear her say it. "*Can* you control yourself?"

The fingers tracing his throat were cold. As hard as stone.

"I can," she whispered. "And I will."

THE DEATHS WERE CREDITED TO WILD WOLVES. AFTER ALL, they'd heard them howling in the forest. It wasn't impossible to think they'd been drawn to their food—or so the crew came to believe.

Nor were they surprised to find a new recruit following the captain around the ship. Had they not all been new recruits themselves at some point? Offered positions on this very vessel after similar jobs and expeditions, a promise for a better life, decent wages, and a chance to see the universe?

True, this new recruit looked too young, her face round and sweet. But her eyes were wise, her features dark and impassive. When she spoke, you knew she wasn't a child. Simply petite. Her black hair was always pulled up into a severe ponytail that tumbled down her back.

She seemed studious. Respectful. If a little distant.

So they didn't question their captain's decision to carry her as far as Prion, where they delivered the castle and commenced their two-week paid vacation.

And it was good timing for a break, the crew thought.

The captain was looking pale.

Perhaps he could use a bit of sun.

SEVEN DEVILS

Six dead brothers held vigil at my bedside. *Wake,* they commanded. *Wake and avenge us.*

My pale body glowed in the gray light before dawn. There was no birdsong, no crackling fire on the hearth. The smoke from an extinguished candle flame rose as silently as a hawk circling in the sky. I did not have a heartbeat, my chest a perfect mimicry of the stillness. The cold hands folded over it a replica of winter lying in wait.

I thought of the queen in her castle. I would see its ancient, scarred walls if only I turned my head an inch to the left and gazed out the gaping arched window. But I could not turn my head. I was not alive.

How can I take vengeance against her? I asked.

My eldest brother, Ronan, stepped forward. Light from the window cut across his cheek, revealing skin much paler than it had ever been in life, devoid of flowing blood and the complexion it lent to the living. His hair was no longer crow-feather black, a gift from our mother to all of her children. Now it was the color of hemlock blossoms. His eyes glowed like embers, and when he turned his gaze just so, they gleamed like a jackal's in the torchlight.

Yet in all other ways he was the same.

I met the eyes of each of my brothers in turn and found them to be filled with the same hellfire. Each changed, yet the same, these boys I'd known all my life.

We come with the sunrise and leave with the sunset. In the hours between we will serve you. But say you do not seek vengeance and we will leave you cold in your bed.

But I did want vengeance.

And even without a beating heart, I knew no wish granted came without its price.

Would I pay that price? Would I accept their offer?

Was the selling of my soul worth it?

For my father, hounded like a mule in the fields, and then whipped to death when the earth could yield no more grain. For my mother, who starved to death with a child at her breast, who scraped her meager portions onto the plates of her children. Vengeance for the infant who also starved without her.

Vengeance against the cruel, war-hungry queen, safe on her alabaster throne, was what I wanted, what I'd prayed for. She'd not only taken my parents and little sister but was also to blame for the loss of these six dead brothers.

Sure, they were demons now, but they had been flesh and blood once.

Ronan and Lux had been slain in her war for more land. Jax, Christian, and Jaden had been imprisoned for false crimes, beaten, and then hanged. One year before my own death, almost to the day, Kaleb was slain before my eyes, his throat slit by her knights, dogs as cruel as she.

I watched the blood pour from his throat onto the earth while each soldier took his turn with me. When they were finished, I was too weak and cold to carry his body home. I buried him beneath the tree's black limbs and said my mother's ancient prayers, to a goddess nearly forgotten.

If our desperation, our starvation, had not driven us to seek that tree, perhaps Kaleb would have lived. It was foolish to risk what little we had left on my mother's fairy tales. Hope was a luxury, and I was no longer a careless child. Yet my mother's stories had always held power over me, and the story of The Crone Tree was no different.

A mere story. Of an ancient tree, as old as the world itself, with roots that stretched all the way to Hell. And within the tree dwelled the spirit of a goddess. A woman who controlled the underworld, granting or barring passage to the souls who passed her way.

If a sacrifice is made to her, a wish is granted, my mother had said.

A sacrifice was made. Kaleb was buried in a nest of The Crone Tree's roots. And here he stood at the foot of my bed as if I had not placed him in the dirt myself. His throat still bore the coarse line of the knight's blade, puckered and gray in the early-morning light. But his demon eyes were calm, placid.

He suffered no more.

You wanted vengeance, Ronan said. He clasped one of my hands in his and turned my chin with the other so that I could not dwell upon Kaleb's scarred throat. Ronan's fingers smelled of sulfur. So that too had changed.

We are your army. You need only accept us.

Over his shoulder, framed in the open window, stood the great castle, its barbed spires pink in the coming dawn.

I met Ronan's eyes.

I accept you.

Fire spread from his palm into mine, through his hand

into my cupped cheek. I cried out, trying to pull away from the heat.

Do not fear the hunger, my brother said. *Hunger is all you have left.*

Then the pain of living was upon me again.

My muscles filled with fire. A pulse stronger than any heart song coursed in my limbs.

I placed my bare feet on the gritty stone floor and saw the world anew. In life, I had despaired of this room: its drab appearance, the curtains darkened with dirt, and the tapestries fraying at their edges. It had been a great house when my father brought his new bride, my mother, here long ago. It was no more.

I thought nothing of these things now flitting through my mind like mice in the kitchen. Little more than darting shadows in the corner of my eye.

Now I had only one desire. One need.

We must go to the castle, I said.

We went straight away. We donned no armor. I did not even stop to slip on the worn goatskin boots sitting by the door. I walked out into the morning, placing one bare foot after another onto the snow.

My hair, kept carefully braided in life, hung long and wild down my back. It blew in the breeze, as worthy a war banner as any we had.

I swore then never to bind it again.

We marched.

Minutes after dawn, we came upon her first knights. I could see by the look in their eyes, I was much changed. Perhaps I looked like my brothers now: pale-skinned with dark orbs burning. Yet I knew my hair had not paled. I could see the black locks blowing about my face, caressed by the northern wind.

It wasn't until Kaleb reached up and tore a squat man from his saddle, hissing into his face, that I recognized the soldier as the one who had killed him. Now his throat was ripped open by my brother's own teeth. I found satisfaction in the wet, sucking sound the wound made as the man choked on his own blood. He coughed, his eyes fluttering, and then he moved no more. His heart pumped what was left of him out onto the snow.

Lux, Jax, and Jaden slayed the others as swiftly as a cat might snap a mouse's neck. Then we mounted their horses. At first the beasts refused us, rearing high on their hindquarters, until Ronan murmured soft words into their flicking ears, his hand on their necks.

Then they went still beneath us, not moving again until we kicked them forward. The gamey smell of their fur soothed me, though I had not ridden a horse since I was a very small child, when my family could still afford to keep them.

We reached the outer walls of the castle an hour after sunrise.

Guards manned the gate that would allow us to pass through the stone wall. My brothers caught and killed each, while I remained on my mount, waiting. Horrid hunger churned in my guts. But I did not fight it. I embraced it. I knew it would see me through this.

And there was only one soul who could quench it.

So I relished the gleeful way my brothers chased each man. It reminded me of happier times, of the pheasants that used to haunt the back fields behind our home. We would crouch low in the high, honey-colored wheat for hours until we heard the soft cooing. Then we would leap up, hands curling into claws. The squawks and falling feathers made us squeal with delight.

I called up to the archers on the high wall of the gate, "Send us all you have, my queen."

The arrows flew true. One tore through my right shoulder, but I felt no pain. No fear. Only that persistent hunger like a stone in the hollow of my throat.

We tolerated this until it seemed all the arrows were spent. Then Lux stood apart from us and raised his arms up, palms out as if he intended to catch an arrow. When he was alive, he had caught rain like this, pulling me from my bed in the dead of night, out into the wildest of storms. We would cup our hands and drink all that we could catch, before putting out buckets to collect the rest. And as they filled, we would hold our arms out and spin and spin and spin.

We had each been happy once.

Until she took that from us also.

A great torrent of wind shot forth from Lux and sailed high over the wall. The archers were blown back, some tumbling like leaves into the water below.

No more arrows came.

By noon, the queen sent her priests. They stood in their thick robes, talismans clutched in their hands. They chanted words I did not understand, throwing their burning herbs at us. This had no effect. Her gods were not stronger than mine.

Frustrated, Jax and Jaden at last climbed the stones. Like twin lizards, they slithered up the rockface and reached the uppermost ledge, where the priests stood spouting their incantations. My brothers tore each from their perch.

All four priests howled on the way down, their robes flapping like kites in a gale about them.

When no one else came, Jax and Jaden opened the gate, forcing the wooden bridge down with their own might.

A small band of soldiers met us in the courtyard. My brothers dispatched them.

Only Ronan stayed by my side as blood stained the stones. A quick movement in my side vision drew my eye.

A woman in gold silks yanked a small boy back as if I'd burned her with my gaze alone. She was no older than I, yet her body was strong, full of life. Her child looked as enchanting as lilac blossoms after a spring rain. Neither had starved a day in their life. They'd never known hunger.

"Do you want them?" Ronan asked into my ear. "They were complicit to our suffering."

I wanted to hold the child. I wanted to cut a lock of hair from her head and keep it. But I did not want them the way he suggested.

"Only she will do," I told him.

I steered the horse away.

It stepped carefully over the corpses of the queen's soldiers.

The courtyard gave way to the garden. Though I had never seen her with my own eyes, I knew the queen the moment she appeared. I dismounted, handing Ronan the reins.

Before I reached her, Christian killed all her guards with a flex of his fist.

I hardly noted this. My eyes were only for her.

For her long red silks splayed like blood around her in the snow.

"What do you want?" she asked. Her eyes were the color of a pond. She looked from me to Ronan as if unsure whom to address. I do not think a man would have had the same dilemma.

"Anything you desire in the whole world, it is mine to give."

"I want your life," I said.

My six brothers came to stand beside me, forming a semi-circle around the queen.

I stepped toward her, crushing snow beneath my bare feet. I took her in my arms as tenderly as one might take one's beloved. I placed a hand on her cheek.

"Please," she said. Crystalline tears pooled in the corners of her eyes. How pretty. "I did not choose to be queen."

Her lips quivered.

I twined my fingers up in her hair. Maybe I would have my golden lock after all.

"I will give you anything. Anything you want."

"I want your heart."

"Or I—"

"You. I want you."

"But—" She could not break free of me though she tried.

I consumed her. First her heart, then her soul.

Her heart was bitter. Her soul sweet cream. Full of her, I knew a satiation I'd never known in life. At last, I was whole.

My brothers stood waiting. Their satisfaction was a drumbeat in my temples.

We are avenged. We are avenged. We are avenged.

I licked blood from my fingers, half delirious with the ecstasy of the moment.

I came to my senses as a bluebird flew through the great windows, swept a curtsey through the cathedral, and landed on a candelabra gone cold. The queen, now as light as her silks, slipped from my grip to the snow at our feet.

I left her there. I didn't even say goodbye.

We walked west from the castle without ceremony. The snow had already begun to glow orange with sunset by the time I first glimpsed the great tree.

When it finally loomed, large and proud, black and gnarled, my brothers stopped before it and knelt as if addressing a queen.

A woman, her skin as black as the tree bark, stepped from

the thick shadows cast by its branches. She had as many limbs as the tree itself.

You have your vengeance, she said, though her voice was unlike any I'd heard before. It was the voice of a crow. And she spoke directly into my mind. *Are you satisfied?*

"Yes," I said, kneeling at last, knowing her for who she was, and the power she'd granted me.

"I am not satisfied," she told me. "My enemies live."

I looked up from the snow to find her standing before me, her breasts bare.

You have a clear mind and strong heart, Vendetta. Would you serve me? Would you give me the vengeance I long for? Will you help me rid this sacred place of them?

I turned to my brothers to find they were my brothers no longer. Instead, above us in the great tree's branches, were six birds. A heron. A hawk. An owl. A peacock. A blue jay. And a sparrow.

The heron had Ronan's eyes.

I was alone now, in body and in choice. I understood that.

Sunset had bled into twilight, and now twilight gave itself over to the night. "I was to die before the day was done. You granted me only today."

I will grant you an eternity so that I may have my vengeance, and all the world shall know your name. For this will you serve me, Vendetta?

I thought of each brother I had loved and lost. A mother and father too, which is nothing to say of my own life and dignity. The unfulfilled dreams of a girlish heart.

Then I thought of the queen's tears on my lips as I devoured her. The taste of her blood as I cleaned my nails with my teeth.

That sweet cream of a soul—the thought that I may have such pleasure again.

Yet no gift comes without its price.

Yes, I said. *I will walk the earth until you have enemies no longer.*

"Then it is done."

The dark goddess threw back her head and laughed, a deep, riotous roar, and at the terrible sound of it, all six birds took flight into the coming night.

V-63

The infection spread so quickly that, after only six months, one in every four residents had tested positive for the V-antigen. And it isn't like I live in Chicago, New York, or hell, even Orlando. Most cities have higher infection rates than we do here in my small midwestern college town.

At least we aren't the only country struggling to get a grip on the virus. Our numbers aren't that far ahead of China's, India's, and Brazil's. And Europe is catching up.

As you can imagine, by the time we realized what was happening, panic was everywhere. Canned goods, milk, bread—and toilet paper, of all things—were snatched from supermarket shelves, and it's not uncommon to walk into a grocery store even now and see the supply chain issues with your own eyes. I don't know about you, but the only thing I bought a ridiculous amount of was wasp spray.

Hear me out.

It burns like mace but the cans are bigger, and they shoot farther.

Businesses are still shut down. Schools are mostly closed.

Friends and families have stopped seeing each other and almost everyone works from home.

We're doing what we can, but people keep getting sick.

People keep dying.

Probably because we know the V-antigen is airborne now. I don't know if it always was—but it definitely is now.

The hospitals are filled beyond capacity, so their parking lots have become overrun with hazard tents full of specialists in hazmat suits trying to tend to the unruly patients.

My best friend, Beth, had the misfortune of living in an apartment that overlooked one such parking lot. After two nights of the screaming—she'd called it *snarling*, actually—she packed her bags and left for Milwaukee. Her plan is to stay with her grandparents until this is over.

Only I'm not sure it will ever be over. I suspect this is something we're going to have to learn how to live with.

Unlike other diseases, there is no cure for V-63. No vaccine.

No wonder we have the mask mandate.

I'm not sure they actually prevent anyone from contracting the virus. But it does keep people from taking a bite out of each other.

The black metal masks, with their mesh air-filtration system and intricate straps, do a good job of muzzling the infected.

People like me.

Not only did I test positive for the antigen six weeks after we got our first case in town, but my results showed *genetic and physiological mutations present*. That's a fancy way of saying that in addition to my body being hijacked by V-63, my eyes have changed. And I've grown fangs. Which hurt, by the way. Imagine burning cuts on your gum that never really go away.

Not that anyone can see them, since I mask 24/7.

And I can forget about my eyes whenever I'm not looking at them. They aren't weird unless I turn them just right and the light gets caught, reflecting back in an animalistic way.

Like a fox in headlights.

But the teeth—they're harder to forget. Even when I'm not looking, I can *feel* them pressing against the back of my lips, rubbing against my skin, making my mouth feel full and grotesquely large.

Over our last video call, Beth asked me why I bothered masking even when I was at home alone.

"For Snaps," I'd told her.

Snaps is my obese tabby cat. A ginger with white-socked feet and baby-blue eyes.

It only took one news report of a sobbing man crying on camera about having eaten his precious dog for me to mask up without looking back.

And that was before I'd gotten infected. Or at least, before I mutated.

I got Snaps as a kitten, just eight weeks old, in celebration of my first period—yes, I have one of *those* mothers who throw period parties.

Snaps has been with me for thirteen years. I'm not about to end our beautiful relationship and destroy that hard-earned trust by eating her.

I'm taking precautions.

But you know what they say about precautions.

They're fucking worthless.

I work in a lab on campus. I know what you're thinking. This is definitely where I caught V-63, right?

Nope.

It's not one of those labs. We only have mice. Small white ones. No vampire bats. No monkeys with creepy, alien eyes.

No mysterious bacteria found under the melting polar ice caps.

Just the mice.

The possibility of V-63 being a zoonotic disease is just a theory anyways.

We still don't know how the infection started.

Besides, these mice are so delicate that you have to feed them and check the temperature of their cages on a precise schedule every few hours or they die.

I don't think they have it in them to bring about the vampire apocalypse.

The routine is simple enough. Feed them. Check the water. Give them their medicine and adjust the heat lamps as needed.

It's an easy gig as far as campus jobs go. Beth has to—or *had* to—work in the dining hall wearing a hair net and spooning nacho cheese into little cups for the students.

I'd rather be in the lab, working with mice instead of people. It's also a hard pass on the hair net for me.

Probably why I've been here for two years, longer than this batch of mice have been alive.

They've gotten so used to seeing me that they jump up and down excitedly when I come through the lab doors, their furry little bellies dragging along the glass of their glorified fish tank as I go about the room, turning on the lights, calling out my hellos.

It's weird to hear my voice in this empty room, even though I know I'm the only one in this whole building. Well, Shaun might be up in his office on the fifth floor. He likes to write up there. He's working on his dissertation. He says it's easier to think here than in his apartment, where his girl-friend remains glued to the news all day. He claims he's unable to work in *those conditions*.

Shaun.

We used to talk all the time, and then I went and had my stupid Christmas party the December before the pandemic started and ruined everything. I can still see him now, standing in front of me in my apartment's window, wearing that ugly sweater and those ugly antlers that light up to the tune of "Deck the Halls." That drunk look in his eyes before he leaned in and kissed me.

How easy it had been to fall into bed with him after everyone left—everyone except Beth, of course, who'd gotten so drunk she'd passed out on my couch.

I guess the whole getting drunk at a Christmas party and having sex with someone from work thing wasn't the *worst* that could've happened on the eve of an apocalypse.

But what I did next was pretty bad.

I'd panicked.

Because the next morning, at a diner, I told him I didn't like him. I told him I didn't see him that way. I told him all of it was just a heat-of-the-moment-drunk-sex thing.

And I'd been lying my ass off.

When I told Beth what happened, she'd called me an idiot. She called me *cold*.

I can't say she's wrong.

I certainly look like an idiot standing here in the science building, staring at the elevator with some kind of paralysis consuming me.

Paralysis because there's what I *want* to do and what I *should* do.

I want to go up to his office and say hi. It's pretty much all I've wanted to do since the moment I pushed him away. But I haven't had the gall to say five words to him since the diner, which is a shame because he's like the best person to talk to. I really miss talking to him.

Every night. For hours.

We used to be friends.

There was even a solid weekend where I wondered if I might be in love with the guy. Even though I've spent most of my life wondering what love even is.

Instead, I turn away from the elevators and from Shaun, and make my way to the labs at the end of the first-floor hallway.

The labs have a way of being eerie at night. Even before the campus became a ghost town it was weird.

During the day it's nothing special. The graduate students make the mice run around their cardboard mazes for the sake of their research. But at night—it's just me, the mice, and possibly Shaun.

If he's up there.

That's probably why I don't rush through the routine. Water, food pellets, heater check. When the other lab attendants do it—Alicia and Chaney—they spend two minutes tops on everything.

Sometimes I linger for twenty minutes or more. I even spent an hour with them once or twice.

I don't want them to feel undervalued. Mice are social creatures.

While they eat, I sit on the stool and watch them. I speak to them in the same voice I use for Snaps, but they seem *way* more into it than my cat does.

Sometimes I take videos of them running around the cage and play them for Snaps later. She bats the screen with her white paw whenever I do.

Once the mice settle down in their shavings again, I take that as my cue to head out for the night.

I check the tank's temperature one more time, bid them goodnight, and turn out the lights, locking the lab behind me as I go.

Outside, the wind is cold and pulls at my hair. I tug my coat tighter and head east toward my apartment.

The gas station at the edge of campus shines like a beacon in the dark. I can see it even though I'm at least three blocks away. Its bright lights fight with the shadows on the sidewalks. The dry branches creak and my phone buzzes in my pocket as I walk. It's my mom asking me for the hundredth time if I'm coming home for Thanksgiving next weekend.

I haven't worked up the nerve to tell her I'm V-positive. She already struggles with anxiety. The last thing she needs to hear is that her precious baby might be a walking vector for vampirism. She cried for months when I told her I was moving away to college—and I'm only ninety miles away.

The gas station lights hurt my eyes, but I pull the door open and step inside anyway.

I want a bag of chips and a couple of drinks before I head back to my apartment. Right now all I've got in the fridge is about twenty pounds of beef and a gallon of fruit punch.

I admit, late-night snacking while watching TV is my guilty pleasure.

Yes, I can still eat and drink normally—for now anyway. No one has been infected long enough to know if that will change with time. Plenty of specialists think that the infected will lose their ability to consume food altogether at some point, but for now, our digestive tracts remain about the same.

But let's be honest here. Even before I'd contracted V-63 I was losing my ability to eat this trash.

All of these processed corn, soy, and wheat products dressed up to look like food had been giving me stomach problems for years. My doctor had recommended an elimination diet to figure out what my food sensitivities were. Beth recommended I go vegan like her, claiming it changed her life.

And honestly, I'd been in enough pain to seriously consider both options.

Me. Vegan.

It almost seems like a joke now, considering I have to eat about two pounds of raw meat a day in order to feel like a person.

It's mostly been cow so far. The thickest, bloodiest slabs I can find.

Apart from the raw meat, the only other real change since my infection is my sleep schedule.

It's clichéd, I know, but V-63 really does make you nocturnal. Or at least it's made me nocturnal. I used to be one of those annoying people who got up at five every day and had everything done before noon.

Now, from dawn until the late afternoon I feel like *absolute* shit. I can get up, check on the mice, but it's definitely like walking around with the flu or the worst head cold of my life.

Once the sun dips behind the horizon, the heaviness, nausea, and brain fog dissipate.

It's like magic.

After peering into the gas station cold cases, I decide on two bottles of iced coffee and some sour cream and onion chips.

The arguing starts up behind me as I'm closing the cooler's door.

"No, man, I'm telling you. It's infringing on our fucking civil liberties."

"How can it be infringing on your liberties when it's a choice? You don't *have* to wear it."

The cashier scowls at the kid buying a six-pack of beer.

If I were the cashier, I'd just nod and smile and let him go on his way. But I can tell by the lines between the guy's eyebrows that it isn't going to happen. He's already in deep.

"It's solidarity, man. I wear this to keep you safe. What if I'm infected? What if I catch the scent of you, go bat-shit crazy, and tear your throat out? I don't want that on my conscience."

His appeal isn't working.

"Don't worry about me. I can take care of myself. All you're doing is letting the government muzzle you, man. Muzzle you like a fucking dog."

I shift the coffees and bag of chips in my arms. I consider abandoning them. An over-sweetened latte knock-off in a glass bottle is *not* worth walking into this argument for.

I'm about to bolt when the unmasked kid grabs his beer off the counter and turns, seeing me for the first time. His eyes fix on the black mesh mask fitted over my face.

He sneers.

"Fucking sheep. Both of you," he says, and walks out, the door chiming as he departs. "You're what's wrong with the country!"

His voice is muffled as he shouts at the large glass windows before disappearing into the parking lot.

I put my snacks on the counter and reach into my back-pack for my wallet. The cashier shakes his head while ringing up my stuff.

"Some people. Don't they realize this isn't a joke? He could die. He could actually die." He slides my purchases into a plastic bag. I used to insist that cashiers use paper bags when I shop, but I stopped once V-63 started.

It just seems a little weird being obsessive over plastic and the environment while the world implodes. But you never know. Maybe this will shake out all right and I'll take up my cause again.

I hand over my card. I don't bother to point out that we could *all* die.

·   ·   ·

MY APARTMENT IS ON THE TOP FLOOR OF A CONVERTED warehouse down by the river. If you ever see it, you'll think, *Ah yes. This is one of those artsy things that rich people do.*

Beth calls it gentrification.

There's even a gallery on the first floor where they have installations or cheese-tasting or something—or they did. Not much has been open in the last few months apart from the gas stations and grocery stores.

I'd chosen the apartment because of the beautiful view. The big living room window looks over the river, and if you're up at dawn, you can watch the sun rise over the water.

It's usually the last thing I see before going to bed for the day.

Snaps starts meowing as soon as she hears my keys clanking against the door.

I use my hip to bump it open, the plastic bag swinging into my legs.

"I'm home."

This is my life, really. Calling out to animals as I come and go.

Snaps winds herself between my legs, rubbing her orange fur against my jeans. I can tell immediately by this affectionate attitude that she wants food.

As I put my bags down, she jumps up on the counter, leading me to her bowl.

"What is it?" I ask in a dramatic voice, knowing full well what it is. "What could possibly be wrong, Gingersnap?"

Sure enough, there's a tiny circle visible on the bottom of her dish.

I gasp in mock indignation. "My poor *baby*. You almost *starved*."

She meows pitifully. I pull her bag of cat kibble out of the cabinet and refill the bowl.

Fifteen minutes later I'm in my pajamas on the couch, my computer open in my lap. A rerun of *Jeopardy!* is playing.

Since Snaps is in the mood to hang out for once, rather than hide in my bedroom closet—her favorite spot—I put the gas station drinks in the fridge and leave the chips unopened on the kitchen counter.

I can snack anytime. Getting my cat to love me as much as I love her—this is a rare opportunity.

Her tail flicks against my shinbones as I get through two episodes of *Jeopardy!* My tongue absentmindedly traces my fangs when I'm not shouting answers at the contestants.

It must be the stress of not snacking that makes me do what I do next—*so stupid.* I know better than to look at the news *ever*, and yet somehow, more and more often lately, I find myself watching the evening update after just a few mindless clicks.

It's a compulsion.

And not even that informational.

It's just four talking heads, arguing over each other while the focus shifts back and forth between them. They're all speaking from their homes, of course, and I can't help but wonder how many of them would be pantless if they stood up.

"The mask mandate is a catastrophe," the blonde says. "If you wear a mask, everyone assumes you're a vampire. Violence against masked citizens has gone up. Not to mention ostracization, prejudice, condemnation, and—"

"If the masking policy were truly a mandate and fully enforced, then no one would feel ostracized. It wouldn't be clear who was infected and who wasn't because we would *all* be wearing them." A brunette's black brows knit together, her cheeks red. "It's this half-ass back and forth that has—"

"It's masks today and what tomorrow? Registration? Restrictions on where we can go and who we can interact with? Are we going to be *branded* like cattle? Will we be required to have a license to *exist*?" A gray-haired man with expansive jowls pushes his glasses up on his brow. "My sister-in-law runs a daycare. It's vital to her community. *Absolutely* vital. She hasn't been able to open her business because of these restrictions and—"

The blonde throws up her hands. "As a mother, I would want to know if there was a risk my child's caretaker was going to hurt her. That's not unreasonable. As citizens, we deserve to be informed. I deserve to know if there's a risk my child will be *eaten* by the very person serving her a juice box!"

The fourth man laughs, putting him at odds with the other three scowling at their respective cameras. "The cases of humans biting other humans have been low—"

"But not zero," the other man interjects. "And there are reports that those numbers have been wildly underreported. Law enforcement divisions are overworked, understaffed, and no one is keeping track of these things. We don't know how many casualties have been the result of—"

The fourth man butts in before momentum can be built. "It's only pets that have been *eaten* at this point. That's what we know."

I catch Snaps looking at me. She blinks.

"Don't listen to them," I tell her. "They're making that up. No one will eat you. Even if you are named after a cookie."

"—if we seek to punish these *accidents*, we all know that the persecutions will disproportionately affect communities of color. V-positive citizens of color will be targeted and incarcerated at higher rates than—"

"It's already happening," the blonde chimes in. "We're already seeing that happen."

The only black man present looks annoyed at being interrupted, despite the blonde's support of his argument.

He barrels on. "There was a bill introduced into the

House *today* that will force all V-positive citizens to register and—"

I escape the conversation by checking the world infection clock. I know I should stop going to this website, but every time the news triggers my anxiety, I end up opening it before I even realize what I'm doing.

The numbers have gone up. At least two hundred thousand more people are infected than when I'd checked yesterday morning before going to bed.

Even as I watch, the numbers of confirmed cases worldwide continue to tick upward without stopping. The countries are color-coded to show their infection rates. If a country is black, their saturation rate is the highest. Then red and orange. Yellow shows moderate infection rates, and yellow-green relatively low infection rates. Gray is supposed to mean no infections have been reported or confirmed.

North Korea is the only country still showing up as gray in the whole world, but everyone agrees that's bogus. For all we know, the entire country is full of vampires right now.

It's just that they'll probably never tell us.

Since this morning, Japan and Mexico have gone from dark orange to red. Argentina, Russia, and several of the African countries have progressed from yellow to orange.

America and China have been black for weeks. Yesterday, Australia moved from orange to red.

I look at the numbers. I look at the colors. I stare at the counter ticking upward as if I can will it to stop. To reverse somehow.

Properly demoralized, I close the computer and head to bed.

Under the covers I spend hours scrolling social media on my phone, yet another failed attempt to self-soothe.

It's a mixed bag.

Some people are replicating the latest dance trend,

complete with four million hashtags. Others are showing off their new fangs, their reflective eyes. Others—mostly scrawny, pasty emos—are glaring into their phones' cameras with their best attempt at a smoldering gaze, goblets of blood in hand.

One guy captions his photo with *Come see me, beautiful, if you're looking for eternity*.

Gross. So cringe.

I write, *No to eternity. I just want a solution for my IBS, thanks.*

My tone is jokey, but I really do feel sick inside.

Sick with restlessness more than anything. Before the pandemic I felt like I was waiting for something to happen.

Something that may *never* come, no matter how much I want it to.

And maybe I'll be waiting forever.

To be clear, I don't think it was a pandemic or a virus I was holding out for.

But something. Something existential.

And I'm still waiting for that one thing that will change my life forever.

I finally get sleepy about the same time the light begins to seep around the edges of my curtains. I'm already too lethargic to get up and go to the living room for another brilliant sunrise.

Sometimes one doesn't need more light.

The darkness is just fine.

I close my eyes.

My ringing phone wakes me. Maybe Alicia is calling because she can't do the morning mice check.

I answer the call with fumbling fingers, eyes still pinched closed against the burning light.

"Hello?"

I'm greeted by someone sobbing.

"Hello?" I try to force my eyes open to check the time but they're resisting. The clock on my phone says it's just after eleven in the morning. God, it's almost high noon. No wonder I feel like shit.

My head is pounding, my vision is blurry. My stomach feels like I've drunk two liters of acid.

"Who is this?" I croak. "Whoever you are, please just tell me what you want."

"Cordelia? Cordy! It's Beth. Beth!"

"Beth?" I sit up and press my back against the headboard. I cradle my aching head, the scratchy mask rubbing against my palm. "What's going on? Are you okay?"

"No!"

"Why? What happened?" I'm already wondering if I'd be able to drive to Milwaukee, as sick as I feel.

"Grandma's been detained."

"Oh shit."

I know what she's going to say before she even says it.

"She ate someone. My grandmother fucking *ate* someone."

I would have laughed if Beth hadn't been so hysterical, and with my luck I'd open my mouth to laugh and puke into my mask.

"Are they charging her?" I ask.

"No. They're calling it an accident."

"How long does she have to stay in detainment?"

"I don't know. They won't tell me anything. They've got her in this cell with fifty other people. It's awful. She's upset and she's confused. She didn't even know she was infected. None of us did. She was perfectly fine until she went and bit Roger."

I don't bother asking who Roger is.

"When did this happen?" I ask.

"Last night. I've been here all night. I haven't slept. My head is killing me."

"Did they make you test?" I ask. Because usually if someone in a household is positive, they require the whole family to be tested as a precaution.

"Yeah." Here her voice falls. "I'm positive."

She sounds scared.

"It's going to be okay," I tell her. "You're going to be fine."

"I'm vegan!" she hisses into the phone. "How the hell am I going to eat raw meat every day, Cordelia!"

"I'm sure we can find you a fascist or two."

This earns me a snort at least. Then the humor is gone as quickly as it came.

"I don't know what I'm going to do. I'm freaking out. I can't do this by myself."

"You aren't going to do this by yourself," I tell her. "I'm right here."

"Are you kidding me?" she hisses, her fury returning. "I can't come near you. I'll never forgive myself if I tear your throat out."

"You won't," I say.

"You don't know—"

"I'm positive—" I tell her. But she doesn't get it. She keeps trying to talk over me. "No, Beth. I'm *positive*. I'm positive for V-63 too. I've had it for months. I've even got the mutations."

"Shut up," she says.

Then she hangs up on me.

It's only a second before my phone rings again, this time with a request for a video call.

I answer it, and she looks worse than I'd expected. Her hair is all over the place. Her eyes are red-rimmed and black liner is streaked down her face. I can see only a sliver of a hallway behind her. I wonder if that's where they're detaining her grandma.

"Take off the mask and show me," she says.

"I can't. You know I'm worried about Snaps."

"Yeah, and I thought you were just a paranoid germaphobe, and yet here you were infected the whole time! Can't believe you didn't tell me, Cord!"

"Focus."

"Close the door then. Lock her out. Hold your breath, open a window. I don't give a shit what you do, but *show* me. I need to see this. It's the only thing that will keep me from killing myself right now."

Well, damn. How do you say no to a demand like that?

I look under my bed, I peer into the closet. I don't see Snaps in her usual hiding places, so I assume she's in the living room, probably sleeping in a patch of sunlight.

I close and lock my bedroom door and climb back into my bed.

I have to set the phone down in order to reach behind my head and undo the straps that buckle back there.

I'm holding the phone up again as I peel it away.

"I was expecting sores or a rash or something, as much as you wear that thing," Beth says, squinting into the phone. "But you look fine."

She's right. My face is a little red and warm to the touch, but it looks okay. I can see myself reflected in the smaller window in the upper right side of my phone's screen.

I have some pretty terrible bedhead and red eyes myself. I guess the apocalypse doesn't look great on either of us.

"Show me the fangs," she says.

I open my jaw and peel back my lips. My face muscles resist. They resent being asked to move after so much time being immobilized. It feels good, actually, to get some air on my face, even if my mouth does feel sticky.

"Holy. Shit," she says, her face right up against the camera. "Turn to the left. To the right."

I do as she asks.

She falls back, her face a normal distance from the screen now.

"Damn," she says.

"Yep."

"Why didn't you tell me?"

"I didn't want you to worry."

"I was already worried!"

"Yeah, I get that." Hell, I get stressed if I leave Snaps alone for too long. I start to feel like a bad cat mom—even though we both know I'm a roommate at best.

"Your eyes don't do the weird flash thing," she says.

"They do," I tell her. "It has to be in the right light."

She wrinkles her nose. "Freaky, man. I wonder if I'll mutate."

"If you do, we'll get shirts made. We'll be weird together."

This earns me a second snort. "We're already weird together."

I fall back against the pillow, swallowing down a wave of nausea.

Someone calls her name off-camera, and she turns away. "That's me!"

They say something else, but I can't hear.

"I gotta go," she says. "I'll call you later."

She hangs up before I can say bye, or remind her to get a mask as soon as she can.

I send her a text instead.

Then, with my messages still open, I send my mom a text too, telling her I won't be home for Thanksgiving. I give her some bogus excuse about no one being able to watch the mice, but really I can't get the image of Beth's little old grandma tearing someone's throat out.

That is *not* going to be me. I can't be the one to infect my mom.

Or kill her.

I reach for my mask the same instant that Snaps jumps up onto the bed.

The second her four white feet settle down onto the cover in front of me, I feel like I've been kicked in the gut. My heart drops right down into the pit of my stomach at the sight of her.

The door is still closed, and I know she wasn't under the bed. How the hell did she get in here?

She must have been in the closet. I must have missed her either because my vision was blurry or because of my pounding head.

"Stay there," I tell her as my fingers inch toward the mask.

I move slowly, deliberately. I'm afraid any quick movement might flip some predator switch in my brain.

"Stay right *there*," I beg her.

She looks at me with her big blue eyes as if daring me to try anything.

I finally get my mask. I press the fabric over my face and fumble the buckles back into place.

Now here we are. Looking into each other's eyes.

It isn't until my adrenaline falls and my heart rate returns to normal that I realize I never had the urge to eat her.

She scared the living *shit* out of me, surprising me like that. But there is no ravenous hunger. No compulsion overtakes me.

I lower the mask again and take a deep breath.

I wait.

And wait.

Nothing.

Huh.

Snaps flops over on my bed, her tail flicking.

I'm still waiting for something to happen, for some switch to flip inside me.

It never does.

I have zero desire to take a bite out of my cat.

Still, I fix the mask in place over my nose and mouth again.

"Better safe than sorry," I tell her, before pulling the covers over my head and willing my throbbing body back to sleep.

I MANAGE TO CONVINCE ALICIA TO ALSO DO THE AFTERNOON checkup on the mice and snag myself a few more hours of sleep, so that by the time the sun dips below the horizon, I feel like a whole different person. I eat my raw steak—locked in the bathroom after triple-checking that the cat is outside. I know she is because she keeps sticking her little paw beneath the door, swiping at nothing.

I feel like I have a toddler.

Once I've eaten, I shower. I brush my hair. I put my mask back on and dress before daring to leave the bathroom and breathe the same air as Snaps.

All evening I've been replaying that moment of her jumping on my bed with my mask off.

I feel like I got away with something.

I have a theory that I feel too sick during the day to be hungry. And I'll be damned if I try the same experiment again now that night has fallen.

The cat gets fed and we watch some television together. I manage to avoid the news and talking heads, but I check the world clock twice before I can stop myself. Both times the shifting kaleidoscope of colors does nothing for my anxiety.

A news article says that more people are dying instead of mutating now. There's speculation that the virus has become more deadly, and less compatible with the human body.

I suppose I should be grateful I caught it early.

But I'm not.

They're also culling a thousand ferrets from a farm after they proved to be infected.

I'm still trying to wrap my mind around the idea of vampire ferrets when it's finally time to go check on the mice. I call out my goodbyes to Snaps and step out into the chilly night.

I'm hoping the walk will clear my head and calm me down. It does.

The lab building comes into view just as I get a text from Mom. She says she understands about Thanksgiving and thought about canceling altogether. She offers to come see me the Saturday after when she's off work, but I tell her it's not safe. Negotiations end when I promise to video chat with her for at least an hour on Thanksgiving because she keeps insisting that she must see me with her own eyes and know that I'm okay.

We seal the deal by sending each other handshake emojis.

I make a promise to myself that I'll tell her about my situation when I talk to her—even if she cries for hours.

She's a good mom. If I keep avoiding her, she's going to show up at my door unannounced.

We can't have that, can we?

THE LAB IS THE WAY I LEFT IT.

The mice do their greeting dance, and while they eat their pellets and burrow through the fresh shavings, I read the notes Alicia left in the morning and afternoon logs.

I linger for almost an hour.

It occurs to me sometime after making Snaps a new video that I'm lonely.

I've been feeling more and more lonely lately. Not sure if

it's a vampire thing or the natural consequence of the world falling apart around me.

Whatever it is, I'm almost in tears by the time I bid the mice good night and turn off the lights.

The only thing left to do about it is go home and cry in bed, I guess. Maybe eat another steak.

I'm considering my options as I leave the building and reenter the night.

Just outside, a group of guys linger by the bike rack. Several of them have beers in their hands, the tops of the cans shining in the moonlight. They expose their long necks to the starless sky as they take long, deep drinks.

At least two cigarettes burn in the dark, though thanks to my mask, I can't smell it.

The heavy metal door to the science building clanks closed behind me and all five heads pivot in my direction. I nervously adjust my bag on my shoulders before I can stop myself.

"What have we got here?" one guy slurs. He's perching on the bike rack.

"A fucking masker," another says, pushing himself to standing. "Are you even a *vamp*, sweetie? Or just a good little sheep?"

I ignore them.

I slip past them up the walkway, hoping I'm lucky enough that they'll let me leave without starting anything.

I'm not lucky.

A rough hand grabs my shoulder and spins me. "I'm talking to you. Don't be rude."

"Yeah," his friend chimes. "Don't be a bitch."

My heart speeds up. Fear floods my veins like ice water, but I refuse to apologize, even if the compulsion to do so dances on the tip of my tongue.

"I'm leaving." I adjust my pack on my shoulder and turn away again.

Slow, calm movements.

I only make it three steps before someone spins me again. My backpack is torn off my shoulder and hits the sidewalk.

Shit. There goes my wasp spray.

"You'll leave when I fucking say you can leave," the guy says. His breath fogs in front of his face, momentarily hiding his glazed and glassy eyes. His lips are wet, and his head is covered by a tight beanie. His coat is too thin for this weather.

His friends circle like hyenas.

"What's your problem?" I try to keep my voice calm despite my tightening throat. I look him dead in the eyes.

"My problem? You're my problem."

"I didn't do anything to you."

"All you fucking maskers are the problem."

I bend to grab my backpack. Before I manage it, someone shoves me. I hit the ground hard. My head bounces off the pavement. Stars spark in my eyes.

Then someone is on top of me, trying to pull the mask off my face. The strap is too tight and his terrible, jerky motions hurt my neck.

"Stop!" I yell, trying to buck him off me with my hips.

"Take it off!" he screams. "Fucking take it off!"

His friends are still laughing. God, they really are like hyenas.

I try to pitch him to one side again but it's no use. He outweighs me by at least a hundred pounds. The first strap of my mask comes loose and a rush of cold air slides across my face.

"Stop! Stop!" There's no hiding my fear anymore. I'm pleading. I'm *begging*. "I'm infected. I'm really infected!"

"Fucking liar," he says.

"Yeah, the virus is a hoax made up by the government," one of his friends says.

I'm clawing at his hands, trying to pull the mask up over my face, but the second strap gives and he snatches it away before I can grab ahold of it. Just like that, the mask slips from my fingers and out of reach.

He holds it over his head triumphantly, waving it like a flag.

I remain on my back, staring up at the night sky. The cold air on my skin would feel great if I wasn't drowning in full-blown panic.

You would think some strange guy straddling me would be the terrifying part, especially while his friends stand around and laugh.

But it's not the guys that are scaring me. It's the *smell*.

I can smell every one of them, and the realization of this keeps me pinned on my back in horror.

I'm scared to move. I'm scared to speak.

"See?" He sneers down into my face. "You're fine, you big baby. You can't believe all that shit you see on television. The government lies. They're just trying to turn us into idiots so we keep buying their bullshit. Capitalism, man."

"She's pretty," one of the friends says.

They sound like voices in a dream. Distant. Echoing.

Reality is becoming soft at its edges. I'm rising from the ground. I feel like I'm flying, floating, up into the night on a dark wave of—

Hunger.

Something—some instinct—has reached inside me and turned off my brain.

It's so fast, I don't even know how it happens.

One minute I'm on my back, stunned, the night sky brilliant above me. The next, I have my hands around someone's neck and my teeth shred his throat like a soft cheese.

Like a fucking *brie*.

Blood gushes into my mouth, too fast for me to drink it all down, but that doesn't stop me from trying. The guy struggles in my grip but it doesn't matter.

I hold tight. I hold tight until he's sagging in my arms.

He's dead weight when I finally drop him to the pavement. I don't know if he's trying to speak or if that gurgling is because of the hole I've made where his neck should be.

Maybe both.

One of the friends is bent over him, trying to cover the wound with his jacket.

Another chooses revenge.

But the fist he throws never connects. I'm on him before either of us knows what's happening.

My teeth remove the chunk of flesh below his ear with one flex of my jaw. I swallow this mouthful of meat without chewing.

"He's dead!" someone screams. "Brian's dead!"

I drop the second sagging body with shaking arms. My stomach feels bloated. I'm starting to feel like a cat lounging in the sunshine.

I turn toward the remaining three guys and find that their eyes are the size of saucers. I take a step toward them, but a hand slams over my mouth.

Someone is covering my dripping, sticky face with a mask.

"Get out of here!" he hisses at the remaining guys. "Get the fuck out of here!"

Now they're running.

"Cordelia," someone whispers into my ear. "*Cordelia*, can you hear me?"

Something about hearing my name—remembering that I *have* a name—brings my mind back into focus.

I look into the eyes inches from mine.

It's Shaun.

He's the one who's holding a mask over my mouth and nose, gripping me firmly with his other hand and using his body to block my view of the guys retreating into the night.

Maybe he thinks I'll chase them.

Maybe he's right.

"Cordelia, say something," he begs. "Please tell me if you're okay."

I burst into tears. Of all the people to find me like this, to see me for what I really am, did it really have to be *Shaun*?

I try to push him away, but he doesn't let go.

"I don't want to hurt you," I choke out. Now that the smell is gone and there's blood drying on my face, the reality of what's just happened is rushing in to fill the space that fear has left inside me.

"You can't hurt me." His voice is clear despite his mask.

"I can! Look at what I did. Look at what I did!"

I'm honestly not sure if I'm talking about the two dudes I just ate or what happened after the Christmas party.

"I know. I saw everything," he explains. "I'm so sorry I didn't get to you faster."

I try to wipe the tears from my eyes but only manage to smear blood across my face. Now it's in my eyes.

Oh my god.

Oh my god.

I've killed someone. And there's blood in my eyes.

Sirens sound in the distance.

"We need to go," Shaun says.

I don't move. I can't pull my eyes off the two bodies lying on the pavement outside the science building. Two bodies lying in sizable pools of blood.

All I can think about is how I want to take this mask off and lap it up while it's still warm.

Christ.

"Cordelia, come on." Shaun picks up my backpack. He grabs one of my arms and pulls me forward. "Come on. I'll get you home."

I let him lead me if for no other reason than I don't know what else to do. My world is spinning.

He keeps to the shadows, probably because I look like hell. I can't see my face, but the front of my clothes are *drenched* in blood. My hands look like they've been dipped in a vat of it. The skin between my fingers sticks together whenever it touches.

But here is my apartment building. Here is Shaun pulling me up the stairs.

He uses my key to open my apartment and ushers me inside.

Snaps takes one look at us and bolts down the hallway into my bedroom, her tail erect, her ears pinned back against her head.

I also feel like hiding in a closet.

"You should shower," he says. "You'll feel better."

"I can't take my mask off again with you here. I'll eat you!"

"You won't," he says. He looks sad. His eyes are big and round with concern.

"I just—"

"I'm positive," he says. "I'm already positive. You can't hurt me."

"Oh." He hasn't mutated then. His teeth are flat and his eyes don't shimmer.

So all this time he wasn't just masking to be safe. He's masking out of necessity too.

"Don't eat my cat," I tell him.

Then I lock myself inside the bathroom.

I'm gone for a long time. I don't want to be. It's weird leaving a guy in my apartment while I cry in the shower, but

I have little choice in the matter. The breakdown is happening wholly without my consent.

I can't stop it.

When I finally get out of the shower, the water has been cold for a long time.

But at least the blood is gone. And something that I strongly suspect was a chunk of a *person* that had been stuck in my hair washes down the drain too.

My clothes will have to be burned though. I leave them in the tub to soak, but I don't think that's going to do a damn thing.

I'm finally dressed, a fresh mask fastened around my face —I don't even bother to peek into the closet and see if Snaps is okay. She probably needs some alone time after what she's just seen.

I give her space.

While I was gone, Shaun was hard at work.

There are little circles of soap where he's scrubbed my bloody footprints out of the carpet.

He's also wiped down my backpack.

"You didn't have to," I tell him.

"It's cool. I don't mind." He asks, "Can I make you a drink?"

"I don't take my mask off when I'm at home," I say.

He frowns. "Why? Anxiety?"

I mean, hell yeah anxiety. "I'm worried about Snaps."

His eyes show no recognition.

"The cat," I say. I look out the window at the river, at the moon hanging in the sky. "So. How long before the police show up and arrest me, do you think?"

"They won't come." He says this with complete confidence.

"I just ate someone. *Two* someones. I'll be in one of those detention centers before dawn."

He shakes his head. He's on the couch now, his back resting against my plaid throw pillow. "The centers are full. We don't have a police force big enough to control this and there's nowhere to put anyone. They couldn't detain any more people even if they wanted to."

"How do you know that?" Because they definitely haven't mentioned that on the news.

He rubs the back of his head. "Because I bit someone too."

I sit down on the sofa beside him. "Did they die?"

"Yeah. And I felt like shit for months about it."

Months. Shaun has been infected for *months*. Maybe even before me.

I try to take this in.

"I didn't even know I was infected until I was covered in his blood. The cops came. They took a statement and identified the guy. They asked me a couple of questions and then they left."

I pull the matching throw pillow into my lap and hug it.

"I tried to go down to the station and turn myself in, and they sent me home. They were actually annoyed that I was there."

"Jesus."

He nods at my phone on the coffee table. "Call and tell them what happened. A hundred bucks says they hang up on you."

I do call. And they don't hang up. But Shaun isn't wrong either.

They ask my name and the location of the incident. They ask if I know the names of the deceased, but I don't. So they end the call by promising to send someone "to take care of it," whatever that means.

The conversation ends with "we'll call you if we have any follow-up questions."

Afterward I hold my phone in disbelief.

We'll call you if we have follow-up questions.

I just killed two people. I murdered them.

And someone is going to get back to me on that?

This is the moment I realize just how fucked we are.

"Wow." I don't know what else to say.

"I know. When it first happened, I hid in the office every night because I was terrified of hurting Heather. We don't bite during the day. Did you know?"

"I wondered."

Heather.

The undergrad girlfriend who wants to be a marine biologist. When Beth told me she'd seen them at a bar together, I'd pretended to be unbothered and unimpressed.

No jealousy here, folks.

I don't think I managed to fool either of us.

"Eventually I had to tell her. I think she knew. She was keeping her distance, and when I finally told her, she didn't seem surprised. She just packed up and left."

"She dumped you?" I hope I sound concerned and not pleased.

"Yeah," he says, running his hand over his hair. "It's fine. We didn't mesh anyway. Even before all this happened."

We sit in the dim light of my living room lamp and say nothing for a long time.

Finally, he asks, "Are you okay? It's okay if you're not okay. I can't believe those assholes. I *heard* you shout that you were infected. They should have listened to you. It's their own fault that they got hurt."

Their fault. "I'll have to keep telling myself that."

I squeeze the pillow harder.

"I just wish I knew what was really going on. Does anyone know? Have you heard one sensible theory?"

"An evolutionary jump," he says with a shrug. "Mother Nature restoring some balance. Somewhere along the line we kept fucking up and this is her decree. That's what I think."

Man, he's such a scientist.

"And we just wait it out until we either destroy ourselves or discover how to live like this? Is there really no going back?"

He rubs the back of his head. "I've run the numbers a million times. The infection rates are too high. Everyone is going to get this sooner or later, or die trying. And the ones who don't get it are going to *wish* they had."

I look out the window at the moon. I feel like crying again.

"I'm going to take you up on that drink now," I tell him. "The fruit punch is in the fridge. The liquor is above the stove."

He goes to the kitchen and helps himself. Seeing him pull down two glasses and raid my cabinets makes me think of that stupid Christmas party again.

To hide my tears, I go to my room, double-check that Snaps is actually in the closet this time. She is, her eyes wide and scared.

I close the closet door and then my bedroom door. Double protection, just to be sure.

By the time I'm back on the sofa, I've managed to blink away the tears.

But Shaun's no idiot.

He hands me a glass, pulling his mask down so it hangs around his throat like a bandanna. I do the same. There was rum and vodka in the cabinet, the only booze I still had.

I take a sip.

Lots of vodka.

Good.

"Thanks for your help tonight," I tell him. "I'd probably have killed all of them if you hadn't stopped me."

"I didn't want to be alone after it happened to me," he says. "I figured you might feel the same. But if you want me to go—"

"No." I say this too quickly. To hide my embarrassment, I peer into the red drink I'm holding, and try not to think of blood. "No, I don't want to be alone."

We drink our cocktails in silence as the moon cuts her path across the cloudy night sky.

"I'm sorry." I toss the words like a grenade into the dark of my living room. The shadows refuse to swallow them up, so they hang in the air between me and the man whose knee is inches from mine.

"They should've never—"

"No." I pinch my eyes closed. "I'm sorry about Christmas. I'm sorry about all those things I said at the diner."

He turns his head to look at me. I can see it happen in my periphery even if I don't have the guts to meet his eyes.

I take a deep breath and say, "I really do like you. I've always liked you, but when I saw you sitting there across from me at the table, it just—I don't know. I freaked out."

"You were scared," he says. He puts his drink on the table. "We're all scared. Even those assholes who attacked you are scared."

I want to wrap my arms around him and feel him hold me back.

"I was lying. All those things I said in the diner. I lied," I tell him.

"I know," he says. He smiles, and it's the goofy grin I love. "I never believed you."

"Then why didn't you call my bluff? Tell me I was full of shit?"

He shrugs. "No is still no. And what I heard was 'no.'"

Damn he's sexy.

Before I can fully consider what I'm doing, I crawl into

his lap. I slide my arms around his neck. Then I get ahold of myself.

"Is this okay? Do you mind if I—"

"I don't mind," he says. He wraps his arms around me as if he's trying to save me. From what? The apocalypse? From myself? I don't even care.

"I've been waiting for this," he whispers into my hair, his lips pressing against my throat.

Me too, I think.

I've been waiting forever.

THE DARK TRICK

Her mother was dying. Eloise understood that this was the way of it. Mothers died. Daughters were left behind to carry on without them. And yet, as she watched her mother gasp in the small twin bed they'd shared since she was a child, sweat beaded on her forehead, her mind refused to accept the possibility that her mother wasn't long for this world. That this woman—the North Star in Eloise's sky—could at any moment suddenly blink out of existence. Go dark. Leaving her alone.

All alone.

Why not me? She wished, not for the first time, that it was she who was dying.

They'd both tended to the Danes family, all of them sick with fevers and red splotches covering their faces. Both had held the baby who'd been carried off to Heaven before its two older sisters, just three and nine, followed suit.

And yet it was her mother that was sick now, and somehow Eloise—apart from an afternoon in which she bore the worst headache of her life—had gone untouched.

"I'll send for the doctor again," Nanny said, wiping her hands on her apron.

"We can't pay," Eloise said.

"He won't charge us. I've delivered two of his babies. He'll remember that."

Eloise squeezed the old woman's hand, a sign of encouragement even though in her heart she knew nothing could be done.

Once alone, Eloise sank into the wooden chair at her mother's bedside and wept.

She woke to a rough knock on the door. As she lifted her head, she found the slanted afternoon light had faded from a cheerful yellow to cool twilight. Nanny, it seemed, had not returned.

Perhaps that is them at the door.

Eloise crossed the uneven floor of their cottage. But it wasn't Nanny or the doctor. It was their neighbor, Mrs. Clark, with another basket full of warm rags and poultices.

"Hello, dearest," she said. "How is your mother?"

"There's been no change, Mrs. Clark," Eloise said, taking the basket from the woman's bent fingers. "I fear the worst. Do forgive me. Would you like to come inside?"

"No, no. I have to get back. Supper is almost done. I just wanted to come by and pay my respects." The woman clutched her collar as if Eloise was going to drag her into the house by it.

She's afraid of getting sick, she thought. And who could blame her?

Not one soul in all of the village's cramped cottages could afford to be ill. All hands were needed to do the work each day. To keep them all alive. Eloise herself had no idea how she and Nanny were going to get by.

Her mother, before she'd become ill, had suggested that

Eloise might find a husband now that she was of age. Someone who was handsome and useful.

But the only eligible bachelor in town was a widower thirty years her senior, Mr. Miller. And Eloise didn't think him very handsome or very useful.

"Thank you for the gift, Mrs. Clark. Your kindness is appreciated."

Eloise moved to close the door.

"Wait!" Mrs. Clark called.

Eloise's brows rose. "What is it, Mrs. Clark?"

"I shouldn't be telling you this—"

"Then do not tell me," Eloise said. She was no gossip.

Mrs. Clark spoke as if she had not heard. "Is the situation dire? Tell me truly, child. Do you believe she will die?"

Eloise spoke the truth, as she'd always done. "Yes. I believe she will die."

Mrs. Clark nodded as if she'd already known this to be the answer. Then she said, "Listen to me and listen well. There is a way to save her, but the price—Lord help me. I do not know if you can bear the price."

"We have no money, Mrs—"

"It is not money he will ask for."

"Oh," Eloise said plainly. "I see."

Eloise knew of women who'd been pushed to sell the only thing they had left to whomever would pay for it. She herself hoped it wouldn't come to it. She couldn't imagine such a thing with a man, even in marriage, let alone in a transactional manner.

"There is one you can go to who will stop death itself."

"No one but God can stop death, Mrs. Clark."

"Or the devil. And I know where you can find the devil," Mrs. Clark whispered. "Do you understand me?"

Witches. Demons. Eloise knew of such things. Was that not why they had a horseshoe nailed above the door of their little home and a bushel of dried rue, oregano, rosemary, and thyme above the bed?

"If you are desperate—truly desperate—I say you go to the house at the edge of Briarwood. Knock on the door and ask for the lord of the house. I do not know what he will ask of you, or what you must pay—all I know is that Agnes Atwood was brave enough to go and her whole family was saved from the brink of death not two nights later. From typhus, if you can believe it."

Agnes Atwood ran away two years ago. No one had seen her since.

"Why are you telling me, Mrs. Clark?"

"Your mother did me a kindness long ago. A true kindness," Mrs. Clark said. "Though she'll never forgive me for sending her daughter to the likes of that lord. That is why I must leave the decision to you. But if you would like to go, go *tonight*. Make yourself up nice. Don't turn up as the filthy village girl you are now, smelling of sick as you do. Make yourself as fine as you can and throw yourself on his mercy. It may be the only thing left that can save her."

And with that, Mrs. Clark spun away, briskly marching to her own cottage door.

Just beyond her, Nanny's hunched form and the tall smudge of the doctor appeared on the horizon. Eloise watched them approach with Mrs. Clark's words echoing in her mind.

THE DOCTOR EXAMINED HER MOTHER FOR NO MORE THAN FIVE minutes before declaring that nothing could be done. When Eloise asked about payment, the doctor waved her away.

In the following hours, she sat at her mother's side, watching her breath worsen and replaying Mrs. Clark's words over and over in her mind.

Finally, she sat bolt upright. "Nanny. Have we water for a bath?"

"Just," Nanny said.

"Let's fill the tub then. I need to clean myself the best I can."

"Why, miss?"

"I heard from—someone"—Eloise didn't want to give Mrs. Clark away—"that there is a place I can go to ask for help. For Mother. But I am not presentable as I am."

Nanny asked no questions. She drew the bath and helped Eloise scrub her skin and ears until they were pink and her nails clean. They put a small dab of orange oil behind her ears and she put on her mother's wedding dress. It was the only decent dress they had in the whole of the cottage, and still, it was plainer than some of the afternoon dresses that the ladies wore in town. But the emerald green drew out the color of Eloise's eyes, and she hoped that would count for something.

And Nanny had taken care to pull her hair back from her face.

"You don't have to do this, my sweet," Nanny said. "Your mother wouldn't want it."

Where does she think I'm going? Eloise wondered. *A brothel?*

"I must try," Eloise said, searching that gentle face. "I will never forgive myself if I don't try."

Nanny only nodded, as if she understood. Then she went to the dresser and dug around before producing a pair of long white gloves.

They were faded with time, but Nanny's face still lit up when she saw them. "Wear these, then, and you'll look like a proper lady."

"Where did you get these?" Eloise laughed, pulling them on one at a time.

"I was a young lady once too, you know. I even went to a

ball and danced with a handsome young man. Though it's true he married another."

Dancing. Eloise did not think she'd ever have time for such a frivolous thing.

She gave herself one last look in the dull mirror before placing a kiss on Nanny's temple. "I don't know when I will be back."

Nanny nodded as if she'd known this too. "Be safe, sweet girl."

Eloise hesitated at the doorway, taking in her mother's shrunken form one last time before stepping out into the night.

The roads were empty.

The windows to the cottages were dark. One had a single candle burning behind the glass, but Eloise could not say what the soul inside was doing. Having a late drink? Reading by candlelight?

It mattered not. She walked on, to the edge of their village and into the woods.

It was work, weaving her way through the trees and low branches by the full moon's light. She was doing her best not to let anything snag her dress or soil Nanny's gloves. It would not do to work so hard on her appearance only to turn up at the lord's door with leaves in her hair like some forest creature.

The darkness too was upsetting. It seemed to press in on her from all sides.

An owl hooted in the night.

A branch snapped nearby, but under what weight, she didn't know. Something howled.

Then she caught sight of the light and followed it until the trees broke open.

The house at the edge of Briarwood was far grander than anything they had in the village. It was like the houses in town, which Eloise had seen only once in her entire life, with more windows than she could count.

Music bled out into the night.

A party, she thought, recoiling. *Am I really going to throw myself at his feet in the middle of a party?*

What choice did she have?

She approached the house only to be met with a furious chorus of cawing. At least a dozen crows sat perched on the roof, and having seen her, they screeched. It was almost like they were taunting her, laughing at her. Daring her to go inside.

She hesitated at the bottom of the stairs.

Be brave, she told herself. *This is for Mother.*

I can do anything for Mother. Because Mother would do anything for me.

Eloise took a steadying breath and went to the door. Before she could knock, it swung open.

She was met with darkness. Complete and total darkness. It was as if no one had lived in that house for a hundred years. Except Eloise had the distinct impression that the darkness was looking back at her.

If darkness could do such a thing.

"Hello?" she called out, a chill running up her spine. Had she not just seen a party from the windows? The candlelight? Had she not heard music? But if so, where was everyone now? "Is the lord of the house available? I've come to—I've come to speak with him, if I may. I have a—"

The door slammed shut.

Eloise's heart took off like a shot. She meant to run then, to go back through the forest from whence she came without a glance backward.

Only the door opened again and now the lights had returned. The music. And a young man was holding the door for her with a smile.

"My lady," he said with a dip of his head. "Come in, if you please."

Eloise still had one gloved hand over her pounding heart as she crossed the threshold into the house.

Did I imagine it? she wondered. Because the house was full of music and laughter again, and she felt as if she couldn't have possibly been looking into that endless dark just moments before. Not now, with this vibrancy pulsing all around her.

"This way, my lady."

Eloise fell into step behind the young man as he led her to a grand ballroom, the heart of the night's affair. It was full of men and women dancing, laughing. There was a piano forte in the corner of the room, and a woman's fingers danced across the keys.

Then the music faltered and all eyes were upon her. Some gazes were curious. Others less friendly.

Be brave, she told herself again. *Be brave for Mother.*

Eloise dipped a bow. "Forgive me for the intrusion. I am looking for the lord of the house. I need to speak with him as a matter of great urgency."

A beat of silence. Then laughter erupted like the taking off of a great many birds, and Eloise was left feeling more than a little stupid, and embarrassed.

Was it something she had said? Or was it her appearance? She'd never looked so fine, and yet it paled compared to the luxurious glamour around her.

She was beginning to feel like she'd made a mistake, as if perhaps she should leave.

But then a voice said, "There is no lord of this house."

Eloise turned to find a woman standing there. Perhaps the most beautiful woman she'd seen in all her life. Her hair was thick and curling, falling down her back nearly to her waist. The black tresses were full of crimson ribbons that matched the red of her full lips. Her eyes were lined with kohl, and her skin as milk white as if it had simply been poured over her bones from a pail of fresh cream.

She stopped just short of Eloise.

"My, you're a pretty thing."

Eloise came to her senses. "Forgive me, my lady. I am sorry if I am intruding."

"You weren't invited, that's true. But we've yet to determine if you're intruding."

Her smile was gentle, if blood red. Perhaps that more than anything gave Eloise the courage to go on.

"I heard from—from a friend—that if I spoke to the lord of the house, he may be able to help save my mother's life. My mother is dying."

The woman arched a dark brow. "Is she?"

"Yes, my lady. And I'm *so* very desperate to save her."

"How desperate?" The woman grinned.

We are speaking of price now, Eloise thought. And yet she found herself a little braver now that she was facing a woman rather than a man. "There is nothing I would not give, my lady. Whatever pleases you, I will pay it."

Laughter circled the room.

"Be quiet," the woman commanded, and the laughter dried up. Her gaze returned to Eloise. "As I said, there is no lord in this house. Only me."

"Forgive me, my lady. I must have been misinformed."

The woman placed one hand on her curving hip. "Do you not believe me capable of helping your mother?"

"I would love nothing more than if you could save my mother, my lady. Please name your price."

That seemed to be the correct thing to say.

"The price for my assistance is that you must stay here with me."

Eloise met her dark eyes. "My lady?"

The woman smiled. "You stay here with me, and I will see to it that your mother does not die. For many, many years."

Her mind raced. It had to be some trick. Perhaps they thought she was some country simpleton, and they were only playing with her.

"I do not think my mother will last until morning, my lady. If—"

The woman waved someone forward, and before Eloise could react a young man appeared at her arm. He took a lock of Eloise's hair between his fingers and brought it up to his nose. He breathed deeply.

Eloise drew back, alarmed. "What in the world are you—?"

"Is that enough?" the lady of the house asked.

The man nodded.

"Good. Find her quickly then." She waved him toward the door. Now she was staring down at Eloise again. "I've sent him to give your mother a special medicine. She will live. And you will stay here with me. Do you understand?"

"No," Eloise admitted. "I am not sure what you are asking of me, my lady."

"Stay by my side. Be my companion. Do as I ask. And when I am ready to retire, come upstairs to bed with me."

She bent and placed her lips on Eloise's throat.

Her heart knocked wildly in her chest as the lips moved from Eloise's collarbone up to the soft skin just behind her ear, trailing soft kisses as they went.

Eloise shivered.

"Is this clear enough?" the lady of the house whispered.

"Yes, my lady," Eloise breathed.

"Good." She pulled back and snapped her fingers. "Let's continue. I would like to dance the waltz next."

Slow, mournful music began to fill the ballroom, and as if

pulled on strings, couples filled the space, spinning around and around in each other's arms.

The lady of the house pulled Eloise into the dance.

"Oh, my lady, I do not know—"

"I will move you," the woman said.

And Eloise found this to be true. The woman turned her this way and that as easily as if Eloise were a child in her arms. More than once she bent, pressing her mouth to Eloise's throat again, each caress sending a fresh shiver down Eloise's back, her stomach tightening.

The couples nearest them watched, unabashedly, their own smiles bright as if they were delighting in the show.

Pray she does not ask more of me here in front of all of them, she thought.

To Eloise's eyes, it seemed the woman's lips were growing redder with each kiss. Eloise herself began to feel dizzy and breathless as she was spun until she had no choice but to cling to her dance partner lest she collapse.

"Yes," the lady of the house purred. "Hold tight to me, little sparrow."

Eloise did. But the candlelight changed, shifting, and the shadows began to play tricks on her.

The smiles around her seemed to sharpen. The lips began to bleed, and the music darkened into something strident and alarming. Once she even thought she'd glimpsed Agnes Atwood herself, sharp-teethed, a wink in her eye, before she twirled out of sight on the arm of a gentleman.

Eloise felt as if she were falling down, down, down.

But no. Someone was lifting her, carrying her like a bride up the carved staircase while laughter from the ballroom trailed after her.

She returned to her senses in the bath.

To find herself naked in pink water was alarming in and

of itself. To find herself thusly with a stranger's eyes upon her more so.

She moved to cover her breasts.

"Don't," the lady of the house commanded. "I rather like looking at you."

Eloise stilled her hand, letting it fall back into the candlelit waters.

"You are so sweet it hurts," she said, turning away.

"I am sorry, my lady," Eloise said. The room was coming into focus now, and she was taken aback by the splendor of it. The candelabras everywhere. The porcelain tub and sinks. The gilded mirror on the wall. In it, Eloise could see her nakedness and the dark shadows collecting across her throat, as if bruised.

"May I carry you to bed now, Eloise? Or do I first need to tell you what I intend to do once we reach my chambers?"

Her heart sped up again. It wasn't that the idea displeased her. In fact, Eloise was struck again by how beautiful the woman was. She was certain she'd never seen such a beauty in all her life. What surprised her was that the woman had an interest in her at all.

"I will go to bed with you, my lady. Only—"

The lady's smile was wicked as she trailed her fingers through the water between Eloise's parted legs. "*Only...?*"

Eloise swallowed. "Only I do not know—"

Anything, she thought. *I do not know anything.*

Her grin turned mischievous again. "You also did not know how to waltz, and yet we managed, did we not?"

"We did, my lady."

"Then let us see how we do in bed." The lady rose. The water began to drain from the tub as Eloise stood, still very aware of her nakedness. Blessedly, her host wrapped her in a large soft towel, covering her.

Eloise did her best to quell the pounding of her heart, the

mounting nervousness as she followed the lady from the bathroom into the adjacent bedchamber.

The room was so large, so luxurious, that it was at least twice the size of the one-room cottage that Eloise shared with her mother. In the fireplace, flames danced, throwing light across the enormous four-poster bed.

The lady was at her back, placing one kiss after the other on Eloise's shoulder. She tugged the towel away.

"You will not need this," she said, her breath sliding along Eloise's skin. "Into the bed with you."

There was no graceful way to climb into a bed so large, so Eloise did her best, sliding across the soft covers until her back rested against the mound of pillows.

At the foot of the bed, the lady of the house undressed. She removed the dressing gown she wore, exposing a form so perfect that Eloise thought she must be an angel.

Or a devil—*For were they not once angels also?*

Then they were in bed together, their bodies close enough to touch. And much to her surprise, Eloise found she *did* want to touch her.

"You may place your hands on me." The lady's eyes suggested that she'd known exactly what Eloise had been longing for

Eloise, despite her shyness, found she could not resist.

She touched her abdomen first. Finding it cold but soft, she moved outward, first to one womanly hip, then the other. She traced the woman's candlelit curves up to her breasts.

"Kiss me," the woman instructed.

And kiss her Eloise did. On the lips. On the neck, the throat, the breasts.

When her hand slid between Eloise's legs, Eloise cried out in surprise, her lower lip trembling against the woman's breast.

"Do you not like it?" the lady asked as she filled Eloise

completely.

"I do, my lady. I do."

And when the woman began to withdraw her hand only to enter her again, Eloise discovered that she liked it so much her legs began to shake.

"Hold tight to me again, little sparrow. For I have not even begun."

Eloise soon knew what she meant by that. As she was moved from her back to her stomach. Her stomach to her knees. As she learned just what the lady was capable of. Just how many places one could be kissed from thigh to throat. How much punishment a body could take before it surrendered completely to the will of another.

Eloise did not even mind the sharp sting of each bite as they came one after the other after the other. How could she, as she tumbled breathless through the waves of her pleasure.

What a lovely price to pay, she thought, twining her fingers in her master's dark curls. *What a lovely price.*

Eloise was never seen in the village again. After her mother made a miraculous recovery, both she and Nanny wrung the truth from Mrs. Clark. Together they tried to retrace Eloise's steps to the house hidden in Briarwood. But when they knocked on the door, it was only darkness that greeted them. No parties. No lord—or lady—of the house.

Not a single soul in sight.

Heartbroken, they had no choice but to abandon their search. But as they turned away, Nanny was certain she'd heard laughter. Faint, but recognizable. She would have bet her very soul that it was Eloise's sweet voice she'd heard, twining with the soft melody of a waltz.

But when she turned toward the house again, she found its windows remained dark.

A VAMPIRE CALLS

With blood and shit drying on the collar of her white shirt, Lettie Cole stepped out onto the concrete porch for a smoke. If this is what one called a *porch*. When she was a kid, they called it a *stoop*. Now more than ever, that's exactly what it was. The earth had shifted underneath and the three steps tilted, giving the impression that at any minute she might be pitched forward onto the cracked and weed-beset sidewalk.

Lettie should've never come back. To Georgia. To this house she'd been born in. But she'd been twenty-two with a baby and no job. And that was the Cole thing to do. Her parents had made it easy. They acted as if Kai, their first grandchild, were a sack of gold rather than a chubby-cheeked girl with ash-blond curls. So when things went bad with Kai's daddy, she'd let them talk her into coming home.

Besides, there was one truth she couldn't escape.

She'd had nowhere else she could go.

But she hadn't been home long before remembering all the reasons she'd run off with the handsome blue-eyed stranger in a motorcycle jacket in the first place. Why his offer had felt like a godsend, a real chance to get her away from Merrick.

No, not everything that was wrong with her life could be blamed on her good-for-nothing brother.

But a great deal of it could be—this bruise on her right cheek for one.

Lettie touched the skin tenderly before slipping her fingers into her shirt pocket. Her heart sank when they found only cloth. Nothing. The ten cigarettes she'd rolled that morning were all gone. She'd have to roll a new one.

Oh, how she missed the days when she could simply tear open a fresh pack of Marlboros. The sound of the cellophane crinkling under her fingers. The comforting tap-tap-tap of the soft pack against her palm. That first pungent whiff of the tobacco when she pulled a cigarette free and slid the paper under her nose for a refreshing, deep inhale. The feel of the spongy filter between her fingers.

But now cigarettes were almost nine dollars a pack. On her mother's social security check and Lettie's disability check, store-bought cigarettes were an expense they just couldn't swing. So they rolled their own. And she'd have to roll one now if she wanted the cigarette she'd been thinking about for the last hour.

Leaning onto one hip, Lettie found the pouch of tobacco she kept in the tight back pocket of her jeans, a faded, nearly white pair provided courtesy of the Salvation Army.

The old woman in the front bedroom howled. If Merrick gave half a shit about his own mother, he'd get up and turn her.

But Merrick wouldn't get up. He'd stay slumped in front of the television, blue-red-white lights flashing across his skin until the comedy featuring Sandra Bullock gave way to an infomercial about a rotating toilet brush.

At least he wasn't harassing her for money.

Come on, Lettie, I know you've got ten bucks stuffed up your cunt.

When the taunting or begging didn't work, he switched to swinging.

That's probably why she preferred him like this, high as he was. At least he left her alone when he had enough heroin in his veins to tranq a horse.

She'd learned to live with a lot worse.

The window rattled over her left shoulder. "Lettie, goddamn you, just want me to die, do you? A helpless old woman and you're just gonna let me rot in here? I know you hear me hollerin'!"

Lettie's teeth clenched, grating against one another. She caught the angry words on her tongue and bit down. She took three breaths before she could trust herself to speak.

"You're not old," Lettie called. And she wasn't, not by today's standards. She was only seventy, but years of hard living had made her look like the mummy resurrected in that old film Lettie liked.

"I'll smoke this cigarette then I'll be back in, Momma. Give me five minutes."

Five minutes of peace and quiet.

"Out there smoking. Smoking! When your own mother hasn't had one all day." The woman howled again, her indignation fresh and furious. Her voice trembled and cracked at its edges. "Probably took my pack out there, too, didn't you? God forbid you let an old woman's cigarettes alone. That's the problem with you, Lettie Cole. You're too much like your damned daddy. Selfish. *Selfish* through and through."

Lettie's teeth came together in a sharp, quick gnashing that made the muscles in her neck stand out. *Selfish?* Then who else cooked every meal, cleaned every room, and wiped that woman's ass?

Yes, I'm the selfish one, she thought with a derisive laugh.

Lettie pinched some of the tobacco between her thumb and forefinger and sprinkled it into the rolling paper. The tobacco somehow smelled both bitter and sweet.

With a shaking hand, she licked the paper closed.

"Lettie, come on in here!"

"Just one minute, Momma," she said, and dug out her plastic lighter. It was black with a red tongue that she depressed with two strikes of her thumb on the flint before it sparked to life.

If Lettie was lucky, her mother's meds would kick in and she'd sleep. Then she could enjoy this cigarette without her nagging voice in her ear.

That first drag on the cigarette after wanting one for so long was one of the few pleasures that Lettie had left. She sucked in a long, slow inhale, letting the smoke roll through her nose and mouth, filling its soft chambers. Then it hit the back of the throat and burned. She didn't care about any of these minor discomforts.

It was worth it to gain the instant calm washing over her now.

Her shoulders sagged. The muscles in her jaw stopped working.

The shake in her hand steadied.

She held in the smoke longer than she needed to—this was no joint.

Then she exhaled in a slow, controlled stream too. She tried to relish it.

The ritual of it.

The smell. The taste of tobacco on her tongue.

The night was complete and total.

The smell of burnt charcoal from someone's grill lingered. Lettie thought maybe one of the neighbors farther down the road had barbequed their supper. As the twilight thickened, three small black shapes darted across the road.

Raccoons, their bushy tails and hunched backs clear in the streetlight for a moment before they disappeared into the thick shadows cloaking the houses on the other side.

Crickets and cicadas began their nightly chorus. The cicadas in particular seemed to swell, and Lettie remembered some fact about how they only emerged from underground once every seventeen years.

It had been seventeen years since her daddy had died, and now her mother seemed to be on death's door. Maybe cicadas weren't the only thing that adhered to an unspoken rhythm.

When the cigarette burned down to her fingers, Lettie contemplated rolling another. Her mother hadn't called out again. The windows to the bedroom remained dark. All the house was dark except the television. She hoped her mother was asleep. One craning look through the front window told her that Merrick was still sleeping too, his chin on his chest as the white-blue light of the TV danced over his sallow skin.

God he was thin, skeletal even, slumped in the over-stuffed recliner as he was.

It was cooler out here on the crooked stoop than inside the dark house. The house was too hot even with the windows open. She didn't want to go inside until she was so dead tired that she'd fall asleep straight away. If she wasn't tired enough, she'd only lie there, on top of her covers, sweating and tossing on the stiff mattress.

She could go around back, over the busted chain-link fence with a flashlight and screwdriver and try to work the switch that turned on the air conditioner manually—but that was both loud and unreliable. Sometimes she banged on that thing for thirty minutes and it still wouldn't kick on. No, it wasn't worth the risk of waking everyone.

She was halfway through her cigarette when the distinct feeling of being watched crawled along her skin. The hair pricked to attention at the back of her neck as sweat slid from her hairline down beneath her collar.

Then she noticed the silence. The cicadas and the crickets had stopped. Even the robins with a fondness for evening songs had shut up.

Her stomach dropped.

She looked up, her eyes sweeping the dark lawn and empty street, and saw nothing. But for a reason she wasn't entirely sure of, her gaze fixed on the large tree in the center of the front lawn. It was an old, mammoth oak with Spanish moss hanging like a shroud from its twisted black branches. It had been here before the Coles came to this part of Southern Georgia and it would probably be here long after the last of them had left.

She stared into the branches but saw no movement. And yet—there was something about the trunk that was different than it was before.

She stared. She stared until a shadow broke away and stepped into the moonlight.

"Fucking shit."

She stood, managed that much but remained frozen on the stoop. Tobacco spilled out onto the concrete.

A pale hand swept the Spanish moss aside as one might part a curtain. For a moment, he was impossibly pale and gleaming. But then a cloud moved and the stranger was cloaked in darkness once more.

Just a man.

Probably another junky looking for a fix. His cheeks were as hollow and gaunt as her brother's.

"He ain't got any," Lettie called out. She tried to look casual. Unconcerned. But her muscles stayed as tight as a wound clock. Only a fool would relax around a junkie looking for a fix. "I just watched him shoot up the last of it.

He'll probably come looking for you or Donnie or whoever when he wakes up."

The shadowed man stopped advancing. He remained ten paces from Lettie, his hands in the pockets of his nice suit.

Nice suit.

She ain't ever seen a junkie in a nice suit before. But who else would he be, coming to the house at this hour, if not one of the guys Merrick ran with? He couldn't be a scrapper who spent his days pawning televisions, radios, or metal, whatever he could get his hands on.

And the man certainly wasn't here for Helen Cole, not unless the woman had gone and hired a lawyer to rework her will.

That only left her. Lettie. But he couldn't be here for her.

Are you sure? that little voice said. *It's you he's looking at.*

He had that indulgent, interested grin that she'd seen on many a man's face. She wasn't the most beautiful woman in the world—life had been too hard. And she'd drunk too much, and that was the reason Kaiya had left. She'd taken off, gone to college, and gotten some decent job in Chicago.

Lettie was proud of her for that. That her girl had escaped a life that still had such a hold on Lettie.

A life that she was ready to fight for even now.

"I don't want any trouble," she said, and noticed, much to her dismay, that her voice shook. Her hands had gone up and closed around a gold cross at her throat. It'd been a gift from Kaiya for Mother's Day and she'd yet to take it off. Mostly because she was afraid if she took it off for even a minute, Merrick would run off with it, pawning it to the first shop that would take real gold.

"If he owes you money or something I've got nothing to do with that."

The stranger continued to stare, the smile widening ever

so slightly, the head cocking an inch to one side. The eyes were flat-water black in the dark. Shark eyes.

Maybe it didn't matter that he was in a nice suit. Maybe he was one of them so-called drug *lords*.

"I came to see you, actually," the man said at last. His voice wasn't what she'd expected. A harsh, grasping voice like Merrick's, that's what she'd expected. But his was sweet and melodic.

"I don't know you," she said. But even as she did, some part of her mind tsked.

"Sure you do," he said, his shoulders relaxed, the smile easy.

"I don't remember meeting you," she said, flicking the end of her cigarette out of habit. Nothing happened. The ash had fallen minutes ago, and the end of the burnt paper sat dark and wilted. "And even if I did, I didn't invite you here. Why are you here?"

His smile spread, a shark grin to match the shark eyes. "Oh, I get around to everyone eventually. Sooner or later."

"Listen, man. I don't know what kind of game you're playing, but I'm not interested. I just put Momma to bed, so don't come up in here causing trouble. I'll call the police quicker than you can spit. I don't need another sick junkie on my hands. The one I got in there is enough."

She jabbed a finger over her shoulder.

This is the part where he begs, she thought. *Come on, just five dollars, or ten. I know you've got that.*

That's what he would say.

Except that they say it every other day until it's thirty or forty a week and hundreds a month, and neither she nor Momma could pull that kind of money from thin air.

The sliding bills that kept growing from month to month could attest to that.

They'd slid so far that now it seemed she paid more *fees*

than *bills*. Late fees, reconnection fees, interest fees, and surcharge fees. Things those assholes slapped on the top to make the bill harder to pay.

Lettie never understood that part. If she could pay the damn bill she wouldn't be stuck with a fee, now would she? But it was not being able to pay that cost more? Now what kind of sense did that make?

"I *am* sick. You're right about that," the man said, the smile faltering at its corners. "But it's not because of drugs."

She relit her cigarette. "What've you got?"

He didn't answer.

"Hepatitis?" she asked. Then on second thought, "AIDS?"

Because she knew about those. She'd lost three friends to the latter and knew two living with the former.

He shook his head. "Let's call it malnourishment."

Malnourishment. That was another one of those paperback words. And she knew it in relation to other words found on the same yellowed page: *hunger, need, desire.*

Not a junkie, her heart said as it began to kick wildly in her chest. A goddamn rapist. She'd been raped before and had no desire in revisiting the experience. But then again, if she screamed, who would help her? The bedridden woman dying in the dark? The comatose addict in the duct-taped recliner?

No one. Not a damn person would make it to her in time.

"How about you come back at a decent hour," she said. "Didn't your momma ever teach you not to be creeping up on women in the dark?"

"No," he said, flashing teeth. "My mother died before she could teach me much of anything. But that was a long time ago. And I have business with you, Lettie Cole."

He might as well have stuck the red cherry of a cigarette to her skin, given the way she started. She leapt up, intent on running inside, locking the door behind her, and reaching her mother's bedroom as fast as she could. She would lock herself inside and call the police. As much as she hated the police, there had to be something, surely *something* that she could use to stave him off until they arrived.

Only she didn't so much as stand before rough hands seized her. She was yanked backward off the porch and pulled up.

Up.

Into the dark sky.

Wind whipped and whistled around her, and when she opened her mouth to scream, no sound came out.

A rock-hard arm had wrapped itself around her, pinning her against a boulder of a body.

All the spit evaporated in her mouth.

All that came out was a dry, desperate wheeze.

Their little piece of Georgia had no more than six or seven thousand people, according to the last census, but she still thought she could make out Highway 44 and the Jackson Road four-way with its corner store advertising tackle, bait, and line on one side and the mechanic across the street, with its cracked, flickering sign.

It was all in miniature now.

So high, she thought, and the terror clawing her throat started to squeeze her all the harder.

Not any higher, she thought. *Please God, not any higher.*

But they still rose until even those few discernible features in the landscape disappeared. All that was left was darkness.

Then they began to descend.

Her guts were replaced by that drop one feels when cresting the hill of a rollercoaster.

She clutched the arm pinning her as if it were a safety belt on such a ride and if it popped up at any minute she would fall out and plummet to her death. She tried to imagine which part of the world she'd hit—the train tracks behind the Pig and Swig? Her brain a mess of bone and pink matter on the rails? Would she hit someone's roof, and would it be enough to send her crashing through a tangle of limbs and broken boards into someone's bathtub or a dark bedroom?

The world caught up to her quickly. They hit the earth, but her hips and legs didn't shatter.

She fell forward on impact, her hands going out in front to catch herself.

The earth was cold and soft. It gave under her palms. Pain still shot up both her arms and into her shoulders. Her arms folded and she found herself cheek to cheek with long grasses.

She smelled death on that warm breeze. The cloistering stench of hot, rotting meat hit her, and with it the clarity that she *would* die here.

"Where have you brought me?" she asked. It was a small voice. An uncertain voice, like the one Kai had used for so many of her questions: *Where are you going, Mommy? Do you know that man, Mommy? Will you really be home tonight, Mommy?*

"I am not one for idle conversation. Instead of trying to convince you of what I am, I simply thought I would show you."

She recoiled.

Shivers crept along her spine despite the heat.

The man who wasn't a man disappeared. So fast that Lettie didn't see him move. One minute he was a white specter in front of her, the moonlit water shimmering behind him, the next, the lake was in full view.

She looked around and spotted him twenty feet away. Something kicked and twitched in its grip.

A rabbit, she realized. A wild gray rabbit with white tufted feet kicked at the man—who was not a man. He brought the rabbit back to where she sat, his one milk-white hand around the creature's throat.

"What are you—" she began, but didn't finish.

He bit the rabbit.

Except *bit* wasn't quite the right word. Once when Kai had been angry with her for one reason or another, she'd bitten Lettie on the hand hard enough to draw blood. Red had filled up those tiny half-moon crescents in her skin.

What this creature did was worse. Savage.

He tore the rabbit's throat out.

Blood spilled down the front of its chest. Wet, sucking sounds accompanied the rabbit's wild kicking.

But the kicking didn't last.

When he finished, he dropped the creature the way a child drops a toy.

Somehow, despite the shock, Lettie found the will to speak. "You're a vampire?"

Because that was the word that rose to her through the shock of her mind.

In books, if something drank blood, it was a vampire. It didn't matter if it also ate your soul or tore you to shreds, blood-drinking was a vampire thing.

"Yes, that's one word for it. And would you like to know what a vampire wants with *you*?"

"Well, *yeah*. If you're going to kill me, I'd at least like to know *why*."

"How sagacious of you, Lettie Cole. I didn't know you had it in you."

"How what?"

"Haven't found that word in your reading yet?"

"How do you know I read?" she asked, still clutching her cross.

"Oh, I've been watching you for some time. I always like to be sure."

The idea chilled her. That some man—who was not a man—had been watching her for God only knew how long.

What had he seen? Surely nothing she would be proud of.

"Why did you bring me here?" she asked. "Is this where you kill people?"

Because he was going to kill her, wasn't he?

"When you are as old as I am," he said, "you know a great many places to hide bodies."

"Answer the question."

She was surprised to realize the idea of dying here, looking up into the stars, filled her with peace.

No more dealing with my mother. No more heroin. None of it. Kai might wonder where I've gone, but we both know she's better off without me.

She loved her girl. Loved her more than anything. Lettie's only regret was that she had not protected her.

"Are you going to make it that easy?" the vampire asked.

"What?"

"Will you make it that easy for me to kill you?" He sounded bored. As if her refusal to become his sport wasn't what he was hoping for.

She threw her hands up to the sky, then swept them toward the surrounding forest. "I can't outrun you. I know how hard you held me. What's the point in fighting if you are faster and stronger?"

He regarded her. "Do you think your daughter would make the same reply?"

No, that knowing voice said. *No, she would hurl rocks at you. She would jump into the lake and swim. She'd rip off one of these branches and try to plunge it through your heart.*

The vampire's smile grew. "Why don't you put up such a fight?"

Lettie said nothing. She let the swell of cicada song fill the air between them.

"I've listened to you for a long time," he said, taking a step toward her. "In your thoughts you think of Kaiya most often. You miss her, but you're glad she's gone. What an odd thought for a mother."

"I want what's best for her. I'm not what's best."

"But you miss her."

"Of course I miss her. I'm her mother. I miss her every day."

I wish I could see her every day.

"Then why not see her? Why not be in her life? Hell, why not *live*?"

"Kai has nothing to do with this," she said, her voice cracked. "You stay away from her."

"I'm not interested in your daughter," he said.

"But you're interested in me?"

"Yes," he replied simply. "I'm interested in you."

A question danced on the tip of her tongue. A dangerous question. "To kill me or ..."

"Or to fuck you?" His smile bordered on a sneer.

Her breath sharpened, and as if he could hear her panic, he laughed. At the end of his laughter he said, "I've never taken a woman against her will. Not once in my *very* long life. You have a choice, Lettie Cole."

"To have sex or not?"

"To be my victim or your brother's."

She wasn't sure she heard him right. "What?"

"Your brother is planning to kill you. The moment that old woman dies—and it will be any day now—he plans to end your life so that he can sell that house and have what's left of her pathetic estate for himself."

"You can't know that."

"I know it as surely as I know you. Your regrets. All the mistakes you feel you've made as a mother. How desperate you are to atone for them and how out of reach such atonement seems."

Lettie didn't know what to say. Was he lying? He was a devil, after all.

But then why did his words ring of the truth?

"I am old and I am hungry," he said, as if this explained everything. "I take life to sustain my own. I will take yours or I will take your brother's. It makes no difference to me."

"You want me to condemn my brother just because you say he *might* kill me?"

"It's just us. Let's be honest," he said. "You've also wished him dead. More than once. The only difference is that your heart isn't in it. Believe me when I say that his *is*."

"I don't believe you. I don't believe any of this."

"When the woman dies, your time is up. Know that."

The bite hurt. It was hard, a momentary jab of pain through her neck and shoulder as if she had turned her head too fast. Lettie cried out. Her whole body went limp in his embrace.

It was the bite, she realized. There was something in the bite that paralyzed its victims, rendering them weak.

It didn't matter. She was being bitten. She felt the warm sucking at her throat and her limp limbs unable to help her. Even her voice couldn't be summoned.

You said I had time, her mind bleated frantically at the creature clutching her. At the beast lifting into the air with her limp body in his arms.

Oh, you have time. A smooth voice slid right through her. *We are only just beginning.*

LETTIE WOKE IN HER BED TO THE SOUND OF HER MOTHER screaming.

"Lettie! Lettie Jean! Why do you do this to an old

woman?" her mother called from the next room. "Gonna let an old woman die in her bed?"

Lettie's heart skyrocketed in her chest, kicking wildly the way that rabbit's foot had twitched.

It was a dream, some part of her mind said. Just a dream. *No strange man showed up here last night. No strange man flew you through the air to his secret lakeside killing ground.*

The twitching white rabbit's foot growing still—*it was just a dream.*

"Lettie Cole!" her mother cried, and the wall vibrated with a sudden, wild thumping. Her mother's fist struck the plaster where their two rooms joined.

You fell asleep reading and dreamed it all, she told herself.

There had been no vampire. No ultimatum to choose her life or her brother's. And yet, she wanted it to be real. She wanted some divine—or demonic—intervention to swoop in and save her from the cursed life that was suffocating her.

From her loneliness.

Until that vampire spoke to her the way it had—dream or not—Lettie hadn't realized just how lonely she was.

"Coming, Momma," she called, and rose from the bed.

All the blood rushed to her head. For a moment, she swayed on her feet. She took two steps and her hip connected with the white dresser, and the mirror sitting on top of it swayed. Something toppled over and skittered across the top of the dresser, but she didn't see what.

She pinched her eyes shut. She stood there, listening to the panicked drumming of her own heart, until the spots in front of her eyes disappeared.

"Lettie, what in the world! Heaven above, I swear if—"

But whatever her mother swore never reached her. The words were lost in the creak of her bedroom door as she pulled it open and stepped into the blaring light. The godawful blaring light. It hit her like a slap across the face.

A migraine, she thought. *I'm having a migraine. That's all.*

Her eyes hurt like hell.

Somehow, with a groping outstretched hand, she found her mother's door handle and opened it.

The stench struck her. No wonder the woman had been carrying on.

"I'm here, Momma," she said. "We'll get you cleaned right up."

Lettie opened the window to let the fresh air in.

Her mother prattled on, cursing and hissing her indignation.

"After all I've done for you, and you have the nerve to sleep like the damned dead and ignore me all morning," she said, her wiry hair matted to the side of her head with sweat.

"I'm sorry. I had a migraine. I couldn't get up."

"Couldn't get up!" the old woman scoffed. "No. *I* can't get up. Last I checked, you still have the two legs God gave you and a mother who keeps a roof over your head."

Lettie pulled back the covers to inspect the damage.

She looked away, as if that would keep her from vomiting.

"Yes, take a good hard look," her mother said bitterly. "Take a good look at what's coming for you, Lettie."

Maybe not for me, she thought as she pushed the wheelchair over to the side of the bed and angled it so that her mother could be eased into it.

She got her down the hall to the bathroom and into the tub.

Even though her mother was lighter than she'd ever been, it wasn't easy to maneuver her around. And the woman's vehement resistance didn't help.

She slapped Lettie's hands as she tried to adjust the taps.

"It's cold!"

"Give it one second," Lettie said patiently, refraining from her desire to stick her shit-slick hand into the woman's face and cry, *Look at this. Look at what I put up with from you, and yet I don't say a damn word.*

The water warmed.

The bathing part was easy enough, Lettie outside the tub, reaching in. Her mother held on to the silver bar the case worker had installed for them after her first round of treatment. She washed and lathered and soaped until the water in the tub no longer ran brown but clear and only white soap bubbles collected around the drain.

As her mother enjoyed the last of the warm water, Lettie washed her hands, wiped down the chair with disinfectant, and stripped the bed. All of it would go into the wash.

"Feel better?" Lettie asked as she returned to the bathroom.

"I'm hungry," her mother said, those eyes cold on hers. "It's got to be nearly ten and you ain't fed me a thing. Trying to speed this along, are you? Can't wait to heave me in the ground, I bet."

"Don't say that," Lettie said. "I told you I had a headache."

She helped her mother to stand and climb out of the tub.

"Likely story. You look like hell. You've been out drinking again, and probably with some man. Just look at your damn neck. And where the hell are my cigarettes?"

She's so thin, Lettie thought as the towel-wrapped crone settled into the wheelchair. She saw every vertebra in the woman's spine, and her wrists felt thin enough to break.

"Look at yourself in the mirror and tell me you weren't with no man last night," her mother hissed, adjusting herself, breathless in the creaking chair.

"What are you—" Lettie began to protest, but as soon as she turned and saw herself in the bright vanity, the words died on her lips.

In the mirror, she saw for herself. The whole right side of her throat was bruised.

She lifted her blond hair, which had gone dark at the roots, off her neck and leaned forward. Mark after mark overlapped on the side of her throat, with the tell-tale red welts of sucking on the raised skin. But it was the bruise underneath. The bruise that had already begun to go yellow around the edges.

"A damn hickey. Like you're in high school," her mother said. "Lord help me, I raised you better than that."

"This isn't a hickey," Lettie said, unable to tear her eyes away from her throat. "This is a bruise. And I haven't had anything to drink in years."

"I didn't fall off the turnip truck yesterday," she replied.

Of course, she hadn't expected her mother to believe her.

All her life her mother had made excuses for the marks left on her body by men.

All her life, her mother had protected everyone but Lettie.

Why in the world would now be any different?

ONCE SHE SET HER MOTHER DOWN AT THE TABLE WITH TWO biscuits from a can and a jar of strawberry jam, she got to rolling the day's cigarettes for them both. It was easier with the machine and without Merrick home to torment her while she worked. She had to admit, she liked the repetitive action of the machine. It reminded her a little of working in the factory back when Kai was seven or eight. It was a steady job and the money hadn't been so bad. And even though it had been hard and sent her home every night with blisters, that mind-numbing repetition had its appeal.

She hadn't had to think when she pulled the swaths of bundled newspapers from the machine and stacked them on the conveyor.

And that's how it was now with the cigarettes. She placed the paper in its place and the tobacco in its place and the filters in their slot and just turned knobs. And there. Perfectly good cigarettes. Except this machine was a little old and sometimes it caught up on the corner and tore the paper and the tobacco would spill into the slot. When that happened, she had to blow it out and make room for the next one.

She rolled thirty cigarettes in the time it took her mother to eat one biscuit and pick apart the other.

"You're quiet this morning," her mother remarked. "Usually you talk my damn ear off and I praise Jesus every minute of it that I'm nearly deaf. But today I ain't seen your lips move but once or twice. You coming down with the flu or something? Or was it that boyfriend of yours keeping you up all night?"

"I don't have a boyfriend, Momma," she said.

Her mother harrumphed. "Yes, you fell and the vacuum hose attacked you, I suppose."

"Where's Merrick?" Lettie asked.

"He came in and kissed me goodbye this morning. Told me he had to meet up with someone. Who knows."

The patched leather recliner with its scuffs and loose stuffing sat vacant. A strip of light came through the open window and illuminated a new scorched black cigarette burn.

He's hunting then, she thought. *For his next fix, maybe. Or for a way to make some quick cash.*

She'd better check around to see if she still had her money. There were enough food stamps in the house to get her and Momma through to the end of the month. These biscuits crumbling on the way to her mother's mouth, the one-dollar jar of generic jelly. All of it was purchased with food stamps.

"You haven't eaten your biscuit," her mother said.

Lettie looked down to see that it was true. The lump of browned bread sat untouched beside a gleaming fork stretching diagonal across the plate.

"I'm not hungry," she said, and was surprised to find it was true. This was the first day she could remember in a very long time when she had no appetite at all.

Her mother's withered brows rose. "Is that so?"

"I told you I'm not feeling well," Lettie said, pushing the biscuit toward her. The woman should eat it anyway. If anyone here was a bag of bones, it was her. "I think it's a migraine."

"Could be. Or a hangover. You're squinting."

"The light is hurting my eyes," Lettie said. And it was true.

Lettie looked down at the rolled cigarette lined up in front of the machine and counted thirty-six in total. They lay in tight little rolls like neat paper sausages.

She slid two cigarettes over to her mother, as well as her own plastic lighter with its red tongue. That left thirty-four.

"Where's your cigarette case, Momma?" Lettie asked.

"My bedside table, I think."

Lettie found the case on the floor by the window. When she inspected the window, she saw a small chip gouged out of a lower pane.

So this is what she threw last night. Probably wishes she could hit me with worse.

Lettie picked up the case.

Back at the kitchen table, her mother was already halfway through her first cigarette.

Lettie watched her enjoy it as she filled the cigarette case with twenty of the ones she'd rolled.

Gray smoke drifted toward the ceiling in a thin, languid stream as her mother tilted her head back and exhaled with all the luxury of a woman who might have been very beautiful before she married two mean, philandering men and gave birth to a brood of reckless children.

A woman who'd kept herself clean of all that and yet had been the one to get sick. *God's punishing me*, she'd said countless times, for as long as Lettie could remember.

God's given it to me good. All of y'all are my cross to bear, and I don't know what I've done to deserve it. Was it feeding you? Keeping you in good clothes? Sending you off to school? I suppose if y'all are demons I should've drowned you in the tub like kittens. Then maybe God would be pleased.

You could be the one to end her suffering, a voice said. *Drown her in the tub if you wish. You have that power, Lettie Cole.*

Lettie startled at the voice. It was the same one she'd heard last night by the lake.

"No, I'm not like her," Lettie said, snapping the silver case closed.

Her mother jerked with a start, her parted lips opening in surprise. "What'd you say?"

I'm not like you.

"Here's your cigarettes, Momma. Let's put your soaps on."

A ROUGH KNOCK ON THE FRONT DOOR MADE LETTIE turn. Her heart went off like a rabbit in her chest. She was in dishwater up to her elbows and her mother wasn't getting up from the chair where she sat watching a young man with pouty lips tell the teary-eyed girl in front of him that he would leave his wife, he promised, he just needed more time. They kissed.

Someone pounded on the door again.

"I'm coming," Lettie called, hoping her voice carried over the blaring vows of the young couple. She turned to her mother. "Turn it down. Someone's at the door."

"Your boyfriend," her mother said, without taking her

eyes off the man squeezing the young woman's upper arms, testing them as if they were fruit to purchase from the market. "He looks like your daddy."

"Who?"

Her mother pointed at the screen with two fingers balancing a cigarette between them. Gray smoke curled and rose toward the ceiling. She wasn't even smoking it. She just liked to hold it.

The hand rapped at the door once more.

"Just a minute!"

When Lettie pulled the door open, she found a man on the porch. But it wasn't the vampire. It wasn't even a police officer. As nervous as the police made Lettie, she'd welcome them right in, feed them a biscuit and coffee and maybe even the last of the chocolate ice cream if they were arriving to tell her, *I'm so sorry, Miss Cole, I hate to inform you that your brother is dead. We found him shot in a drug deal gone wrong.*

That's the kind of thing they said on television, but Lettie frankly didn't care where they found him. They could find him in a drug den or a ditch or even in their mother's rusted-out van which he drove around town.

Without Merrick, maybe her mother would finally appreciate all that she did for her. And Lettie herself would never have to worry about her brother's fists again.

"Hello, ma'am, good day."

"Hello," Lettie said, warily eyeing the man in the white polo and clipboard. It was an election year. If he wanted signatures he'd come to the wrong house.

"I'm with the city department," he began.

"Is there a problem?" she asked.

"Your meter's stopped," he said. He gave her an apologetic smile, as if this news was his fault. His eyes slid down the side of her throat before looking away. "We'll have to send someone out here to replace it."

A stone dropped into her stomach. "How much does that cost?"

"Oh, nothing," he said. "The city pays for the replacement and maintenance of the meters. It was likely damaged in a storm. But I wanted to show you something before I leave."

"Nothing serious, I hope."

He flashed her another one of those good ol' boy apologetic grins. "You aren't the squeamish type, are you?" he asked, trying again not to look at her neck. "Your husband or someone home?"

"I live here with my mother and brother," she said.

"Is he home now?"

"No."

"Well, would you mind stepping outside for a minute to have a look?"

"What the hell is going on?" her mother croaked over the blaring television.

"Just a city person, Momma," she said. "Something's wrong with the meter."

Lettie stepped out of the house and pulled the door closed behind her. "Make it quick."

He waved her toward the back shed. The backyard sloped upward toward a dense tree line. The woods beyond stretched on for a mile or more before running into the back of a shopping center. As children, they used to walk through those woods and come out on the other side, where they traded their dimes for soda and penny candy. But Lettie hadn't been in there since she came back to Georgia with a baby.

"It's just back here," the meter reader said, and led her to the space behind the white garden shed where the trees began.

If he was going to rape her, kill her, and leave her for dead, this would be the place to do it, she thought. Just pull her into the woods and be done with it. No one would know for a long time. He'd get into his company truck, drive away, and her momma would probably tell the police that she'd asked for it.

"When I was tracing the lines, looking for storm damage, I came across this," the man said, crouching down in the weeds.

This is it, Lettie thought. *I'll kneel down beside him and he'll attack me.*

But the man didn't move. Instead, he pointed at the patch of dirt four or five feet ahead of them.

She saw the bright splotch of red. Then the white fur.

The rabbit. *My god, he brought the rabbit and left it here behind the shed for me to find.*

"Awful, I know. You got dogs, Miss Cole?"

"No," she said. "None at all."

"Ah well, I thought maybe a dog got ahold of these and tore 'em up. They don't look eaten. Most of the meat is still there but not much blood. Maybe a raccoon? They'll eat anything they can get their little paws on. My sister had a whole coop of chickens torn apart by a pack of them raccoons. Heads bit off and everything."

Lettie's stomach turned.

"Sorry, I'm not trying to be graphic."

"It's okay," Lettie said, but it didn't sound okay. She sounded like a little girl on the verge of vomiting up her breakfast. Only Lettie remembered she hadn't had breakfast. Or lunch either. "So you think there's something in the woods?"

"Got to be," he said. "I found four more just like it."

Five dead rabbits in the yard. It felt like an omen. Like that old song her daddy used to sing. *One crow silver, two crows gold...* Was that how it went? Or was she confusing it with the story about a king and his pies?

"Anyway, I just wanted you to know in case you've got a little dog or something. You don't want to let it run loose in the yard at night. It could get hurt."

I've been watching you for a long time, the vampire had said.

Had he? Perhaps right here at the edge of the woods, looking into her house at night while the lights were on. Seeing straight into her world while he ripped open the throats of whatever pitiful creature he had captured.

Lettie turned toward the house, and sure enough, there was her bedroom window. Clear as day.

Anyone standing here in the dark shadows between the shed and the trees—well, they could see in just fine.

JUST PAST NINE THAT NIGHT, HER MOTHER FELL ASLEEP IN THE battered recliner with a cigarette still smoldering between her index and middle fingers. The minute Lettie plucked it from her grasp, the woman's eyes snapped open, rolling in their sockets before locking on hers. The pupils were narrow and that hateful grin twisted her face, aging her ten years in an instant.

"Quit stealing my cigarettes, damn it," she rasped, her throat dry from sleep.

"I'm not stealing it. I'm trying to keep you from burning the house down," Lettie said, and rubbed the red-hot end of the cigarette into the ashtray gingerly so as not to crush it. Then she laid the remainder against the glass rim. "Come on, let's get you into bed."

"But I was watching that." Her mother gestured at the television.

Lettie moved so that her mother could see the riveting infomercial about a robot vacuum. "This? Think we need this, do you? Come on."

Lettie got her mother into the rickety wheelchair with its

big silver wheels and pushed her out of the living room, down the hall, and into her bedroom.

It smelled of grass and Lysol.

Lettie had given the room a rub-down after dinner. Once the sun had set, she'd felt marvelously better.

"There you go," Lettie said. "Fresh clean sheets. Doesn't it feel nice?"

Her mother grunted something that could almost be mistaken for appreciation and scooted in between the sheets that Lettie held open for her. White sheets with gray triangles in alternating patterns to match the gray comforter on top. Lettie rolled the comforter down past the old woman's knees because even with the overhead fan going, swinging wildly as it had always done, and both of the windows open, the room would stay warm.

"Fold it nice," her mother clucked. "Don't rumple it like you always do."

I should let him take you, Lettie thought. *Let him take you so you don't suffer no more.*

A cold voice laughed. *So she doesn't suffer? Or you?*

Lettie shook these thoughts away. "Goodnight, Momma."

In her bedroom, she turned on the light and began to undress for bed.

The wind through the open window licked her bare breasts and stomach. And as she bent down to grab an over-sized t-shirt that said *Maui* in an arrangement of tropical flora across the front, it struck her.

The smell of death. She thought of the rabbits. Of the wide-open view of her bedroom from the dark tree line.

Lettie froze. Heart racing, she remained bent over the drawer, the t-shirt crushed in her hand. Without standing, she pulled it over her head and wiggled her arms through.

I'm being stupid, she thought. *If he's seen my tits, he's seen them already.*

Yet, she found herself turning, giving her back to the open window as she pulled her night clothes into place.

A sudden wild and panicked certainty overtook her then. She knew if she turned toward her bedroom window, she'd see his skull-like face there, staring at her with those shark-black eyes and red rabbit blood smeared across his lips.

She turned slowly.

The window was dark.

Still she battled with the childish urge to run to her bed and throw herself under the covers, pulling them up over her head so they could work their ancient magic, a magic that every child instinctively understood.

You're losing your damn mind, she told herself. *There are already too many crazies in this house. No need to throw your head in the toilet too.*

She wasn't sure when she fell asleep, but she woke to her brother shaking her.

"Where the fuck is it!"

Lettie began screaming. This startled him. Had she ever expressed confusion, anger, or distrust when he snuck into her room? Certainly. But she'd never come out of a dead sleep screaming bloody murder.

Except Lettie had thought it was the vampire. That was reason enough to scream.

"Shut up!" he snapped. "Shut up or you'll wake Momma!"

She clutched the covers. "Christ, Merrick, what are you doing?"

"I said, where the hell is it?"

She sat up. "*What?*"

"The money, where is it?"

Not *your* money. *The* money. That was his way of rewriting the story, evading the fact that he was taking what didn't belong to him.

"I don't have any," she said.

"You're lying. Where is it? It was in the sock drawer yesterday and—"

She didn't hear the rest. Nothing after *yesterday*.

Yesterday. He was in my room, stealing my stuff. It must have been in the morning while she'd slept, before she'd gotten up to care for their mother.

No wonder he'd left early.

"If it's not there I don't know where it is." And this was true.

True or not, he still struck her. And when her answer didn't change, he struck her again.

She fought back. She always did. Even if it meant more pain, she struck out, she kicked, and she pulled his hair when he pulled hers.

A weak fist hit the wall. "Stop it in there, you two! I said stop it! Why can't y'all ever get along?"

"She started it!" Merrick called, his pockmarked cheeks puffing and deflating with his heavy breaths.

"The hell I did, you fucker!"

Merrick lunged for her again, his hands closing around her throat.

As her vision began to darken, a crash came from her mother's room. Something toppled. The old woman let out a choked cry.

It was the cut nature of that cry that stopped Merrick. The spell of the moment, of his rage, evaporated as surely as it came. He stumbled back from Lettie, pushing her away from him as if she had been the one attacking.

"Momma?" he called.

Nothing. The old woman remained silent.

"Momma!"

He disappeared from the room, leaving Lettie in the dark, chest heaving, trying to catch her breath.

Merrick began screaming in earnest then. "Momma! Momma! What's wrong?"

Lettie stumbled to the doorway of their mother's bedroom and peered into the darkness. Merrick was bent over the old woman. Her eyes were gaping at the ceiling, showing more whites around those milky-blue irises than ever before. And her fists were curled in front of her chest as if she'd try to claw at something.

Merrick wouldn't stop screaming. "Call an ambulance!"

Lettie didn't. She was looking at the closet door, at the slit of darkness there. Lettie was sure it had been closed when she'd put her mother to bed.

Are you in there? she thought. *Hiding in the dark, watching us?*

Did you kill my mother?

"For fuck's sake, Lettie, call someone! She's not breathing!"

Lettie picked up the phone and dialed 911, but she kept her eyes on the dark closet, half expecting the monster to come out and kill them too.

But the door never opened. Not before the ambulance arrived. Not before the paramedics entered the room and collected the body that had once belonged to her mother. Not before Merrick had climbed into the back of the ambulance.

The paramedics said there was only room for one of them. Lettie didn't insist it be her.

She watched the ambulance, sirens blaring and lights swirling, drive off into the night, leaving her on the porch.

Alone.

That's when the tears came.

Tears for her mother. Tears for herself.

She was still crying when the vampire finally showed himself.

"I thought you had to be invited into the house," she said.

"I was invited," he told her.

"By who?"

"You."

"Me! I never told you to hurt my family. Why are you doing this?" She wiped her tears away.

"You prayed for this, Lettie."

"I—"

"You prayed for this every night. For years. That someone would come and liberate you from this hell of a life."

And that's the thing about prayer. You can't ever be sure who will answer you.

THEY CALLED IT A CEREMONY OF LIFE, THE SMALL GATHERING at the funeral home. Lettie had found this to be absurd, given that whatever they had been doing for the last fifteen years in that shell of a house, was by no stretch of the imagination what Lettie could call *living*.

People who went out into the world. People who saw things, did things. They were alive.

Lettie—she didn't know what she was.

And that's what troubled her most as she sat there looking at the remains of her mother in a plastic jug, the so-called urn, and gave halfhearted nods to the handful of people who came to the funeral home to pay their respects. People from church, who hadn't spoken to her mother, let alone visited her, in years. Two distant cousins who were— undoubtedly—just sniffing around to see if there was any money to be had. When they discovered there wouldn't be unless the house was sold, they left without so much as a goodbye.

Merrick had been there the whole day. And he'd even been kind to her—kinder than he'd been in ages. Lettie might have died from shock at such treatment if she wasn't lost in the fog of her own grief. Everything seemed like a dream. And the worst part was she felt as if she was waking up to a terrible, terrible reality, worse than the awful dream she'd been having.

It wasn't until her mother was gone, the one fixture of her days so completely removed, that Lettie was left with a terrible truth. She didn't know who she was without her family. She didn't know who she was if there was no one to look after. She had derived her entire reason for existing from caring for that hateful old woman. Without her—

"How are you holding up?" Merrick asked.

He was still wearing the mask of concern he'd plastered on his face since he returned from the hospital to tell her what she'd already known—their mother was dead.

Lettie said nothing.

"Listen," Merrick said. "I don't want to fight. Momma wouldn't want that, and now that she's gone there's just us. You know that, right?"

There's Kai, a little voice said.

"So I don't want to fight," he said.

"Me neither," Lettie said.

He clapped her on the shoulder as if she'd just passed some difficult test. An empty reassurance. It took everything Lettie had not to recoil.

"Good," he said. "Then let's go home."

Lettie moved through her days only half connected to the world. This out-of-body experience was exacerbated by Merrick, who continued to be kinder to her than he'd ever been. It made her feel as if she'd stepped into some adjacent reality where brothers didn't hit you, didn't steal from you, or lie to you.

Then to make things more bizarre, Merrick announced he had a new job.

"It's just driving a forklift, but we need the money now that Momma's social security check ain't comin' in."

He wasn't wrong about that. When their mother died, she took the bulk of their income with her. Lettie was still supposed to get her monthly disability check, but not for weeks.

"I'll be gone every day from six to three. Will you be okay here by yourself?"

Will I be by myself? she wondered, looking toward the shed in the backyard, where all those dead rabbits were decomposing out of sight.

"Sure," she said. "Don't worry about me."

"When I get back, we should talk about the house. I'm thinking we should sell it and get a smaller place. Something cheaper and easier for us to take care of. Max tells me we can get a lot of money for it."

"Who's Max?" Lettie asked.

"A friend."

A druggie friend, she thought. But she didn't say so.

Merrick stooped and placed a kiss on her check and went out into the sunlight. A piece of her hoped this was how it would be always. That they could have peace between them after everything. That maybe he could get clean and stay clean this time.

Then the vampire's words came back to her.

Your brother is planning to kill you. The moment that old woman dies—and it will be any moment now—he plans to end your life so that he can sell that house and—

"You don't know that," she said to the empty house.

But I do, a voice answered.

"So you're still here," she said to quiet rooms. "Why?"

The vampire made no reply.

And he went on saying nothing long after the sun went down, the moon rose, and Lettie was alone in a dark house with only the chorus of crickets outside her window for company.

Then she was dreaming. Or at least, she thought she was in a dream.

Why don't you speak to Kai?

She was by the lake again, with that monster who called himself a vampire. She had no memory of being transported there this time. No dramatic lift into the sky. No bird's-eye view of the shrinking town below.

It was straight to the nighttime chorus of frogs and cicadas and something rustling in the long grasses. She really hoped it wasn't another rabbit.

"She left because I was drinking," Lettie admitted. "Because she was tired of watching me get beat up."

"But you've stopped drinking," the vampire said.

He was beside her on the embankment, overlooking the moonlit water lapping gently on the shore.

"I did."

"Do you miss her?"

"More than anything," Lettie said. "I love her more than anything. She was the only good thing in my life."

"You're not the only one who prayed," the vampire said. "She prays too."

"Don't you—"

"Relax." He dismissed Lettie's fear with a wave of his hand. "She is not in danger from me."

The fist around Lettie's heart unclenched.

"She prays for me?"

"Yes," the vampire said. But his smile was too big. Those sharp teeth too white.

Lettie realized at the last minute, once his face was

already too close to hers, that he was leaning toward her. He was burying his face in her neck again.

His breath was hot on her throat when he said, "She prays for you to live."

Lettie woke to a pinprick of pain between her toes. She sat up, her heart racing. She thought it was the vampire. She thought the bastard had decided her blood wasn't enough and now he was going to start eating her alive from the toes up.

But it was Merrick who stood, rising from the foot of her bed like some fairy tale monster.

That's when Lettie saw the syringe in his hand. One of his filthy fucking heroin needles.

"No," she said. "My god. *No.*"

"Shhhh," he said. "Don't worry. Everything's okay."

"What did you do, Merrick! What the hell did you do!" She lunged for him, but her body wouldn't cooperate. Her muscles were weak. The world slowed down.

He's given you a large dose of it, the vampire whispered in her mind. *Large enough to kill you.*

"Why?" she begged.

Before he could answer, before Merrick could explain all that cold rage on his face, a shadow separated itself from the corner of Lettie's room and fell on him. Merrick fought. He writhed and twisted in the creature's arms, but it was no use. He went as limp as those kicking rabbits had. Until he was motionless on the carpet beside her.

The dark figure bent down over her where she lay on the bedroom floor.

"Do you want him?" the vampire asked. "If you want him for yourself, Lettie, I won't kill him tonight."

But Lettie didn't want her brother's life. For all that he

had done to her, for all that he was—he was still her brother. And in her mind's eye she saw him as he had been when their mother had placed the swaddled bundle into Lettie's arms and proclaimed her a big sister.

I can't. I could never.

"Then if you're sure," the vampire said, and sank his teeth into her throat for the last time. And it was different this time. In that moment, Lettie realized the beast had handled her with some care in the past.

He was not careful now. He tore at her throat with the hunger of a desert cat, parched and half mad for relief.

The strength left every muscle in her body. Her vision darkened to a sea of endless black.

But what he took, he gave back.

Hot blood flooded her mouth and fingers vigorously rubbed her throat, coaxing it down.

"Drink, Lettie," the vampire said. "Drink and you just might live after all."

WHEN LETTIE WOKE THREE DAYS LATER, SHE WAS BURIED IN the dirt behind the shed, the remains of half-eaten rabbits rotting on top of her. Still, there was police tape around the house when she rose and walked toward it, looking into the dark windows. Later, in the newspaper she found a brief byline saying that the deaths of Merrick Cole and his sister were thought to be the result of a drug deal gone wrong.

She'd laughed at that.

Lettie lifted the crime tape, broke her bedroom window, and climbed inside. She washed the dirt and blood off her body then packed a small bag of clothes, two of her paperback books. The remainder of the cash she'd hidden under her mattress.

Then she went to the bus station and bought a one-way

ticket to Chicago. It was hard to say why she felt so bold now, after being unable to leave her mother's house for all those years.

Had it been her encounter with death itself? Had it been losing the only two people who'd held her back?

Or did it have something to do with the blood coursing through her? This vampire blood working its magic, making her into something brand new. Something that Lettie had never imagined she could be.

It wasn't hard to find Kaiya's apartment. It was on a quiet tree-lined avenue near Logan Square.

For several nights she only stood outside her daughter's apartment, in the shadows beneath the trees. She watched Kaiya through the windows. Followed her through the streets when she went out to dinner, when she walked her large, goofy dog.

She kept her eyes on her daughter until the hunger was so great that she had no choice but to take the nearest prey, pulling someone into a dark alley for—what looked like to passersby—a passionate kiss.

She slept her days away beneath the nearby basilica only to return to her daughter the next night.

The vampire found her on her sixth night in Chicago.

He'd been waiting on the steps of the church as if he knew where she'd been all along.

"Let me walk with you," he said.

And so they did. They walked the mile and a half to Kai's apartment and stood together outside, shoulder to shoulder, looking into the lit windows where her girl sat at the kitchen table, eating noodles, while the dog's tail slapped at her legs. Then suddenly her face crumpled, and she began to cry.

It hurt Lettie's heart to see it.

"She thinks you're dead," the vampire said. "The police

called her and told her what happened. Or rather, that they *think* happened."

Lettie had assumed as much.

"Don't you want to tell her the truth?" the vampire asked. He seemed less like a monster now, nearly human. That made Lettie wonder just how much she'd changed herself.

"No," she said. "Let her think I'm dead."

"Why?"

"I'm more useful to her this way."

And I want her to be free.

"I saw what you did in the park the other night. When you took that man."

That man. He must have meant the one who'd been following Kaiya home from the corner store. Lettie had recognized the hungry look in his eyes. Had known what his intentions had been. It had been an easy decision to kill him before he got too close.

"You could have revealed yourself to her then," the vampire said.

Lettie watched her daughter wipe her tears away before giving her dog a sweet little pat on the head. Then she smiled, cooing something to the creature.

"She wanted you to live. She wouldn't want you to be out here forever trying to atone for whatever happened," the vampire said.

Atone. Lettie supposed that's exactly what this was. An atonement to the daughter she loved so much but who she'd failed so terribly.

"It won't be forever. Just for the rest of her life," Lettie said.

Lettie wanted to always be here for her girl. No one was going to hurt her the way she had been hurt.

Lettie was going to make sure of it.

NIGHT SHIFT

Vampires actually make excellent nurses—or at least I do. You might think that the blood would bother me, but I haven't lost control of myself in *centuries*. Besides, it isn't blood that I smell when I walk the eighth floor of St. Elizabeth's Memorial Hospital. The scent is there, to be sure. To one degree or another. But mostly what I smell when I walk those halls is death.

Or sometimes I feel it.

That's what happened last night.

I was with Agatha Gomez in 804 when you arrived. Mrs. Gomez needed a new catheter and had asked for me specifically.

She's the only one who doesn't hurt me, she had said. So sweet.

It is probably because I can insert IVs and catheters quicker than is humanly possible.

When *I* do it, there is no digging. No forcing. No mistakes.

I'm so fast and precise that often the body doesn't even

have a chance to register pain before I've finished with my intrusion. My patients can thank evolution for that.

You think I'm bragging?

I suppose I am.

I've been a nurse for one hundred and seventy years and have worked in that particular hospital for the last twelve. Before you walked through those lobby doors, I had been wondering, for a while now, if I should give it all up.

Perhaps move away.

Some of the other nurses have commented on my unchanged appearance. I lie and say it's Botox. Lots of sunscreen. A healthy diet. But we both know the lies will only carry us so far.

No matter. Nurses are needed everywhere. It wouldn't be difficult to find a hospital in this country, or another. Only, I'm rather fond of this city. I've been here since the towers fell, you know. I arrived just the week before.

It had been the same for World War II. I hadn't had the slightest interest in returning to Europe before 1939. But I'm often drawn to places before catastrophe strikes.

No, it's not just me.

I met another, nearly a century older than I am, if you can believe it—and he also finds himself longing for a place shortly before disaster strikes it. That's why he spent all of 1918 in Chicago, which is where we crossed paths.

Who knows why we're drawn to the carnage. Some survival trait, I suppose, the gravitational pull we feel toward an abundant food source.

So yes, I was half ready to leave that hospital, this city, if I'm being honest.

But what you did last night—it's changed things.

It was after I stepped out of Ms. Gomez's room that I sensed you.

My nose prickled. My skin tingled. My scalp itched.

There's a weight to the limbs, too, when death is close.

It was because of this weight that I made no sudden movements. I simply reached out and pressed two pumps of sanitizing foam into my palms—as if there were a disease in all of this building that could kill me—and rubbed my hands together until the substance began to evaporate.

What do you mean you can't sense death?

Really?

Well, you are much younger than I am. How old did you say?

Sixty. And you look no older than twenty-five, so less than a hundred years old when all is said and done?

You're practically human.

No wonder you did what you did. Only a child would make such a fatal error.

Yes, you said you're sorry, but *I said* you're going to shut up and listen or I'll pull out your other fang.

Didn't I say that?

No, no. It's all right. I got a little distracted there.

Now. Where was I?

Oh, yes. I was on the eighth floor, halfway through my shift, when I caught the scent of death. I felt it like ice on my cheek.

I didn't know then that it was *you* who was to blame. After all, death is not uncommon in a hospital. I only knew that death had arrived.

With the sanitation foam still drying on my hands, I turned toward room 813, knowing that was where death awaited. I took my time. I pretended to check my pockets for gloves. I took a fresh mask from one of the dispensing stations.

I said hello to the charge nurse behind the desk. She barely looked up as her fingers flew over the keyboard, her eyes fixed on the screen in front of her.

Someone is dying, I'd wanted to say. *Someone is dying in room 813.*

Knowing Rita, she would have said, *Someone is always dying.*

She's a pistol, that one. I'm rather fond of her. I've daydreamed of eating her just to see how much of a fight she puts up. But as you can see, I haven't. *Some* of us have self-control.

I hadn't expected when I stepped into room 813 to find you bent over Mr. Knapp, your fangs buried in his throat.

And you were *so* careless about it. Poor Samuel. You know that old throats tear more easily, don't you? It's the skin. It's delicate. And you'd ripped through Mr. Knapp like wet paper. It was simply a—a—*disgrace.*

Well, no, of course you didn't hear me come into the room.

I don't walk like humans do. Sometimes I add a bit of weight to my steps to blend in with the others, but why would I do that when creeping up on death?

I *still* can't believe you hissed at me.

Hissed. At *me.*

Yes, of course, I grabbed you by the back of the neck. What else was I supposed to do with such behavior? You'd already half emptied Mr. Knapp of his blood. As far as I could tell, I had two choices. I could raise the alarm myself, fill the room with nurses, and corner you. Or I could grab you by the back of the neck, open the window, and toss you out into the night before anyone saw you.

Oh please, it was only eight stories. And I wasn't going to bring attention to what you did just so we could end up on the ten o'clock news.

Man Fatally Bites Patient in St. Elizabeth's. Can you imagine?

No, thank you.

That rings a bell, actually. Was it '97? '98? I think it was.

Who knows if the biter in that case was actually one of us, but the attack made headlines nonetheless.

That's not the sort of thing I can allow in *my* hospital.

So yes, sue me. I threw you out the window.

Then I cleaned up Mr. Knapp, reconnected all the machinery you disabled—which was tiresome, by the way—and snuck out before the nurses came running.

He still died, you know.

I admit I'm a little annoyed by that.

Don't you have any respect for the rules?

What do you mean, *what* rules?

The rule about hunting in each other's territory. When *I* was reborn these rules were far stricter. You were beheaded on the spot for such things. But now that there are so many of us, I suppose there's no helping the overlap.

Still.

I find it rather inconsiderate.

There's not much I miss from the old world, or the centuries past, but I *do* miss the sense of decorum from time to time. Nothing is sacred anymore. It's a shame.

Anyway. Are you trying to distract me? Keep me talking until dawn in hopes that you'll be spared? You think maybe I'll fall asleep and you can sneak away?

I'm sorry to tell you that I don't enter stasis during the day anymore.

Why would I lie about that?

You have no idea how old I am, do you? Or perhaps even what a nurse's night shift is.

Seven to seven. It's light when I walk in and light when I walk out.

True, I don't feel my best when the sun is up.

But no, the stasis part of our condition phases out in

the... fifth century? Sixth? To be honest, I can't quite remember.

No, wait.

The Black Death was spreading through Asia. I remember that. When was that? The 1300s?

If that's the case, I was nearly seven hundred when the day sleeping stopped. My point is that stasis is a requirement only for the young ones. *I* can walk about anytime I like and there's no bursting into flames. No boils and blisters.

No, that's not how I found you. Stasis or not, I do like to sleep during the day.

Actually, I waited until my night off to hunt for you. You weren't hard to find. You still smelled like poor Mr. Knapp. You *still* do.

It wasn't that hard to follow your scent to the downtown bar district. It didn't matter that it's nearly sixteen miles from the hospital. All I had to do was drive around the city with the windows down until I caught your scent.

I suppose that girl you had on your arm doesn't know just how lucky she is.

She was cute. I'm sorry to have interrupted. But when I walked into the bar and saw you leaning against the pool table, holding that beer bottle and laughing, well, I guess it really pissed me off.

Here you were four blocks from my apartment, *still* hunting my territory, and not looking the least bit remorseful about it.

Yes, yes. *I know.* If you say you're sorry again I'm going to pluck your eyelashes one by one.

You're young. It's true. But you have a nose, don't you? Couldn't you tell I was close? Didn't my mere presence strike a chord of terror in you?

No?

No, no. Don't take it back now. Of course I'm insulted, but you can't *uninsult* someone.

Honestly.

I suppose it was for the best you couldn't sense me. It did make it easier to grab you when you stepped out into the alley with the girl. And it was nothing to render you unconscious and carry you back here.

It doesn't *matter* that I'm small. I'm a *nurse*. Don't you know how laborious that occupation is?

Nurses are very strong.

So, yes, as I was saying, I guess you changed things with your little stunt last night. I'd been nearly ready to leave the city, to start a new life somewhere else. It was beginning to feel like time.

But after what you did to Mr. Knapp, now I know that's not possible.

I simply can't walk away now. I can't abandon my patients. They're my responsibility. And I take my responsibilities very seriously.

At my age, they're really all I have left.

Don't worry.

I won't kill you until the sun comes up and you're soundly in your stasis.

After all, if nursing has taught me anything, it's mercy.

GRAYSON'S STORY

From Night Tide

The night air cooled the back of Grayson's neck as he walked away from his parents' house and deeper into the neighborhood. With his hands stuffed into his pockets, he didn't look back until he'd reached the stop sign at the corner.

His dad was still on the porch, watching him go. He was frowning, but he lifted his hand to wave all the same. Grayson met this wave with one of his own, hoping it would reassure him.

He didn't want to scare his parents or put them through undue stress. Grayson understood he had it made in the parent department. They respected him, trusted him, and treated him like an adult, which was more than a lot of his friends could say.

But he also understood that the phone call they'd received tonight must've scared the hell out of them.

It was a good indicator of their self-restraint that they were willing to let him go out and celebrate his birthday despite what had happened. Surely they must have wanted to lock him in his room for the rest of his life to keep him safe.

After all, a kid had died tonight. It might not have been *their* kid, but there was a dead kid all the same.

It was a sharp reminder that this town, for all its magic and mystery, had an underbelly. Here the monsters were real. And after Landon's death—his best friend, of all people— maybe they *should* be afraid.

Grayson wasn't really sure where he was going, but the night air felt great on his face. It was warmed by the collective heat rising from the pavement.

It had become a proper summer night.

But Landon should be here. He should be celebrating my birthday with me.

He trudged north-northeast until the narrow streets of Midtown opened up in the North Quarter, or what the kids at Castle Cove High liked to call Red Light.

This strip of town was known for its dark bars and raucous nightlife. The chances were high that Grayson would encounter more vampires than humans if he went down this road. Every bar had to be full of blood drinkers. He knew a few other supernaturals must be mixed in, too.

Werewolves, shifters, and demons.

Usually his sense of self-preservation kept him from wandering around these parts of town late at night. But he was eighteen now, and his best friend was dead.

It's about time I see the place for what it really is.

Because Landon didn't have a clue, another voice chided. *And look where it got him.*

Grayson turned left and walked toward the thickening crowds.

There seemed to be a bar for every type of partygoer. He passed several upscale establishments with would-be drinkers queued at the door, dressed to kill. He passed a couple of pubs that seemed more casual, with patrons wearing jeans or shorts.

Then Grayson stopped dead in his tracks.

A Victorian mansion loomed in front of him. It was massive, taking up half of the block on the north side of the street. It looked like a frat house going through a moody, gothic phase. Spires stretched skyward from its roof and sharp slopes. Rock music blared through the open windows into the night. There were people lying on the grass in the yard talking and laughing. Grayson could smell the pot from the sidewalk where he stood.

The sign read *House of the Setting Sun.*

A half-naked guy stood guard at the front door. His chest was bare except for the fringed leather vest hanging open. The vest matched his ass-less leather chaps. And he was barefoot, which struck Grayson as odd for a bouncer.

For several moments, Grayson only stood there, looking at the house and wondering if he had the gall to go in—and what might happen if he did.

After taking a deep breath, Grayson mounted the wooden porch steps.

"ID?" Leather guy held out a long, slender hand toward Grayson, expectantly.

Grayson hesitated. Maybe he had to be twenty-one. "How old do you have to be?"

"Eighteen."

Grayson slipped his hand into his pocket and pulled out his wallet. It took him a moment to get the plastic card out of its holder and pass it over to the waiting hand.

"Happy birthday," the doorman said with a mischievous grin. Grayson caught the glint of fangs in the moonlight and his heart stuttered in his chest.

The vampire took Grayson's hand in his and drew two

large black X marks across his skin, one on the back of each hand.

The light brush of his fingers made Grayson's heart beat faster. The vampire's smile only widened.

Because he can probably hear your heart in your chest, he thought, and wondered if that rumor was true.

Apparently, what a vampire could—or couldn't—do depended on whether they were a living vampire or an undead one. Or at least, that's what his friends had told him.

They were different, living vampires and undead vampires. The living vampires were those who had not died during their transformation. Their hearts never stopped. Therefore, the virus living inside them had more of a symbiotic relationship with its host. It gave them strength and eternal youth. They were not allergic to sunlight. They simply preferred the night. Their bodies emitted pheromones that attracted and disoriented their prey. They were warm and had a pulse.

The undead were a different story. Unlike their living brethren, who seemed to rely on their physical attributes to attract prey, the undead relied on magic. The undead died during their transformations, and it was at that moment of death that a demon entered their body and took residence.

Most of the person's previous life and human connection were instantly forgotten. They were also strong and fast, but they didn't spread a virus from their bite. Their powers—the ones humans knew about, anyway—included telepathy, mind-control, telekinesis, and flying, depending on how strong the demon that inhabited their body was.

The undead were very clannish, too. The oldest vampire in that lineage was usually the strongest, with the most connection to the demonic power within. Those created further down the line deferred to their matriarch or patriarch since, essentially, they were sharing the same demonic connection.

Living vampires seemed to be more democratic. They were free-spirited loners who answered only to themselves.

Grayson didn't know just by looking at him if this vampire guy was alive or dead.

The doorman handed the license back. "Birthday boys get a free drink at the bar."

Grayson's brows rose. "Isn't that illegal?"

The doorman smiled even wider. His eyes held and reflected the light like an animal's. "I'm not talking about alcohol, Grayson."

A group of five or six girls, probably CCU undergrads, stumbled up the walkway, laughing and calling out to the doorman, "Oli! Is Liam here tonight?"

"Somewhere." Oli, the doorman, nodded toward the house. "Off you go. Be careful in there, birthday boy."

Grayson put his wallet back in his pocket and stepped across the threshold.

The music swallowed him whole. The crush of bodies was overwhelming but not complete. With a few polite words, he could navigate fine. People stepped aside for him. A few eyes lingered on his, which surprised him. But what surprised him most was how easy it was to tell the humans from the vampires.

The humans dismissed him almost immediately. It was as if they knew he wasn't what they were looking for. Probably the giant black X marks on his hands. By contrast, the vampires seemed to watch him closely. Some smiled, some looked away. Grayson suspected there was a whole exchange happening here, a subtext he wasn't following.

Instead, he made his rounds, getting the lay of the land so to speak. It was like a large house with rich wooden banisters and high ceilings. Bodies filled most corners and a great deal of the throughways. Eventually, he found a ballroom complete with a bar and a dance floor. At the head of the dance floor was a band playing some kind of dark rock music.

Grayson didn't feel bold enough to visit the bar and see what Oli had meant by a free drink, so instead, he decided to check out the upper floors.

He was on the stairs when he locked eyes with a young man that looked about his age. He had soft brown hair and sharp blue eyes. His thick lips quirked into a smile when he saw Grayson. In one hand, he had a cocktail of some kind. He saw Grayson looking at it.

"Can I buy you a drink?" he asked, pausing on the stairs two steps above Grayson's.

"I'm only eighteen," he said. He held up his X-marked hands. "But the guy at the door said I could have a free drink for my birthday."

"Oh, he didn't mean a cocktail. He meant blood. You can have a free shot of vampire blood on your birthday. House policy."

"*Oh,*" Grayson said. He wasn't sure what to do with this information.

"You're cute," the guy said. His lips quirked into another smile. "I'll open a vein for you if you want."

He turned over a pale wrist in offering.

Vampire blood. Grayson's stomach turned. "No, thanks."

The guy placed the hand on his hip. "Good call. It can be addicting. For humans, anyway."

Grayson leaned against the banister.

The vampire mirrored his movement, leaning his weight on the opposite banister. "What's your name, birthday boy?"

"Grayson."

"Happy birthday, Grayson. Why did you pick the House for tonight's celebrations?"

Grayson wasn't sure how to answer this question. He didn't want to talk about the accident or Landon's death. He didn't want to explain that his grief had sent him running out into the night as if his own house were something that could suffocate him.

He simply said, "I wanted to try something new."

The vampire seemed to sense his dark mood. "Are you here alone?"

"Now I am. I was with my friends earlier."

"Birthdays *always* depress me," he said, taking a casual drink of his red cocktail. The liquid shimmered strangely in the martini glass. "Of course, it could just be that I've had too many."

"How old are you?" Grayson asked.

The guy crossed the staircase to Grayson's side, standing just one step above him. "That's a rude question, Grayson. Didn't your mother teach you not to ask about a lady's age?"

When Grayson looked apologetic, the vampire laughed harder.

"Oh, you're too sullen for me, birthday boy. Lighten up. I'll be ninety-eight this year."

The guy looked no older than twenty.

"How old were you when you turned?"

"You go right for the jugular, don't you?" The vampire smiled. "You're like a puppy who has no idea how cute he is, you know that? You could've at least asked me my name first."

Grayson felt his face flush. "Sorry, I—"

This only seemed to encourage the vampire. "I'm Daniel, and to answer your question, I was twenty-six. But I've always looked young. I didn't mature much after the change, either. Some do." He gestured at a guy on the landing above them as if pointing out a friend in the crowd. "Liam was changed when he was a kid and matured through his late twenties. Now he looks like that. It can go either way, you know what I'm saying? Well, if you're a living vampire, that is. If you're undead, you're stuck with what you've got."

Grayson recognized the name Liam. Wasn't that who the girls at the door were looking for?

"Who is he?" Grayson pointed at the vampire leaning against the wall talking to a group of girls. They were crowded around him, cornering him, and laughing at every word he said as if he were the cleverest guy in the world.

"Liam?" Daniel asked. "He owns this place. He's kind of a big deal in town. I'm guessing you've never heard of him, otherwise you'd probably be chasing him like all the other groupies."

Liam was beautiful, and Grayson felt the strange allure that seemed to emit from him, almost like an aura, if one believed in such things. But he couldn't imagine walking up to the guy and saying, *Hey, bite me.*

Daniel took another sip before going on. "Oh, don't get me wrong. He'll show you a good time, but he's not on the market, if you know what I'm saying. And he's not what you want for your first time. *Heartbreaker* doesn't even begin to cover it. Of course, you could do worse. There are some real freaks here. I'm very vanilla by comparison, you know what I'm saying?"

Grayson couldn't say he did. There was something about this guy that made Grayson's mind fuzzy around the edges.

Living vampire, he thought. *This one is definitely a living vampire. I'm reacting to his chemistry or something.*

He searched for the word. It came to him.

"Pheromones. Are you a living vampire?" The words were out of Grayson's mouth before he had a chance to consider the propriety of his question.

The vampire didn't seem offended in the slightest. "Oh

yeah. That's all you'll find around here. The undead have their own haunts."

"Like ghosts?"

The vampire laughed and leaned his body into Grayson's. "You're killing me. If you get any cuter, I'm going to lose it. You wanna go somewhere else? We could head up to the Heights—"

"No, not the Heights," Grayson said, pulling back to look into his eyes. Perhaps not the smartest thing to do with a vampire. Weren't their eyes supposed to be hypnotic or something? He couldn't remember. The closer the guy stood to him, the harder it was to think.

But he knew about the Heights. Vendetta Heights was a glorified make-out spot on the edge of town where vampires and humans hooked up. But it was also where people went missing sometimes. Going there in the middle of the night was beyond stupid, especially after what happened to Landon in the cove.

"Okay, not the Heights," the vampire said, his lips quirking. "There's also my apartment. It's three blocks from here."

"Toward Midtown? I live in Midtown."

The vampire's lips pressed together. "Do you *really* want to be telling some strange vampire where you live? You know we're predatory, right? We like tracking people down. Especially people we *want*."

Grayson felt the heat in his face and throat.

The vampire's eyes seemed to dilate in tandem with Grayson's growing flush. "So what do you think? You want to get out of here or not?"

Grayson tried to clear his head.

"What would we do?" he asked. "If we went to your place."

The vampire's smile widened until both upper fangs were visible. "Only what you consent to, birthday boy. It's your party."

Grayson wasn't sure if it was the pheromones or his desire to lose himself in anything but his grief, but either way, the choice was easy.

"Sure. Let's go to your place," he said.

Daniel tilted his head. "Let's."

When he stepped around Grayson to take the lead, he took his hand.

Only they didn't make it far before Liam stepped into their path.

Liam held Grayson's gaze with dark, curious eyes. Looking into those eyes, Grayson suspected he understood what Daniel had meant by heartbreaker. There was a soulfulness there that hurt a little bit just to look at.

Liam spoke, but his eyes remained fixed on Grayson. "Daniel."

The vampire froze, his hand tightening on Grayson's. "Yeah?"

"Be careful tonight." And with that, he broke the gaze and turned away. Grayson felt all the heat in his body leave in a single *whoosh*. His knees nearly buckled underneath him.

What is it with that guy?

"Of course," Daniel said to Liam's turned back. But Grayson heard the hollow click in his throat.

Daniel pulled Grayson down the staircase and across the foyer. They stepped out into the night together.

"You can't take the glass," the doorman said, snatching it from Daniel's hand before he was even off the porch. He did it so fast that Grayson barely saw the doorman's hand move.

Daniel forced a pouty face. "Oli, come on. Let me finish it at least."

He plucked it back with a triumphant grin and threw back the alcohol. That's when Oli seemed to register Grayson's presence.

He looked from Grayson to Daniel and grinned, flashing fangs. "Not bad. You could've done worse."

"Thank you for the endorsement, Oliver." Daniel snorted, handing the doorman the empty glass. He reached for Grayson. "Come on."

Grayson followed him off the porch onto the sidewalk. His sneakers scuffed the pavement as they headed east toward the university.

"Does the birthday boy have a birthday wish?" Daniel asked. He was walking close to Grayson, their shoulders brushing every few steps. "Everyone gets a birthday wish."

For my friend to not be dead.

Grayson shrugged. "I don't know."

Daniel pointed at the adjacent street, and they cut across after a baby-blue Volkswagen Beetle passed.

"Gentle, rough, role play—I mean, I can do just about anything."

Grayson's face flushed. "It's my first time."

Daniel stopped walking. "*Ever?*"

Grayson laughed. It was a high, nervous sound. "No. I mean with a vampire."

Daniel placed a hand over his chest. "I'm honored, Grayson. What do you usually go for?"

"Human girls."

Daniel snorted as if Grayson was making a joke. Grayson wasn't sure he had. It was true he'd never slept with a man before, but he had found plenty attractive. He'd wondered if it was the supernatural element. When it came to humans, it was mostly women he noticed. But when they weren't human, he seemed more *fluid* in his choices.

"Then perhaps I should take the lead on this one?" Daniel stopped outside a brick apartment building and removed a key from his pocket. It jingled on the ring. He was watching

Grayson's face carefully. "Assuming you still want to come up?"

Grayson nodded.

"Just checking." Daniel pushed open the door and hit the light switch. "I'm on the top floor, 303."

Grayson followed the carpeted stairs up to the top floor. There were two red doors on the level, one on each side. Number 303 was on the left.

He waited for Daniel to fish out another key.

The apartment door opened with a creak, revealing a wide, open floor plan. The kitchen was small, with gleaming stainless-steel appliances and a dark granite countertop. Daniel seemed to follow his gaze. "Yeah, it's a tragedy that this place has such a nice kitchen and I'll never cook in it."

He went to the fridge. "But I do have some drinks if you want something. Coffee, tea, OJ."

"Water is fine." Grayson realized he was hovering in the doorway and Daniel was waiting for him to move so he could shut the door.

"Sorry." Grayson stepped into the apartment. "You have a nice place."

Opposite the kitchen was an open living room with a large TV and a blood-red couch. Between them, on the far wall, were sliding doors to the balcony. He crossed and looked out at the courtyard below.

"Thank you. Do you live by yourself? I'm guessing not since you turned eighteen today." Daniel slid a cold glass of water into Grayson's hands.

"I live with my parents," Grayson replied. "And my little brother."

"Going to college in the fall?"

"I was accepted to UCLA and CCU. I haven't decided which one I'm going to attend."

Daniel nodded once, as if Grayson had made a point.

"Castle Cove is a special place. There's nowhere else like it. I should know. I've done quite a bit of globetrotting."

Daniel settled onto the sofa, reclining back against the pillows. His eyes seemed to beckon Grayson to join him.

He took a sip of water and placed it on the coffee table before settling down beside the vampire. Their knees brushed.

"I'd heard that there were other towns like Castle Cove," Grayson said, draping an arm along the back of the sofa. His fingers brushed Daniel's arm.

He felt pretty safe here, comfortable. He wasn't sure that was how one was supposed to feel in a vampire's apartment.

"There are," Daniel admitted. "Let's see. There's the one near Kyoto, and the one outside Prague. There's another near Seville and one in the South of France. Oh, and the London underground. Hmmm, what else? Two in Canada. Mexico City. Rio. South Africa. Morocco. Gosh, I know I'm forgetting some of them."

"If there are so many then how can you say Castle Cove is special?" Grayson felt his mind coming alive again. It was his curiosity about Castle Cove and its true nature, but also Daniel. He was easy to talk to. Maybe it was how relaxed he looked there, reclining on his sofa.

"I don't know," Daniel said, looking at the ceiling as if the answer were written there. "There's just something this place has that the others don't. Maybe it's Vendetta."

"The Heights?"

"No, not the place, the person," Daniel said.

"I didn't know there was a person," Grayson admitted.

For the first time, Daniel hesitated. It was a noticeable contrast to the chattiness Grayson had experienced until this moment.

Grayson felt like he'd said something wrong. "You don't have to tell me if—"

"Oh damn. Not those puppy dog eyes." Daniel tilted his head. "Okay, I'll tell you, but keep this to yourself. It's not the sort of thing you're supposed to be whispering among the humans, all right?"

Grayson scooted closer. And Daniel smiled.

"I'm being rewarded. I like this," he said. He opened his arms so that Grayson could move in as close as he wanted. Grayson did, until he was in the crook of Daniel's arm.

"Vendetta is the woman who started it all, or so it's said. She was—hell. I'm not sure exactly what she is. A goddess, maybe? The first vampire, first demon, and first witch, all rolled into one."

"I don't understand. How could she be all of that?" Grayson liked watching Daniel's jaw move as he spoke.

"The story goes that she wanted revenge on the queen who killed her family. And she prayed to an old god, a dark god, in order to get the power she needed to exact that revenge."

"Which god?" Grayson asked. Because his mother taught mythology and she'd filled his head with stories from all the world's cultures since he was a kid.

Daniel began pushing his fingers through Grayson's hair. "I think the word we're looking for here is primordial. The kind of god who lived in the darkness before biblical times, if you get what I'm saying. I don't remember how she got imprisoned in the tree though. I've forgotten that part—"

Grayson laughed. "A tree?"

"Don't ask," Daniel said, seemingly pleased to have made him laugh.

"All I'm trying to say is that Vendetta is supposed to be here, somewhere in Castle Cove, in stasis. She sleeps, waiting for the ancient god to wake up. Which if you ask me sounds *terrifying*. But, according to the stories, Vendetta still serves her mistress, so she stays here with the tree, and so it's either

Vendetta's presence or this magical tree goddess, *something* that gives this place a special vibe. Even the castle ruins overlooking the cove—that's supposed to be what's left of the evil queen's castle."

The cove. Grayson didn't want to think about the cove, about where Landon died.

Grayson felt warm in Daniel's arms. Ease washed over him. Despite being in the den of a killer, a hunter, he wanted to be here. "Maybe you just like Castle Cove."

"You think so?" Daniel turned so that he could look into Grayson's eyes. Grayson's stomach dropped. Daniel touched a finger to his lips. "I wonder."

A shiver ran up Grayson's spine.

"Do you mind if I kiss you, Grayson?" Daniel asked. He was watching him carefully. Because Grayson was looking into his eyes, he saw the pupils dilate. Black overtook most of the clear blue.

"I don't mind." Grayson wet his lips.

His tongue was still on his bottom lip when Daniel moved in. Their tongues brushed and something tightened in Grayson's stomach. Heat seemed to rush through his core and warm him from head to toe. Fingers trailed up the back of Grayson's neck and into his hair. A strong, firm hand fixed there, trapping him in the kiss. Grayson didn't mind. Until he couldn't breathe.

He pulled back gasping.

Daniel was smiling. "Sorry, right. I forgot you have to breathe. Honest mistake."

He turned his head and placed a kiss on Grayson's throat.

"Your heartbeat has the sweetest rhythm. Did you know that?"

"No, I didn't," Grayson said. "Are you going to bite me?"

"Would you let me bite you?" Daniel asked. His warm tongue trailed up the side of Grayson's neck and into the notch below the ear. Grayson shivered again. This seemed to delight Daniel as his embrace only tightened.

"Yes," Grayson said. "I'd let you."

Daniel let out a moan. "You're *killing* me."

Grayson pulled back to look into his eyes. Seeing the vampire's excitement only intensified his own.

"How am I—?" he began.

Daniel didn't let him finish. "Living vampires have venom in their bites. If I bite you, it's very possible that you'll be infected. So I can't bite you unless I want to chance changing you. Even though I really, *really* want to bite you, that's not on the table tonight."

"Oh. Right. I knew that, actually." Grayson felt a little stupid.

"Blame it on the pheromones." Daniel grinned. "It's hard to remember things in the heat of the moment. And we're having a moment, aren't we?"

"Yes." Grayson softened as more kisses were brushed along his throat and the line of his jaw.

"If I were undead I could bite you all I wanted to and there'd be no danger. *But* as a living vampire, we have to be careful."

"How can we—" Grayson wasn't sure he could finish. "How, uh—"

"Oh, we can still fuck," Daniel said, chuckling into Grayson's throat. "And I *can* drink your blood, if you'll let me. But no fangs. Unfortunately, that means a bit of pain for you. How do you feel about pain?"

A strange excitement fluttered through him. "How much pain?"

"This much," Daniel said, and then there was a quick prick in the side of his throat. A second later, the prick was replaced by a burning.

Daniel held up his thumb, showing the metal cuff capped

on its end. It was like a pointy thimble with a strange design on its side that Grayson couldn't make out in the low light.

Grayson forgot all about the thumbnail ring that had cut open his throat when he saw the vampire's eyes.

"May I kiss it and make it better?" Daniel asked. His voice was low. It was almost a growl.

Grayson tilted his chin slightly away, offering himself to the vampire. A warm slick tongue flicked across his collarbone, and upward across the cut.

The throb that had been building in Grayson's groin hardened until his erection pressed uncomfortably against the inside of his jeans. There was nowhere for it to go, but the pressure only intensified the sensation.

Daniel moaned into the side of his neck, his lips locking around the wound. It burned as the vampire sucked, but the sensation wasn't altogether unpleasant.

"You're sweet," Daniel whispered into his ear.

"Thank you?"

"It means you're healthy," the vampire replied, licking his lips. "Clean living."

Whatever he wanted to say next was swallowed up by a moan as the vampire locked his lips around his throat again.

In that instant, Daniel's hand had also undone Grayson's pants and freed his erection. Daniel had Grayson's cock in his hand before Grayson had a chance to think about what was happening.

"How about this?" Daniel asked. "Are you okay with this?"

"Yes," Grayson forced out. He was more than okay with it.

Daniel stroked him, building a steady, teasing rhythm, all the while never removing his mouth from Grayson's throat.

He's mimicking my heartbeat, Grayson realized. Because as soon as his heart sped up, responding to the mounting desire, so did Daniel's rhythm.

"Don't come on me yet," Daniel said, pulling back. His lips

were red with Grayson's blood. "Your blood isn't the only thing I want."

The vampire slid off the couch and knelt between Grayson's legs so fast that Grayson hadn't been able to track the movement with his eyes. One minute they were entwined on the couch, and the next, Daniel was between Grayson's legs.

He was looking up at Grayson with dark eyes. That's when Grayson realized he was waiting, again for consent.

"Please," Grayson said.

"Of course." Daniel wrapped his mouth around Grayson's erection, pulling a long, deep moan from his throat.

The suction was unbelievable. The iron-clad pressure sent him over the edge. The vampire swallowed and didn't seem to want to let go. Grayson fisted the cushions around him.

Then, when he thought he could take no more and would surely die if he wasn't given a break, the vampire released him.

"Too sweet," he said again, rolling his eyes up to meet Grayson's. Some of the blue had returned.

Grayson felt lazy with pleasure. His limbs were heavy on the couch, somewhere between spent and wanting more.

Daniel's eyes roved Grayson's body. "I've made a bit of a mess of you. Do you want a shower?"

"What about you?"

"The only danger of getting in the shower with me is that I will want more," the vampire said, his smile once again wicked. "Would you mind that?"

Grayson found himself shaking his head before he thought better of it.

"Well," Daniel said, standing. "Let me start the shower then."

Before he left, he put the glass of water in Grayson's hand. "Drink this first."

Grayson obeyed as the vampire disappeared through the door. It stood open, revealing the end of a bed. The shower was adjacent. How easy it would be to end up in the shower and then fall into the bed together.

And did he want that? Yes. In fact, the longer he lay on the couch, sipping the cool water in his hand, the more desire built inside him.

He was bouncing back rather quickly.

Daniel appeared in the doorway and beckoned Grayson forward. "You ready?"

Grayson stood, holding the front of his jeans up with both hands. He crossed the moonlit bedroom, past the queen-sized bed that looked soft and inviting. The bathroom was bigger than he'd expected. The shower was a stand-in stall rolling with steam.

The vampire pulled him into the hot water the second his last piece of clothing hit the floor.

"You okay?" Daniel asked, pushing his head back under the hot water. There were two showerheads, Grayson realized, pouring from each direction.

"Yeah. It's just a little disorienting when you move so fast."

"Right," Daniel said. "Sorry about that. My excitement is showing. Do you mind if I drink from you again?"

"No."

As soon as the word was out of his lips, Grayson felt a prick on his chest. He looked down in time to see the metallic thumb drag across his pectoral and a line of red welling there. Daniel's tongue lapped at the cut and the sensation sent Grayson's casually building desire into over-drive. His erection was rock hard again.

"Why does that keep happening?" he murmured.

Daniel looked up with bloody lips, soft laughter rumbling in his throat. "It's the pheromones. Living vampires create arousal in their prey. If you stay aroused, you stay *around*. For feeding. So unfortunately, it will keep happening as long as we—"

"Because I'm the prey?" Grayson asked. His head rested against the tile as hot water beat down from above.

"Do you mind?" Daniel asked. The humor was gone.

Grayson didn't like this touch of seriousness. Everything about this encounter was meant to wash away the horror of Landon's death.

Grayson wanted to lose himself in this oblivion. There could be no seriousness tonight.

"No. I like it." He pulled Daniel into a kiss. "I want more of it."

Daniel's hand found his erection before he broke the kiss. He moaned into Daniel's mouth, but he wouldn't let him go. He worked Grayson until he came again, lapping up the blood from his chest as he did.

The actual showering seemed like an afterthought. When he finished for a second time, Grayson's legs were weak.

"Do you want to move this to the bed?" Daniel asked with wet lips.

Given the tremor in his quads, Grayson needed the relief. "Yeah."

Daniel moved them to the bed in a heartbeat.

Grayson hit the pillows with a gasp of surprise.

Daniel hovered above him, holding himself above Grayson. The vampire searched his face. "Listen, if you don't want something, or you want me to stop at any point, you just have to tell me. I'm not a mind reader."

"Okay," Grayson said.

"No matter how into it I am, I *will* stop."

Grayson softened into the bedding. "All right."

He was dragging his thumb across Grayson's neck once more.

"Why did we shower again?" Grayson laughed.

Daniel grinned. "Maybe I wanted an excuse to get your clothes off you."

Grayson snorted. "Smooth."

Daniel rolled onto his back, pulling Grayson on top of him. Grayson looked down at the naked vampire and felt his erection stirring again.

My god, he thought. *Really?*

"I'm sorry. You're just too cute. It's the shock and surprise for me. Every time. I'm guessing you don't usually bounce back this quickly."

Grayson shook his head. "No. Not at all."

Granted, Grayson hadn't had a ton of sex since losing his virginity at fifteen, but even so, he felt there was certainly something remarkable—or ridiculous—about what was happening here.

He was still marveling at his insatiability when he realized Daniel was speaking. His words barely penetrated the fog of Grayson's mind.

"I've got a condom."

Grayson looked up. "What?"

"I have a condom if you'd like to try something else. The kind of thing you'd do with a human girl, for instance." When Grayson only frowned, he added, "Penetration. I'm talking about penetration."

"Oh." Grayson's face warmed. In that case, of course he wanted to try something else.

Daniel handed him the condom with a smile. "Show me what you can do."

"But what if my erection doesn't—what if—because of the pheromones?" Grayson asked as he slipped the condom on. "What if it doesn't stop?"

"I can handle it." Daniel was beautiful, with the moonlight falling across his cheeks and his bright eyes. "Come here, birthday boy."

Grayson obeyed, lowering himself down, finding that he was the same height as Daniel and that made it easier. He entered him, slowly, carefully. Perhaps he was going too slowly, because Daniel grabbed his hips and thrust him in deeper. Grayson moaned in surprise.

"You won't hurt me," Daniel said, hoarse. Then Grayson felt a fresh cut spring up on his arm just before Daniel wrapped his lips around it.

Grayson found that he could in fact go as hard and fast as he wanted, and Daniel only seemed to enjoy it more. Daniel's lips vibrated against Grayson's skin where he fed.

When he almost came, Daniel's grip on him tightened.

"Don't you dare," Daniel growled. "Come on."

Grayson tried to think about anything except the feel of Daniel's lips trailing over his skin until he couldn't hold back any longer. His rhythm faltered and his head swam. Daniel flipped him onto his back before he could collapse.

"Oh Gray," the vampire said, continuing to stroke his own erection as he leaned over him. "I like you."

"Let me," Grayson said. He took the vampire in his hand. It was strange, holding a dick that wasn't his own. But he knew what he liked, so he started there. Daniel didn't seem to mind.

When the vampire came, he collapsed beside Grayson, his eyes bright.

"Are you okay?" Daniel searched Grayson's eyes and pressed his fingers to his neck as if checking for a pulse. "How do you feel?"

"A little light-headed, but good. *Really* good."

Daniel grinned. "Yeah, me too. I hope I didn't take too much."

"I'm not sure if it was the sex or the blood-drinking—"

"Both," Daniel said. "But you've got quite a bit of stamina, you know that? Oh, to be eighteen."

Grayson blushed. "I didn't do nearly as much for you as you did for me," Grayson said. "Do you want me to—"

Daniel pushed his fingers through Grayson's hair, a satisfied grin lingering on his face. "I'm more of a *giver* by nature. And I took plenty, don't worry."

"But I want you to be satisfied, too," Grayson said. "It's not nice if we don't both—"

"*Gray.*" Daniel grabbed him and kissed his lips. "Keep going like this and I'm going to want to keep you."

Keep me, Grayson thought. *Keep me in this part of Castle Cove where the magic is beautiful. Keep me away from the parts that hurt.*

Daniel glanced toward the window. "We've still got time before dawn. Will you drink some juice if I get it for you? It'll help."

"Okay."

Daniel was back with the juice before Grayson even had a chance to sit up and situate himself against the headboard. He took a few sips gingerly.

"So..." He searched for the words. "Were we safe enough?"

He wasn't sure if the vampire virus could be transferred in other ways, like sex.

"Actually, I think I'm pregnant," Daniel said, taking the empty juice glass and setting it on the side table. "And I'm keeping it."

Grayson nudged him with his elbow. "Be serious."

"There's nothing you can catch from me except vampirism," Daniel explained. He crawled in between the sheets and placed his warm body against Grayson's. "The condom was just for your peace of mind."

"Oh," he said.

Daniel reached up and brushed his hair off his face.

"And I didn't catch vampirism?" Grayson asked.

Daniel's lips quirked to the side. "No. Your blood would taste different. I'd know instantly. But maybe I should check one more time just to be sure?"

Grayson loved that devilish glint in his eyes. "Just to be sure."

A quick prick on his shoulder and then Daniel's tongue was lapping at his skin. The shivers were instant, and Grayson began to worry he would get another erection. Fortunately, Daniel stopped before the arousal could take root again.

"You're safe."

"Good to know. It's close to sunrise, isn't it?" Grayson had noticed the vampire's eyes fluttering closed with the lazy, satisfied look in them.

"You *are* a clever boy," Daniel said. "I *am* feeling the sunrise, but I've got enough left in me to walk you home if you want."

"No, it's okay," Grayson said. "I don't live far from here."

"Tsk, *tsk*," Daniel said, his eyes closed. But the playful smile was still in place. "I've told you. You shouldn't tell vampires where you live."

"I'll take my chances," Grayson said, and bent to kiss his lips again. They were soft and full. But that delirious passion had faded. Maybe vampires didn't emit pheromones during the day. It seemed that way. Because while Daniel was still very attractive, it wasn't driving Grayson out of his mind anymore. It was like the air was clearing and the delirium had left him.

He felt quite sober as he brushed the hair off Daniel's face, regarding him one last time. "I'm going to head out. Uh, thank you. Thanks for everything."

Daniel snorted. "Any time."

Grayson stood and dressed as quietly as he could.

"Hey, Grayson?" Daniel called, rolling over in his bed to give Grayson one more gracious smile.

Grayson hesitated in the doorway. "Yeah?"

"Happy birthday."

"Thanks." Mirroring the smile, Grayson closed the door.

He walked home in a delicious haze. The morning sun gave everything a dewy glow and warm shine. He felt exhausted but wonderfully happy. Too happy. It was a borderline crime to be this content in the wake of his best friend's death.

The pheromones, he realized, had also suppressed that sad part of him, the part that was grieving a terrible loss.

Now that the vampire was well out of reach, his reality was pressing in on him again.

By the time he was at his front door, he was nearly in tears.

He slipped into the quiet house and mounted the stairs as slowly as possible to avoid creaks. He didn't have it in him to face his parents or their questions.

In the coming days he thought of little else. Grief hung like humid fog in the air, pervading every moment, every experience. But the clouds also parted and a sunburst of light broke through whenever Grayson thought of Daniel. Of his gentleness. Of how much care he'd put into making sure Grayson was safe, comfortable.

Maybe that was why he went looking for the vampire again just two weeks later.

Grayson stood outside the three-story apartment building trying to slow his heartbeat. At this rate, he was going to work himself up. He wanted to handle this right. He really did. And yet he found a small handful of gravel on the sidewalk and scooped it up into his hand. Chalk residue stuck to his sweaty palms as he paced the sidewalk, trying to find the right window.

"Here goes nothing."

He took a deep breath and threw the smallest pebble at the third-floor window, the one he thought overlooked Daniel's bed. As soon as the rock clipped the glass, he felt incredibly stupid.

What am I even doing?

He could've gone to the bar. He could've hung out at the House of the Setting Sun and tried to run into Daniel that way. He could've been *cool* about it. He didn't need to be standing here at sunset throwing rocks at someone's window like a total creeper.

He dropped the remaining pebbles and turned.

That's when the window creaked open and a familiar face appeared.

"Grayson?"

"Hey." Grayson wiped his sweaty palms on his jeans. "How are you?"

Daniel laughed. "I'm fine. How are you, Romeo?" He gestured at the window. "You going to recite some poetry now or something?"

Grayson shook his head. "No. I'm no good at poetry."

"You better come up then. Go to the front. I'll buzz you in."

Grayson walked around to the front of the building and stood nervously outside the glass entrance. Several excruciatingly long heartbeats later, a buzzer sounded, and Grayson pulled the door open.

Daniel stood on the third-floor landing, bare-chested and barefoot with only black silk pants on. He smiled when Grayson appeared on the landing below.

"Come on in." He held open the apartment door.

Grayson found it was the same as it had been on his first

visit. The impeccable kitchen. The inviting sofa. The soft glow of lamps well placed in the corners of the room.

"Can I get my hopes up that you're here for my company alone?" Daniel asked. There was no hunger in that gaze tonight, only curiosity.

Grayson slid onto a kitchen barstool. "Yes."

Daniel leaned one hip against the counter. "Can I get you something to drink? As you know, I don't have any food in the house, but if you give me thirty minutes I can take you out for dinner if you want."

"I imagine it would be pretty boring watching me eat," he said.

"You'd be surprised." He went to the fridge and pulled out two see-through blood bags.

Daniel misunderstood his gaze. "Does blood gross you out? I get it from a blood stand near Hyde's Park."

"I know," Grayson said. When Daniel frowned, he added, "My father's lab manufactures and distributes a lot of the blood in town."

"Really?" Daniel looked genuinely surprised as he cut the corner off the blood pack and poured the contents into a pot on the stove. "So your father is a scientist."

"Biochemist."

"And your mother?"

"She teaches folklore at CCU."

"Good genes," he said with a smile, pulling a metal spoon from the drawer. "That explains you."

Blush spread across Grayson's cheeks.

"Forgive my frankness, but I never thought I was going to see you again, Grayson. I'm more than a little surprised you're here."

"If you want me to go—"

Daniel put a pot on the stove and turned back. "No, I didn't say that. I just said I'm surprised."

Grayson bit his lip, unsure of how to answer.

"I was under the impression that I was just playing the role of hookup for a curious guy." He pressed a hand to his chest dramatically. "Are you telling me that I'm *mistaken?*"

Grayson picked at his sleeve. "Maybe."

"Maybe?" He emptied the blood bags into the pot on the stove and stirred. "How about we play a game? Do you know Hot or Cold?"

"My little brother loves that game."

With steam rising from the pot, the vampire reached for a ceramic mug on the counter and poured the blood from the pot into the mug. He set it down, untouched, and turned off the stove. He came to stand in front of Grayson.

"I hope he doesn't play it like this," he said.

Daniel stepped forward and grabbed Grayson's hand. He pulled him from the stool, forcing him to stand in front of the vampire. Then he placed a hand on Grayson's hip. "Is this what you came for? Hot or cold?"

"Warm."

Daniel moved closer so that the entire length of his body was flushed against Grayson's. "Now?"

"Warm*er.*"

The vampire enveloped Grayson in his arms and pressed his lips to his throat. "And now?"

"Warmer."

Daniel's smile spread as he kissed Grayson's throat.

"Hot," Grayson breathed.

"So you came back for kisses?" Daniel asked, chuckling into his throat.

Be brave, Grayson thought. *You didn't come all this way just to chicken out now.*

"No," he said, his heart knocking in his chest. "I came back for you."

Daniel stepped back, regarding him with an amused

expression. "For *me*? Are you sure that's not the pheromones talking?"

"Yes."

Because the truth was that Grayson needed this. Grayson needed a reason to stay in Castle Cove. He needed a reason to connect to its mysteries, its magic. He couldn't go back to the world where best friends died and monsters tore the people he loved apart in the night.

Daniel was searching his face.

"I know that vampires have this mysterious, sexual vibe going on, but you should know that I'm the monogamous type. I am, in fact, rather boring as far as vampires go," Daniel said. "So be clear. When you say you came for *me*, are you saying you want to keep hooking up with a vampire, like *any* vampire, or is it actually *me* you want?"

Grayson managed to breathe despite the pulse in his throat. "You. I want more time with you."

"I-want-to-be-a-vampire more or I-want-a-boyfriend more?"

Grayson rubbed the back of his head. "If you're already with someone—"

"I'm not."

"Donors or—"

Daniel shook his head. "No donors. Or boyfriends."

"Okay. Then would you be open to—" He searched for the words. "Seeing where this goes?"

"Seeing where this goes." Daniel ran his fingers down Grayson's chest. He bent and placed a kiss on his throat, where the jaw and ear met. "I have a feeling I know where this goes."

"And?"

"And yes, Grayson. My answer is yes."

CURFEW

Harper pushed her bike along the craggy road with her little brother trailing behind her.

"Harper, wait!" he whined.

But Harper couldn't wait. If Carter's bike hadn't gotten a flat to begin with, they wouldn't be in this mess. It was supposed to be a simple ride down the river trail. He'd wanted to see the swans nesting in the reeds.

But now they were still a mile from home and moving at a snail's pace while the sun faded from yellow to orange. As she watched its descent, her stomach clenched tightly.

"We can't wait," she called over her shoulder. "We have to get home before the—"

Her voice was cut off by the wail of the sunset siren.

That was their thirty-minute warning.

Thirty minutes to get indoors or they would be dead.

"Is it curfew?" Carter asked, his voice filling with alarm.

And of course he was scared. Why did the sirens have to sound like that? Like something out of that nightmare movie *Silent Hill?*

"Forget your bike," she told him.

"But Harper—"

She left her own in the street and went to him, pulling his bike out of his hands.

"Hey!"

"It's slowing us down." She pushed it across the road to the closest tree.

"But I just got it. I just—"

"We'll come back for it tomorrow," she promised. *If they don't take it.* "But we have to get home *now.*"

"Okay." His quivering lips said he was trying not to cry.

"Get the lock out of my basket. Hurry."

He ran to her bike and grabbed the lock. She did her best to secure the bike against the tree, but she knew this was all for show. They could just rip it off the tree if they wanted. Hell, she was half convinced they could rip up the whole tree. Or at least some of them could. But she also knew she needed to do this, if only to hurry Carter along.

Once the bike was chained up, she gave the lock a rough tug. "See? Nice and tight."

He pulled at the lock, but nothing happened. His hands were too small.

"Now come on," she said. "Climb on my back. You're going to have to hold on tight the whole way home."

She bent down and hefted Carter up onto her back, feeling him clasp his little hands at her throat as she used her arms to hoist his butt higher. Once he felt centered, she lifted her bike and threw one leg over the seat.

"Hold on to me," she told him again.

The last thing we need is for you to fall off and scrape yourself. The smell of blood will only get us killed quicker.

It was hard to get her balance just right, but once she got the hang of it, the bike built speed. Sure, her calves burned like hell and her chest ached, but she peddled on, her eyes transfixed on the orange horizon now fading to red.

The second siren started bleating just as their little white house came into view.

Carter jumped at the sound of the siren, his grip tightening around her neck.

She whipped the bike into the driveway and screeched to a stop. "Get in the house. Run!"

He slid off her back and hit the mulch bed on his side. But then he was up, bolting for the house while their mother stared at them through the glass storm door, furious.

Harper threw her bike into the open garage, pulled the cord to slide the door down into place, and ran up the walkway.

As soon as she crossed the threshold, her mother started in on them.

"You were supposed to be back two hours ago, Harper Marie!"

"I know, I'm sorry. He got a flat."

Her mother waved her away. "We can't do this right now. Check the windows. I'll get the back door."

Harper did as she was told, going from window to window, making sure that each one was locked and the security wire was stretched across each frame. Then she covered them with the locking shades to make sure the view into the house was completely obstructed.

She moved through each room, slowly, carefully, making sure not to miss a single window or a single step in the security process.

After she'd cleared the upstairs, she turned to find Carter just behind her. She jumped.

"Jesus."

"Where's Dad?" he asked.

"He's not home?" Harper bent and picked the kid up, carrying him down the stairs to the kitchen. "Mom?"

The basement door opened and her mother appeared

holding a flashlight and a mallet. She handed the flashlight to Harper.

"Where's Dad?" Harper asked.

"He got stuck at work," she said, her face drawn. Harper thought the dark circles under her eyes were worse than usual.

"But it's curfew."

"I know." Her mother's eyes pinched shut. "I know. He's going to shelter at the Ninth Street garage tonight."

Harper knew a lie when she heard one, but she didn't press her mother on it. She didn't have the time. She could already hear the wings beating.

Carter began to cry. "I hate that sound."

"I know, baby," their mother said, and pulled him into her arms. "Why don't you watch some television while I make you chicken nuggets?"

The three of them moved through their evening routine as if nothing was wrong. They ate dinner, watched TV. Then came the baths. The teeth brushing.

As Harper was putting Carter in his dinosaur pajamas and hefting him into their parents' king-sized bed, a loud thump sounded on the roof above their heads. All three of them froze. Carter looked at Harper, Harper looked at their mother, who stood at the mirror, brushing out her long hair.

"Where are your headphones, sweetie?" she asked.

Carter pointed at the nightstand.

The roof thumped again.

Carter stared at the ceiling. "Mom?"

"Here." Harper lifted the noise-canceling headphones and slipped them over his head, checking twice that they covered his ears on both sides.

Then she tucked him beneath the covers.

"You don't think—" Harper began, but her mother cut her off.

"Why don't you head to bed? It's been a long day. We're all tired."

That was the understatement of the century.

"Are you sure you guys are going to be okay in here?" Harper asked from the doorway. To be honest, she wanted to climb into bed with them. Her bedroom at the end of the hallway suddenly seemed very far away.

"We'll be fine," her mother promised, and gave Harper a kiss on the cheek. "Sleep tight."

Harper was sixteen. She was too old to say she was scared to sleep alone. So she said the next closest thing. "I love you, Mom."

"I love you too, honey."

Harper left her bedroom door open. It was crazy to her now that so many of the teenagers in movies always insisted on keeping their doors shut, in maintaining defiant distance between themselves and their parents. Harper wanted her door open in case Carter or her parents screamed—or more importantly, she wanted someone to be able to hear *her* scream.

Harper crept through her dark room and climbed beneath the covers. She wanted to turn on all the lights, but that would draw them to her. Early in the change, before people began to figure out what was happening and what could be done to keep safe, lights were often left on.

People felt safer in the light. Seeking it was a basic human instinct.

But light only attracted them. A house with glowing windows stood out in the night like a beacon. In the early days, before they started turning off all the lights at sundown, Harper had been certain that hundreds of them were crawling along the roof of their house.

Crawling. Sniffing. Listening.

Now, despite her desire for the light, she slept in the dark like everyone else.

Or at least she tried to. It was hard to doze off to the sound of the wings beating. To the creaking of a settling house. To the tapping on the windows.

She'd been only nine years old when the trouble started. The first night she'd heard tapping on the window, she had thought it was a bird. She'd been certain, one hundred percent convinced, that there was a bird outside, just as scared as she was, and it was begging to be let in.

When she'd lifted the curtain to find her neighbor—Mrs. Hurst—suction-cupped to the side of their house, she'd screamed. A good thing too. Later she would hear other stories of people who'd been kind enough to let in their neighbors, their friends, only to have their whole family slaughtered.

Georgia French at school thought the vampires preferred eating kids and that's why they targeted them. But Harper thought it was just because they were easier targets. They could still be fooled, tricked because of their kindness.

Everyone else stopped being kind a long time ago.

The window screeched.

Harper sat bolt upright in bed. For a terrifying moment, she thought the window was opening on its own. But it remained locked in place. The curtain fastened over the glass.

The screech sounded for a second time.

What was that? *Fingernails?*

She didn't want to think about it.

She reached across the nightstand and grabbed her own noise-canceling headphones and slipped them over her head.

If she didn't wear them, she wouldn't get any sleep, and she had an exam in chemistry the next day.

The only bad thing about the headphones was that they

worked. All she could hear was her own shaky breathing. If something did break into the house, Harper would never hear it coming.

HARPER WOKE TO HER MOTHER SHAKING HER.

She pried her eyes open and pulled the headphones off her head. "What? What is it?"

"I have to go. Can you make your brother breakfast and get him off to school?"

She pulled up the curtain, throwing sunlight across Harper's face.

She squeezed her eyes shut. "What time is it?"

"It's twenty past seven. Sunrise was ten minutes ago."

7:20. That meant they only had an hour to get up, get ready, and get to school.

"We'll miss the bus," Harper said.

"I'll leave the keys to the Prius on the counter."

"What are you going to drive?"

"The SUV."

The SUV was Dad's. If it was back, that must have meant he'd made it home okay. Harper's chest relaxed. "Yeah. Okay. I'll do it. Is he up?"

"He's watching toons on the tablet." Her mom pushed twenty bucks into her hand and brushed a kiss across her forehead. "I'll see you after school."

Then she was gone, leaving Harper in the light of early morning, sleep still clinging to her.

Dressing the kid, getting all his homework and books into his bag and into the car, was the easy part. Feeding him was usually a battle. Carter was pickier than she had ever been.

So she promised him a breakfast burrito and hash browns from the drive-in, and it made both of their lives easier.

It also helped that the elementary school was next to the high school.

"I'll pick you up here at three," she told him, waiting until he crossed the threshold into the school, a spot of ketchup still on his cheek.

Harper was ten minutes late for homeroom, but no one cared. No one seemed to care about much these days except for being indoors at curfew.

The adults were distracted by the world ending. They *tried* to act like all was well or that they had things under control. But Harper knew that chemistry exams and talk of the SATs were just their last-ditch attempt at keeping anyone from looking too closely at the dumpster fire burning around them.

What the hell did an SAT score matter when monsters crawled the city every night waiting for a chance to tear their throats out?

The bell rang and Harper shuffled to first period. Then second, and third. The day passed in a haze. Lockers opened and closed. People held hushed conversations in the hallways. She said hi to her friends, and acknowledged her teachers, but the details of the day slid over her, dream-like.

It wasn't until her last period—study hall in the library—that the world came into focus again. This was partly because she loved the library, everything from the smell to the quiet, and partly because the promise of the end of the day always brought a fresh surge of energy.

There were six other kids in this study hall period. Each sat at one of the long tables in the center of the surrounding stacks. Their books and papers were spread out on the table-tops before them, heads bent in conversation. Everyone seemed focused on their work. Everyone except Dana Barton.

The circles under her eyes were deep and her face was

red. She'd obviously tried to clean herself up in the bathroom before class, but it didn't matter. It was clear to anyone who looked she'd been crying.

Since there were no other open tables, Harper pulled out the chair cattycorner to Dana's.

"Do you care if I sit here?" she asked.

Dana looked up, her blue eyes shining. She managed a nod before looking away.

Harper went through her homework. She did a chapter of trigonometry and read the Kate Chopin short story assigned by their English teacher, Mrs. Simfield.

Harper was rereading the same page of "Desiree's Baby" for the fifth time when she caught sight of Dana's trembling shoulders in her periphery.

Harper put her pencil down and slid around the table to the other empty seat. Once beside Dana, she whispered, "Are you okay?"

Dana looked up, wiping her running nose. "I'm sorry."

"Don't be sorry," Harper said. The two guys at the closest tables were pretending not to listen, but she could tell they were. "What is it?"

"My sister didn't come home last night," Dana said.

Harper remembered watching Dana run the hundred-meter dash for field and track last year, and she was so fast. So strong. Now she looked small and defeated. Seeing her like that made Harper's heart hurt.

"Maybe she had to stay in a lockdown shelter. Have you heard from her at all?" Harper asked.

Dana shook her head. "I tried calling her phone this morning before school, but someone picked it up and said he'd found it in the park off Broadway. That's where she meets her boyfriend sometimes, and so I called him, but he didn't answer either."

"Maybe they sheltered somewhere together," Harper said. "And she just dropped her phone and can't call you."

"Then why isn't she here?" Dana asked, swiping at her red nose again. "Even if they sheltered somewhere or went back to his place, why didn't they come to school?"

Harper didn't have an answer to that.

And her silence seemed to be enough to send Dana running from the library, crying, her books and bag abandoned at the table.

"Fucking crybaby," Frida said as the doors swung shut behind Dana's retreating form.

"Give her a break," Harper said. "Her sister could be dead."

"We could all be dead right now," Frida said, turning the page of her Spanish textbook. "It's only a matter of fucking time."

Harper wanted to yell at her for that. Tell her not to be such a shitty person at a time when things were bad enough. But Harper had heard a story just two weeks ago from Zack Bennet—Frida's ex—in which he claimed that the reason Frida always had an attitude now was because her mom was caught outside after curfew a month ago.

Now she was one of *them*. And every night she came back to the house and tapped on Frida's bedroom window all night, begging Frida to let her in.

It's making her crazy, man, Zack had said.

If that was true, Harper couldn't blame her.

CARTER WAS WAITING AT THE EXACT SPOT WHERE HARPER HAD told him to be that morning. After Dana's story, Harper found she was relieved to see him standing there, safe and sound in a bright patch of sunlight. Sometimes she looked at that kid and felt so much love for him it hurt.

"Hey, kiddo," she said. "You wanna go get some ice cream before we head home? I still have some of Mom's money."

"Yeah!" His eyes sparkled and his tongue pressed against the little gap in his front teeth.

"Okay. Give me your bag."

She bent down and pulled his heavy pack off his back, throwing it over her other shoulder.

"What about my bike?" he asked.

"We'll go back for it after the ice cream," she said, taking his hand.

She thought he might pull away from her, tell her he was too big to be holding his sister's hand. That it wasn't *cool*.

But he didn't. He held tight to her fingers as if it were the most natural thing in the world.

The ice cream stand was busy when they arrived. Mostly it was kids that Harper knew from school, hogging the picnic tables out front.

A few threw Harper a wave as she parked their mom's Prius in the lot and marched her little brother up to the window. She had to lift him up on her hip so he could read the menu. He always insisted he read the menu even though he always got the same thing—a hot fudge sundae with extra whip cream, sprinkles, and a cherry on top. Chocolate ice cream instead of vanilla. Harper went with her usual strawberry crunch milkshake.

By the time their order was up, a table had become available. Just as they sat down on one side of the bench seat, Nick York, Donovan Graves, and Trish Beaumont sat down on the other side.

"Is this cool?" Nick asked, gesturing at their side of the table.

"It's fine," Harper said. "Just watch your language." She nodded toward Carter, who in just three bites had as much chocolate on his face as in his cup.

She felt like such a loser having to ask, but Donovan had one of the filthiest mouths. She expected them to make at least one snide comment about it, but Nick just pushed back his golden hair and lifted his chin.

"No problem, Harris," he said, using her last name as if they were cops or something. Then again, he played almost every sport their school had, so maybe it was just habit.

Donovan swallowed a spoonful of his cookie blast and added, "Yeah, Harris. We can control ourselves. We're not animals. *Yet.*"

Trish laughed at his joke. Nick didn't. He was still looking at Harper. "How've you been, Harris?"

Harper shrugged. She didn't know how to answer the question. How did anyone answer that question nowadays?

"The same as anybody," she said.

"Awful," Carter said, putting his spoon in his cup and reaching for a napkin. "We had to leave my bike tied to a tree."

Harper pushed two paper napkins into his sticky fist and said, "We went for a ride yesterday and he got a flat. We had to ditch it or we wouldn't have made home by curfew."

"That's too bad, buddy," Nick said. "Did you get it back?"

"We're going tonight," Harper said. She checked the clock on her phone. "We've got plenty of time."

"You want company?" Nick asked. "I can come with you."

"I thought you were coming to the arcade with us, man," Donovan whined.

Trish elbowed him hard in the side, giving Harper the impression that she was missing some subtext here. "We go to the arcade all the time. Maybe he wants to hang out with Harper. He hasn't seen her since the observatory."

That was true. She and Nick had been assigned as "buddies" for the field trip three weeks ago. It was honestly the most fun Harper had had in forever. She couldn't remember ever laughing so much in her life.

Harper looked at Nick. His hazel eyes were still heavy on hers.

"You don't have to say yes, Harris," Nick said, his gaze falling to his hands. "I just thought you might want help with the bike."

Carter's bike probably weighed all of twenty pounds, but Harper didn't think that was what was going on here. She was starting to suspect—much to her surprise—that maybe Nick York liked her.

Harper turned to Carter. "What do you think? Do you mind if Nick comes with us?"

"Will you play basketball with me? Like we did in the park?" Carter asked.

Harper had forgotten about that.

"Sure thing. You guys have a hoop at your place?"

"We do," Harper said. She'd played all through junior high before giving it up for track in high school.

Carter's whole face lit up. "Let's go play."

He clambered off the bench, his melted ice cream abandoned.

"Is it cool if I ride with you?" Nick asked.

"Sure," Harper said, gathering up the sundae and wadded napkins. "You guys want to come too?"

Donovan looked ready to say yes, but Trish's hand tightened on his arm. Whatever words he'd been about to say folded into a little screech.

"No, we're going to head to the arcade to meet up with some of my friends," Trish said, her smile still in place. "You guys have fun though."

"Yeah," Donovan said, obviously defeated. "Have fun."

. . .

Nick didn't say anything as they drove through the side streets between the ice cream stand and where they'd abandoned Carter's bike the day before. But that hardly mattered. Harper was very aware of his presence in the passenger side of the Prius. Part of it was his smell. He wasn't soaked in cologne like some of the guys at school, which always made her want to gag, but he did have a scent that was hard to ignore.

Then there was the size of him. He was too tall to be sitting in this tiny car, the top of his head nearly brushing the roof.

"I'd forgotten about the time we played basketball," Harper said to break the silence. "How long ago was that?"

"October," he said. "It was right before Halloween."

"Oh, that's right." Because they'd had trick-or-treating in the park beforehand and all the families had met up to lead the kids around in a "safe" circle of candy booths. And it had to be done in the middle of the day, of course. When Harper was little, trick-or-treating was something they did at night.

Carter would never know what that was like.

"We played with Kevin!" Carter cried. "Where's Kevin? Can he play today?"

Nick stiffened at the mention of his little brother, his gaze turning toward the window. But even though he was trying to hide how he was feeling, Harper saw his hand flex on his knee, squeezing it tight.

"Not today, buddy," Harper said.

Thankfully, Carter didn't ask anything else about Kevin. Instead, he pointed out the window at the tree and screeched, "My bike! There's my bike!"

"It sure is," Harper said, grateful for the distraction. "You stay in the car and Nick and I will get it, okay?"

He kicked his feet excitedly. "Okay."

Harper shifted the Prius into park and threw open the

driver's side door. It took her a minute to dig the keys for the bike lock out of her backpack.

Nick was already bent down in front of the bike by the time she walked up.

He held up a nail as she approached. "This was in his tire."

"Explains the flat," she said, shoving the key into the lock. "Probably too big to patch."

"Nah," Nick said. "I can patch it for you if you want. I've got mechanics for fourth period."

That was right. Harper often passed him in the hallway on that side of the school on her way to her fifth-period woodworking class. He always said hello.

"Can you?" she asked. "If you're working on something else—"

"It's no problem," he said. "It won't even take me a whole period."

"Then sure," she said. "He'd love that. Thanks."

"You're welcome." Nick flashed her a smile before standing. He turned back toward the car.

"Wait," Harper said. She'd almost grabbed his arm but let her hand fall before her fingers brushed his skin. "I'm sorry he brought up Kevin."

Nick looked away. "He's just a kid. He didn't mean anything by it."

"Still," she said. "I'm sorry."

He looked like he was going to say more, but instead he turned his gaze toward the horizon. Harper didn't need him to say anything. What was there to say anyway? When someone's little brother is murdered, there's nothing *to* say.

"Let's head to your place," Nick said, adjusting his grip on Carter's bike. "We don't have a ton of time before dark and we haven't played basketball yet."

"Okay." Harper gathered up the chain and lock.

She followed him back to the car without comment, but

her mind kept replaying the moment she'd heard about Kevin just before Christmas. Rumor was it had been Kevin's best friend from class who'd changed into one of *them*—who'd come to Kevin's bedroom window and had asked him to come outside and play. Kevin had been about Carter's age at the time. So young. He didn't know any better. He'd crept out of his bed and out into the night without a second thought.

Rumor also said that it had been Nick who'd found the body in the yard, torn apart.

Harper's mother had said it was a small mercy that Kevin hadn't turned, but Harper wasn't sure which was worse—having someone you love become one of *them* or losing someone altogether, knowing they were so brutalized in their final moments that there was nothing left to turn.

THE SUV WAS STILL GONE WHEN HARPER PULLED INTO THE driveaway. She parked the Prius on the left side of the garage so there was still room to play basketball in the driveway—if what they were doing could be called basketball.

Harper watched them while she used her dad's tools to remove Carter's flat tire. She'd just put all the tools away and had laid the tire against the side of the house when she got a text from their mom.

We're running late but we'll be home before curfew. Are you home?

Harper replied, *Yep. Nick is here playing ball with Carter. Ok?*

As long as his mom knows.

"Your mom knows you're here, right?" Harper called out.

"Yeah," he said. "I texted her before we left Custard's. She said she'll pick me up at six when she gets off work."

His mom is supposed to pick him up after work.

Her mother sent a string of emojis in reply. A kissy face. A heart. A thumbs up.

Harper sank onto the top step of the porch and watched Nick and Carter play as the afternoon light faded, lulled into something that could be mistaken for happiness while listening to the basketball strike the concrete again and again and again.

Then the curfew siren blared and any good feeling she'd had evaporated.

Nick had been about to throw the ball, his knees bent in anticipation, when he froze, straightening.

He pulled his phone from the back pocket of his jeans and frowned at the screen. "It's almost seven."

"Maybe she got held up at work," Harper offered.

"Maybe," Nick said, his thumb flying over the keyboard of his phone.

"But I want to keep playing," Carter whined.

"You know we can't," Harper said. "Do you want the bats to get you?"

Bats.

That was the lie they'd fed Carter since he was old enough to ask questions about the sirens. About the need to stay indoors at night. They'd filled his head with terrifying images of rabid bats so they didn't have to tell him the truth about what was really scratching at the windows at night.

And Harper had only made the story scarier after hearing about Kevin. She'd told him sometimes the bats borrowed people's voices.

They call your name to get you to lift the curtains and look at them—but if you ever do, then they know you're inside for sure and they'll keep attacking the window until they break through it and gobble you right up.

That had been enough to keep him away from the windows. In fact, he'd slept with their parents ever since.

Harper only hoped the lie would hold until he was old enough to understand the real danger.

And to think, people used to only lie about Santa Claus. Of course, now they didn't, lest children get the idea that it was okay for strangers to crawl down the chimney or make noise on the roof.

"Let's go inside and start your homework," Harper said. She helped them put away the basketball and clear the right side of the garage of bikes so that the SUV would have somewhere to park. They'd just gotten everything out of the way when the SUV swung into the driveway and her father stepped out of the passenger side of the vehicle with his briefcase in one hand.

Upon seeing him, Harper's chest lifted with relief.

She hadn't realized until that moment just how worried she had been. But here he was, standing in the last of the sunlight, looking tired but otherwise intact.

"Hey, guys," he said, giving Harper's shoulder a gentle squeeze. "How's it going? Are—"

Whatever else he'd meant to say was cut off by the second curfew siren, marking the moment the sun reached the horizon. Their last warning before full darkness fell on them.

They all turned toward the orange glow spreading on the horizon.

"My mom's not answering my texts," Nick said, still frowning at his phone.

"It's too late to run you home," Harper's mother said, taking Carter by the shoulders and spinning him in the direction of the front door. "You can stay with us tonight, Nick. We're making tacos for dinner."

"Thanks." Nick offered a weak smile. "I promise to stay out of your hair."

"Don't be ridiculous," Harper's father said. "You're not going to bother anyone. Come on. Let's do the windows."

Harper reached the door first and held it open for everyone as they crossed the threshold one by one. Her parents went upstairs to change into their house clothes—what they did every evening when they got home. Carter went straight to the television to turn on his cartoons.

Nick hesitated by the door. "Are you sure they won't mind?"

"It's okay," she told him. "Get in here."

Harper showed Nick how they did the windows, checking the lock on the storm glass, and then again on the inner pane. How to secure the tight-mesh wire over the glass before locking the curtains in place.

"Wow," he said. "Your windows are a lot more intense than ours."

Together they latched the four windows in the living room, then the two in the dining room, and the one in the kitchen. Four in the den and also the window above the back door. Then they went upstairs and did the windows in the guest room and Carter's room.

She trusted her parents to do their own windows—and even as they passed the door, she heard the rattle of the mesh clicking into place, barely audible over their hushed voices.

That only left Harper's room.

She wasn't expecting the wave of shyness that washed over her as she moved to the first window, leaving Nick at the doorway. He didn't cross the threshold. Instead, he leaned against it, watching her.

"I've just got the two," she told him. "It'll only be a second."

"Is this your inner sanctum then?" he asked.

She laughed. "Yeah, I guess."

"It's nice," he said, nodding his approval.

"*Thanks*." She locked one window, then the other. "That's it."

"That's all the windows?" he asked.

"Technically there are six more in the basement, but my parents put bars over them last year."

"I guess no *bats* will be getting in there then," he said.

"Yeah, it's weird," she told him. "We should tell him the truth but—"

"No, I get it. We told Kevin the truth and it still didn't help." Nick rubbed the back of his head. "Whatever you can do to let him be a kid—I get it."

Harper felt like a fist was squeezing her stomach. "Are you okay sleeping in the spare room?"

His smile returned. "I was prepared to sleep on the couch. Anything above that is an upgrade."

"My dad probably has something for you to sleep in and we have extra toothbrushes. My uncle's a dentist, so we end up with like a hundred a year."

"Harper," he said.

His name on her lips was enough to shut her up. But it was that look in his eyes that nearly killed her.

"I'm happy with whatever," he said. "You don't have to worry about me. I'm just glad I'm here with you."

"Cool," she choked out. Her face felt like it was on fire. She hadn't fully recovered when her mother appeared in the doorway with sweatpants, a long t-shirt, and a toiletry kit. Harper was pretty sure that was her dad's travel kit, but she didn't say so.

"Here you go, Nicholas," her mom said. "The guest room has its own bathroom. So you should be all set."

Harper swore. "I forgot about the guest bath window. I'll close it now."

As Harper worked on latching the window tight, she heard her mother come into the guest room with Nick.

"The sheets are clean and the Wi-Fi password—if it holds

up through the night— is on the little card here in the drawer. Do you need a charger for your phone?"

"No, Mrs. Harris."

"Okay. Well if you need anything, just ask Harper."

"Yes, Mrs. Harris."

When Harper came out of the room, she found the spare bed had been turned down and the pillows fluffed. The clothes and a fresh towel had been laid out for him on the foot of the bed. There was even a pair of noise-canceling headphones. Her mother had thought of everything.

"I'm going to go start the tacos. Harper, keep an ear out for your brother," she said.

"What about Dad?" Harper asked.

"He's got a headache. He's going to lay down until dinner."

Then it was just the two of them standing in the guest room. Nick nodded at the clothes and supplies on the foot of the bed. "I see where you get it from."

Harper snorted. "I am my mother's daughter, if that's what you're saying."

"It's not a bad thing," he said. "I stayed close to you on the field trip because you had all those snacks. Well, to be honest, that's not the *only* reason."

And just like that the heat was back, burning her face and making the room soft in its focus.

"Did you hear back from your mom?" Harper asked.

He shook his head. "But you can't get a good signal in lockdown."

"I'm sure that's it," Harper said. Because she didn't like to think of the alternative. His mom was all that Nick had left. His dad had died of cancer a few months before all this madness began. Kevin had been born using the sperm he'd stored when he'd been diagnosed.

At first, Harper had thought that was hella weird—using a

dead guy's sperm to make a baby. But Kevin was—had been —a great kid.

But without him, that meant Nick and his mom were all that was left of his family. It felt like that was the norm. Everyone had lost someone. For Harper's family, it had been Uncle Tony, her dad's brother. That single loss seemed like a miracle compared to how many other families had been decimated.

Her mother was always saying how lucky they were, but it was hard to feel lucky when every day another classmate disappeared.

"I'm sure she's okay," Harper said again. "Try not to worry."

He nodded, rubbing the back of his neck. "Should we go check on Carter?"

They found her little brother on the couch with the remote. He bounced his legs up and down on the cushions while singing along to the lyrics scrolling across the bottom of the screen. A girl with multicolored hair and sparkly cheeks danced, waving her magic wand, while her backup dancers—all of them brightly colored ponies—executed a similar choreography.

Nick and Harper joined him on the sofa, but Harper had the distinct feeling that neither of them were actually watching the show.

When the dance number ended and it cut to a commercial, the house vibrated as something large struck the siding. It reminded her of how thunder felt sometimes, the way it rattled the floorboards when it was close.

"Whoa." Carter pressed himself closer to Harper's side. A nervous laugh escaped him. "That's a big bat."

Over Carter's head, Nick was searching her face.

"Don't worry, buddy," Harper said. "As long as we stay inside, we're safe."

"I bet he could eat me in one bite," Carter said.

Nick pushed the hair back from Carter's face. "That won't happen."

Harper's mother appeared in the doorway, wiping her hands with a dishcloth. She saw the three of them together, her mouth opening in question. Before she could ask anything, the house shuddered again. It was followed by the distinct sound of feet walking across the roof.

Still looking at the ceiling, her mother said, "Turn off the TV. And Harper, go wake your father. It's time for dinner."

Ten minutes later they were all seated around the dining room table. The curtains were drawn tight, and Harper was suddenly grateful that her parents had spent a fortune on soundproofing the windows four years ago. Even with a window not six feet from her seat, she couldn't make out the difference between the tapping on glass and the scraping of salsa-laden tacos across their plates.

"Which shelter did you end up staying in last night?" Harper asked.

Her father was sitting across from her, his dark eyes on the taco he was unsuccessfully stuffing. For every spoonful of meat and cheese he managed to get into one side of the shell, an equally large spoonful tumbled out the other side.

"I didn't," he said. "I stayed in the lab."

"Your father has a cot at work," Harper's mother said. She was looking at her husband with displeasure. "He seems to think it's safer in his lab than in lockdown."

"Is it safe?" Harper asked.

"Being a workaholic?" Her mother huffed. "No, I'd say not."

Her father said nothing.

And that's not what Harper had meant anyway. She was asking if the lab was as safe as a house.

She wasn't sure why that one superstition had proved to be true about the vampires anyway, but they seemed hung up on thresholds. They never entered someone's home without an invitation.

Public buildings were a mixed bag. Libraries, schools, courthouses, stores, post offices, hospitals—buildings where anyone was allowed to enter seemed to be the rule no matter if the person was living or undead.

Hospitals were one of the weirdest examples. Vampires could walk right into the lobbies and reception areas. But they couldn't enter the closed wards—even when the wards were only separated by a doorway.

Maybe that was how her dad's lab worked. Maybe they didn't try to pass into the offices for employees only on the upper floors?

That still left her with the nagging question of *why* did it work that way?

Technically the lockdown shelters were public, but they were solid concrete and completely sealed—no windows, no doors—by sunset each night.

As for the other superstitions, things like crucifixes, holy symbols of any kind, and garlic proved useless pretty quickly.

A stake through the heart didn't do anything. In fact, their healing capacity seemed so intense that there had been a video that circulated the internet for *years* in which some guy blew out a vampire's brains every night for more than one hundred and eighty-four nights only to watch it regrow its head each time. Complete dismemberment seemed to be the only way to kill these things. With the exception of a vampire-on-vampire kill.

It was rare, but there had been a video of one vampire

sucking another dry, from which it didn't resurrect. Her dad said that food scarcity in that area had probably caused it.

Vampires showed up in mirrors and on security cameras just fine. They absolutely wanted to drink blood but also seemed happy to eat organs. The heart, the liver, brain, lungs.

It was disgusting to think about.

Her father hissed, drawing his hand back suddenly. Blood spilled over the side of his finger, running along the knuckles of the second hand trying to pinch the cut closed. He'd been trying to cut a lime in half when the blade slipped.

"Oh no, Dad!" Carter cried, reaching out for him.

"No! Don't touch me!" His father pulled back.

Carter recoiled, his face crumpling.

By the time her father had left the table clutching his hand, Carter had begun to cry. Harper's mother moved over to her husband's seat and began consoling him.

"Don't cry, honey. He didn't mean to yell at you."

Harper stole a glance at Nick. But Nick was looking at the bathroom door where her father had disappeared. From where they sat, they could hear the sound of a running sink.

"Is he mad at me?" Carter sniffed.

"No, baby. He's just under a lot of pressure at work. It has nothing to do with you. Nothing at all."

Her father reappeared with his finger wrapped in a fresh bandage.

"I'm sorry, kiddo," he said, and placed a kiss on the top of Carter's head. "I shouldn't have yelled. But your mother is right. I didn't want to get blood on you. Do you forgive me?"

Carter's eyes were still wet and shining, but he nodded.

"What if I give you a bowl of chocolate ice cream?"

Carter's face lit up. "Yeah!"

Her father and Carter disappeared into the kitchen. Ice cream bowls clattered against the counter. The freezer door opened and closed.

Harper turned to her mother, who was finishing off her last taco.

"He's already had ice cream today," she said.

Her mother shrugged. "Sometimes it's a two–ice cream day."

Nick squeezed her leg under the table and Harper's heart leapt. "I think I'd like a second ice cream too."

GIVEN THE KID'S EARLY BEDTIME AND THEIR FATHER'S lingering headache, by ten o'clock it was just Harper and Nick in front of the television. It played in the background, the volume turned low, while they did the last of their home-work—if what Nick was doing could be considered homework.

Harper wasn't sure he'd accomplished much. He'd kept refreshing his phone, clearly hoping to hear from his mom before he finally gave up. Harper had quit trying to placate him with empty reassurances hours ago.

She thought it was likely his mom didn't have service inside the lockdown facility, whichever one she was in. There were two by the cosmetics store she managed, and surely she could have made it to either one before it locked itself up tight for the night.

Harper was finishing up her last math problem when he'd asked, "What's your dad do? I mean for work."

"He works in the New Day labs," she said.

"They're the ones trying to make a cure, right?"

"Yeah," she said. "But Dad says that there's no such thing as a cure for a virus. The best we can hope for is a vaccine or a weapon."

"No wonder he's stressed. He's trying to solve the unsolv-able," Nick mumbled, checking his phone for the millionth time. "Ever since Kevin died, I've wished there was something I could do."

She reached out and took his hand and squeezed it. He covered it with his other one.

For a long time, he didn't let go.

They'd called it quits at midnight, saying goodbye at the door to the guest room before Harper sidestepped into the bathroom to do her pre-sleep routine.

Now, as she lay awake in her bed, teeth and hair brushed, staring at the ceiling while her headphones played Nine Inch Nails, she wondered if she should have said something—anything—to let Nick know that it was going to be okay. That even if it wasn't okay, they would figure something out. He wasn't alone in this.

The bigger and more pressing question, of course, was why did she care about consoling Nick at all?

He'd always been nice, but Harper just assumed he was like that to everyone. She couldn't think of a single person who hated Nick or spoke ill of him.

She'd always thought him handsome. That was true.

He'd hit puberty before half the guys at school and had shot up a foot over the last year. He'd been hard to miss even before he got the muscles, thanks to his freckles and sandy hair. The hazel eyes.

There was no question why *she* liked him. He was super cute. And it was endearing how much he loved his family. How strong he'd been after losing his dad, then Kevin. He wasn't a showoff or a braggart. He was respectful. He was smart. Capable.

The only mystery was why in the world he liked *her*. She wasn't sure he'd been around her enough to have developed feelings for her.

And yet they'd had so much fun at the observatory that day. And he'd been so kind to her since.

Stop obsessing and go to sleep, she thought. *It's not like I'll ever have the guts to ask him anyway.*

Her eyes fluttered closed. She was almost asleep when her mattress began sinking beneath her. She shot up, a scream half formed in her throat.

A hand covered her mouth.

It was Nick.

"I'm sorry. Please don't scream," he whispered. "I didn't mean to scare you."

Harper's heart pounded in her chest.

He took his hand off her mouth. "And I'm sorry about covering your mouth. I just didn't know if you would freak out if I woke you up."

She pulled her headphones off.

"Good call." She placed a hand over her heart and drew a deep breath, trying to slow its beating. Even though it was bouncing out of her chest, she knew that the only reason he would have crept up on her was if he had something to say. "What's wrong? Did you hear from your mom?"

"No," he said. "I've left a million messages. If she could have called me back, she would have."

Harper couldn't imagine. If she couldn't get ahold of one of her parents, she'd be losing her mind.

"I'm so sorry, Nick," she said.

He looked down at his hands. "I woke you because I can't sleep. I was wondering if it was okay if I stayed in here with you. I can stay in that chair. I'm not trying to be a creep. It's just every time I doze off, I wake up and don't know where I am, and it freaks me out all over again. I think it would be easier if I were with you. At least then I'd know where I was instead of waking up in a dark room by myself."

She couldn't make him sit in that old armchair all night. But she also wasn't sure how her parents would feel about coming into her room in the morning and finding a boy in bed with her, even if it was a big bed. They trusted her, but Harper felt like there were probably limits to what they could handle. She was pretty sure that a vampire apocalypse didn't leave room for even the average level of teenage rebellion.

"You'll never fall asleep in that chair," she said. "You can stay in the bed, but can we do something with the blankets so my parents don't think—"

She wasn't even sure how to finish the sentence.

"Oh yeah. Of course." He stood up and took several steps back from the bed.

"There's an extra blanket in the closet." She pointed at the door across the room. "On the top shelf."

Nick went to the closet, pulling the chain to illuminate the small space. For a moment he stood there in her father's sweat pants and baggy shirt, his hair mussed. Before the light clicked off again, she thought she saw tears drying on his cheeks.

But he didn't let it show in his voice, she thought.

Before she could be sure, he'd grabbed the blanket off the shelf and turned off the light.

There was a pause as he bent and plugged his phone and charger into the wall. Then he was at the bedside again.

"Is it okay if I lay on top of the covers like this," he said, stretching out on her comforter. "You're not trapped or anything, are you?"

"No," she said. She moved her legs under the covers to demonstrate. She pushed an extra pillow toward him. "Are you comfy enough?"

He positioned it under his head and snuggled deeper under his blanket. "Yes, thank you."

She could only see his eyes peeking at her over the edge of the blanket.

God, he was cute.

She was about to ask him if he needed anything else when a sound stopped her cold. A haunting, melodic voice was passing by her window. It was a woman—or something *like* a woman—singing.

"That's the other reason I couldn't sleep," Nick said. "She was singing right outside my window for what felt like hours. I think she even tapped on the window a couple of times."

Harper swore. "What about the headphones my mom gave you?"

"I didn't wear them. I was afraid I wouldn't hear my mom call or text," he said.

She should have thought of that. "You can wear them now, can't you? Surely wherever your mom is, she's asleep."

"Yeah, I guess you're right," he said, but didn't put on the headphones.

So Harper didn't put hers on either. It seemed like time stretched on forever, with the two of them lying in the dark, listening to the creature outside her window singing. It was Harper's window it was tapping on now, and she wondered how it had known that Nick had moved to this part of the house.

At least there's no beating wings, she thought as sleep began pulling her down. *The wings are the worst.*

HARPER WOKE TO HER MOTHER SHAKING HER SHOULDER. "Honey, it's time to get up."

Harper already had an excuse forming on her lips. Before falling asleep, she'd rehearsed what she'd say to her parents as to why Nick had spent the night sleeping in her bed.

Except that when she looked over, her bed was empty.

"Where is everyone?" she asked. She hoped this question was vague enough not to imply she was asking about Nick.

But her efforts were unnecessary. Her mother looked as if she'd barely slept herself.

"Your father is waiting for me in the car and Nick and Carter are in the dining room eating cereal. I'm leaving the Prius with you again. Nick asked if you could help him look for his mom today—"

Did he? That was bold.

"—I told him that's fine, but you've got to get Carter to school first," she said. Her phone buzzed and she pulled it from her pocket. "That's your dad. I gotta go."

She bent and kissed Harper on the cheek. "I'll see you tonight. Keep me posted on Nick's mom."

"Okay," Harper said. "Be safe."

"You too. Love you." Her mother kissed her again.

Harper showered, changed, and found Carter in front of the television watching cartoons thirty minutes later.

Nick was in the kitchen making sandwiches. He smiled when he saw her. "I asked your mom if you could help me today. She said it was fine, but are you okay with driving me around?"

"I want to skip school!" Carter called from the dining room.

"Mom said no, buddy," Harper called over her shoulder before turning back to Nick.

She didn't have any exams or anything that couldn't be made up. And their teachers were pretty flexible when it came to homework assignments. Everyone had to be flexible these days. And the truth was she didn't want Nick scouring the town alone. What if he came across his mom's body—or what was left of her?

"Of course I'll help you," she said.

A relieved smile lit up his face. "I thought it might be best if we pack lunch just in case. I made us both ham and cheese sandwiches. That's what you like, right? It's what you brought on the field trip." He held up the jar of mayo and the tub of mustard. "But I wasn't sure how you dressed it."

Harper arched a brow. "Lots of mayo and lettuce. Usually. Once in a while, I get a weird craving for mustard."

Why was she telling him this? Why in the world did it matter?

He took a butter knife from the drawer and began smearing mayo on her sandwich. "I also packed a couple of root beers. And your mom insisted we take this."

He held up a liter of water.

Harper's phone buzzed. She checked it. It was a neighborhood alert. She only read the headline, but it was enough to sink her heart.

Woman's body found near Lake and 37th Street. Unidentified due to the condition of the remains.

Her phone prompted her to open the alert and read more. She didn't want to, not with Nick standing right beside her. But when she looked up, she knew it was already too late.

"We can go there first," he said, his face colorless. "After we drop off Carter."

"Okay," she said, all of her reassurances evaporating on her lips. Instead, she took her sandwich and slipped it into the lunchbox he'd started for her. "We need to leave in about ten minutes if we want to get him to school on time."

It only took them six minutes to get Carter's shoes on and the three of them into the Prius. Nick waited in the car as Harper walked her little brother up the sidewalk to the elementary school, stopping just short of the glass doors.

"Okay, buddy. You have a great day, okay? We'll pick you up right here at the end of the day."

"Okay!" He slapped her a low five before running through the doors. Harper followed his retreating form until he disappeared from sight.

Nick was still looking at the school when she climbed

into the car. "Can we go by her work first? I'm hoping maybe she just forgot her phone there."

"Of course." Harper was glad he'd changed his mind about going to the body identification site first. She turned the car in the direction of the shopping center on the west side of town. They drove past clothing boutiques, the electronics store, and a bookstore before the cosmetics store where his mother worked lurched into view.

As Harper circled the lot looking for a place to park, Nick said, "Her car's not here."

"Do you want to try somewhere else?"

"Just let me run in for a minute," he said, opening the passenger door before Harper brought the car to a full stop.

He was inside for five minutes tops before Harper spotted him running across the lot toward her. As he collapsed into the passenger seat, he said, "She's not here. They can't get ahold of her either. They say she left late, after they did."

"Do you think she went straight home?" She hoped her voice didn't betray her doubts. "Maybe she's there and she just lost her phone. Or forgot to charge it."

"I guess we should check," he said.

The silence was thick as they drove to Nick's house. Harper kept racking her brain for what to say but nothing came to her. All possible encouragement felt wholly inadequate. She was left stealing glances at Nick, whose eyes remained fixed on the world beyond the car window.

Her heart sank when his house came into view but there was no car.

"Maybe she parked in the garage," she said.

"Wait here."

"Okay." She put the car in park as he dug his keys out of his backpack and ran up the steps to the front door.

He was inside for a long time. At least it felt like a long time. But when she checked the clock on her phone, only fifteen minutes had passed since she'd turned off the car and watched Nick go into the house alone.

When he finally came out, he didn't look happy or relieved. The skin between his brows was scrunched.

"What is it?" she asked as he slipped back into the passenger seat.

"She's not here."

Harper gripped the steering wheel. "Did you just call her name or did you look around and—"

"I looked everywhere."

Harper felt like an asshole for asking, but she couldn't forget about her classmate Lydia Butler, who'd thought her dad was in lockdown for the night only to realize, come nightfall, that he'd been turning into a vampire and had spent the day sleeping in the attic. Once he woke, he slaughtered Lydia, her three sisters, and her mom. The whole thing was recorded on their home security cameras.

"I want to check the lockdowns next," he said.

He must know as well as I do that it doesn't look good, she thought. *No point in me saying it.*

She drove him from one lockdown facility to the next until they'd checked all six on the route between the cosmetics store and his house. Despite their efforts, Nick said nearly the same thing upon returning to the car each time.

"She's not on the check-in roster. They haven't seen her."

"Should we call the hospitals? Or the other lockdowns in town?" she offered.

"Maybe we should head over to 37th and see if the body they found is hers."

They both felt relieved—and perhaps a little guilty—that the woman who was missing two of her limbs and the entirety of her throat was not Nick's mother. What was left of her face told them as much.

They also went to two other scenes that Harper had found on the community alert boards, but those turned out not to be his mother either. Harper thought that the body on South Street had been Dana's sister though. And she hadn't had the heart to text the girl and ask if she'd checked.

Out of ideas, they pulled over and ate their sandwiches in the park—the last one she'd seen Kevin in alive. While they ate, Nick made calls to all the lock-ins and hospitals to see if his mother's name, or anyone that fit her description, had turned up in any of the systems.

But there were no matches. It seemed like no one in the entire city had seen so much as a glimpse of her after she'd left work.

And they were running out of daylight. Harper hadn't realized how much of the day had gotten away from them until the phone buzzed with a message from her mom.

We picked up Carter early and grabbed a pizza. Are you still with Nick?

Yeah, sorry, she wrote. *He hasn't found her. We've been looking all day.*

Where are you? her mom asked. *How far away?*

Thompson and Lilac.

She tried to do the math. Even if they left right now, she wasn't sure they'd make it back to her house before dark. She swore inwardly. She should have been paying more attention to the time, but as Nick's concern had escalated, so had hers, until she'd become more focused on helping him than keeping track of the time.

Her mother must have made the same conclusion. Her phone rang a moment later.

"You need to shelter tonight," she told her. "Don't try to come home. Go straight to the shelter."

"Which one?" Harper asked. Her eyes were on Nick, who

stood just outside the car, speaking to yet another hospital attendant on the phone.

"Abbot and First," her mother said. "It's pretty close to you. Ten minutes, I think."

Harper knew which one it was because they'd checked it earlier. It was the one nearest to Nick's house.

"Okay. We're going now," Harper said, turning the car on.

"Call me when you get there," she said. "Let me know you made it inside okay—"

The first siren blared.

"I promise. I love you," Harper said, unsure whether her mother had heard her.

Nick pulled open the passenger side door. "I'm so sorry. I wasn't—"

"My mom wants us to go to the Abbot Street shelter."

"I'm so sorry. I should've been paying attention to the time," he said. He pulled the seatbelt across his chest.

"It's okay," she said again. Because the fact remained that they hadn't found his mom. She understood why Nick had been so desperate to use every second of daylight they had regardless of the risk. If it were her parents out there, or God forbid *Carter*, she'd have done the same.

She drove on.

Harper was still a block away from the Abbot lockdown when the second siren went off, vibrating the steering wheel in her hand. She jumped in her seat, prompting Nick to issue another round of apologies.

"We'll make it," she said.

At least she hoped so. She was already driving well above the speed limit. Not that it mattered. There wasn't a cop in town that was going to pull her over right now.

Still her heart leapt with relief when the Abbot Street lockdown came into view. She'd never been so happy to see one of the dull, featureless buildings in her life.

She threw the car into park outside the building, yanked off the seatbelt, and leapt out. They sprinted across the lot toward the entrance.

But much to her horror, the concrete barrier meant to seal the building shut began to slide into place.

"No!" she cried, running faster. "Wait, please!"

But it didn't stop. And no one came out to help them. The barrier slid into place, leaving Nick and Harper locked outside. Their frantic hands slapped the concrete, pleading.

"Oh my god, oh my god, oh my god," Harper said. She stepped back from the wall and looked at the sky sliding from orange to the first hint of purple twilight. "We're too far from my house. We're too far!"

"Let's go to mine," Nick said, pulling her back toward the car. "Come on! We have to try, come on!"

Even as she followed him to the car, her mind was doing the math. Yes, his house was closer, but it was still at least two miles away.

We're not going to make it. We're not going to—

Harper climbed back into the Prius and turned on the car.

"It's quicker to go down Main," Nick said, not even bothering with his seatbelt. He was leaning toward the dashboard as if he could urge the vehicle forward with his will alone. "Down Main then left on Maple."

Harper barely registered when the car began beeping, crying out that they weren't wearing seatbelts. Her mind was devoted to the road.

There was no one. No people. No moving cars. They were the only ones in motion. The birds had vanished from the sky. Harper had felt certain that when she was a child—before this nightmare began and the world devolved into this unending hellscape—she remembered birdsong in the warm evenings. Robins would sit in the magnolia tree outside her bedroom window and sing prettily long into the twilight.

Now nothing sang. The world was silent except for the incessant beeping of the seatbelt alert and their panicked breathing. Distantly she could also hear the faint whine of the tires on the road.

Main. Then Maple.

Main. Then Maple.

The buildings were awash in violet light by the time Nick's house appeared in the distance.

"It's that blue one there on the left. Two down."

Nick turned, looking over his shoulder out the back window. "Faster. *Faster, Harper.*"

Harper looked in the rearview and saw the approaching mass of darkness.

Her foot smashed the gas pedal harder than she'd meant to and the Prius lurched forward. Nick was rummaging in his bag, his hands shaking.

"Shit, shit, shit, shit." It was like an invocation of protection pouring from his lips. "Oh thank god."

He pulled out a small remote and pressed it. The garage door began to roll open, revealing the vacant interior.

A watering can. A push mower. Tools hanging on the walls. Lawn bags half filled.

"Pull into the gar—" His voice was cut off by something slamming into the side of the Prius. The window shattered, throwing glass across Harper's face. Instead of the brake, Harper smashed the gas and the car lunged forward, across the garage's threshold.

The roof scraped against the bottom of the rising door.

She braked too slow and crunched the mower against the far wall. But the car was inside the garage. The car was inside and *they*—those creatures—weren't following them in.

Nick was smashing the buttons again, the remote aimed

over his shoulder. By the time Harper looked in the rearview mirror, turned around, all she could see were legs pacing outside the closing door, the animalistic screech of their frustration making her insides quake. A flash of bat-like wings.

And so many legs.

So many. My god. How many were there? Twenty pairs? A hundred?

"It's okay," he was whispering over and over again. "It's okay. It's okay. They can't come in, remember? They can't. It's okay."

Harper didn't know if he was whispering for her benefit or his own.

She couldn't blame him. Her eyes were huge in the rearview mirror. Some part of her brain had disconnected, noting this terror and shock on her face as if it were happening to someone else. Some other girl.

"Harper?" Nick was searching her face. "Are you okay? Did it touch you? You're bleeding."

One more look in the rearview confirmed he was right. There was a cut across her cheek. It was a clean line. She was pretty sure it had come from the flying glass. She hadn't been bitten.

"I'm okay," she managed. "That just—that just scared me."

"No kidding!" A nervous laugh escaped him, half choked. "I think I just shit myself."

Harper looked around, trying to regain her bearings. There was glass on her lap, her clothes, shimmering as she moved. The cut on her face was still bleeding. It was bleeding more than she'd expect, but that was the least of her worries.

Something outside howled, and the sound chilled Harper's bones.

They can smell me. My blood.

"I have to call my parents," she said. "They're going to freak out."

"Let's get inside first," Nick said. "We can't stay in this garage all night."

She agreed. They grabbed their bags out of the backseat and stepped out of the car. The feral growling and hissing outside the garage door grew louder.

They're not even trying, she thought. *They know we know what they are and they're not even trying to pretend they're human.*

No singing. No sweet calling or laughing. The horrifying sounds they could hear now revealed exactly what they were.

In the kitchen, Nick put his keys on the hook by the door and kicked off his shoes. Harper put her bag on one of the kitchen chairs and pulled out her cell phone. She needed to call her parents before they lost their minds with worry.

"Do you want something to drink or—" A loud thump sounded overhead. Nick's voice broke off.

The thump came again.

"Is that inside the house?" Harper asked.

His eyes were as wide as saucers. "It sounded like it, didn't it?"

No sooner had the words passed his lips than a dark figure appeared at the end of the hallway.

"Mom!" Nick said, relief washing over his face. "Oh god, Mom, I was so worried. We—"

The woman stepped into the light, revealing the mutilated remains of her throat. No one with that level of damage should be alive, let alone have enough strength to saunter down the hallway toward them with a grin on her face. Her eyes liquid black.

"Your room, now! Where's your room?" Harper yanked him away.

"This way." Nick bolted through the kitchen, the dining

room, across the living room, and down the first-floor hallway to the room at the end. Harper was close on his heels.

As soon as they crossed the threshold she commanded, "Call out, 'This is my room! You're not allowed in here.'"

"What?" Nick's face pinched in confusion.

"Say it!" Harper screamed. "Say it now!"

"This is my room, you're not allowed in here," Nick said.

"Louder, like you mean it!"

"This is my room, you're not allowed in here!"

"Tell her she's not allowed," Harper breathed again.

"Mom, you're not allowed!"

The woman with a gaping hole in her neck where her throat should have been stopped just short of the doorway. "Nickie, baby. I'm your mother."

Nick shook his head.

Harper went to the door. No sooner than she put a hand on the handle did the woman snarl at her.

"No! Don't touch her!" Nick threw himself between Harper and the creature that had once been his mother. But he was too close to the threshold, past it even. And the creature took hold of him.

Nick moved at the last moment but wasn't quite fast enough. His mother's nails raked across his arm, raising three lines of bright blood.

"No!" Harper slammed the door in the monster's face and locked it.

Nick sank onto the side of his bed, covering his bleeding arm with one hand.

Harper wanted to go to him, console him. But her phone began to ring. She fumbled in her pocket until she pulled it out.

Her mother's voice sounded over the line.

"Harper? Where are you?"

"We didn't make it to the shelter," she told her. "They locked us out."

"Oh my god. *Where are you?*"

"We're at Nick's house. We made it, but we have a serious problem."

"What do you mean, a problem? What's going on?" Her mother's voice was high and tight.

"I have to talk to Dad. *Now.* Where is he?"

It had been her father who had taught her about the bedroom threshold trick, after what had happened to Lydia's family. That if something should ever happen in the house—if any one of them turned—they could treat their bedrooms as a second threshold.

There was a rustling sound, and then her father's voice was on the line. "Harp, what is it? What's happened?"

"Nick's mom turned. And we're trapped in the house with her."

A beat of silence.

"We're in Nick's room and—"

As if for emphasis, the woman chose that moment to let out a blood-curdling scream. "Nick, how could you? How could you do this to me? How could you do this to your own mother?"

"Jesus Christ," her father said over the phone.

"You heard that?" Harper asked.

"I heard it."

"I would never hurt you, Nickie." Nails raked across the closed door. "Be a good boy and give me the girl. Come on, Nickie. I don't want to hurt you. I just want to talk to your friend for a minute. I'll be nice. I promise."

"I don't know how long—" Harper wasn't sure how to finish. What she *wanted* to say was, she didn't know how long Nick would last. How long before he lost his nerve and opened the door? Would he feed her to his mother? Would he sacrifice himself now that he had no one left?

And there was the matter of his arm. It didn't look great. Had any of the virus gotten in? Had any of his mother's blood mixed with the cut?

She certainly hoped not.

"Dad," Harper said. "What do we do?"

"She's on the other side of the bedroom door? She's not trying to cross?" her dad asked.

"Right. She's staying on the other side like you said she would."

"And neither of you was bitten?"

"No, but we have scratches."

Her father gave a sharp exhale. "Okay. Harper, listen to me. You're going to stay in that room. I don't care what she says, what she promises. I don't care if she tries crying or threats. Your only goal is to keep Nick away from her. Don't let him do anything stupid."

"Okay," she said, hoping that Nick hadn't heard that. "But don't do anything heroic, okay? Don't try to come over here like Brittney's dad did. There's too many of them outside. They're all over the house."

"What do you mean?" he asked.

She told him first about Brittney's dad, who thought he could simply fight his way through four blocks of vampires to save his daughter from the treehouse where she'd been cornered. Not only was he turned, but he was the one who took Brittney's life two weeks later.

Then Harper told him about the shelter locking them out, and the harrowing rush to get to Nick's house. "We cut it really close. A lot of them followed us here. If Nick didn't have his garage opener in his bag, I don't think we would be alive right now. You'll have to break it to Mom that the Prius took some damage."

Her father swore again. "You will survive this. You hear me?"

A swell of affection rose in her. "We will."

"And I will be there as soon as the sun rises, okay? We just have to get through the night. Now tell me about these cuts."

"I think mine was from the glass, from when they hit the car. Nick's mom scratched him."

A beat of silence rang on the line.

Finally her father said, "What can you do for Nick to help stabilize him? Emotionally."

"Let me figure that out and I'll call you back."

Harper ended the call.

"What did he say?" Nick asked, his eyes red-rimmed.

"To stay in the room until dawn and they'll be here first thing. We just have to get through the night."

Of course, a lot could go wrong in the next ten hours, and they both knew it.

"Do you have headphones?" she asked. He did, but only one pair. "You wear them. She's not going to bother me as much as she will you."

Nick took the headphones, but he didn't put them on.

"What about a phone charger?" she asked.

He had two. An old one and the one he used every night. Fortunately, they had the same brand of phone. So Harper plugged hers into the wall socket and let it charge.

"Weapons?"

"Maybe," he said weakly. He got up from where he'd been slumped beside the bed and went to the closet. He rummaged around for several minutes but only came up with an old aluminum baseball bat. Still, it was better than nothing.

He returned to her, pressing himself into her side with their backs against the wall. For a long time, they just sat like that, not moving, not speaking.

"I suppose it's stupid to tell you to get some sleep," she said finally.

He only shook his head.

Her mom texted her. *Update?*

Nothing to report. Will call back soon.

Fists pummeled the closed door, rattling it in its frame. "How could you do this to me, Nicky! How could you? I'm your mother. I'm all you have left. They're dead, all fucking dead, and this is what you do to your own mother!"

Nick pinched his eyes closed.

Harper took his hand and gave it a good squeeze. "That's not your mom. She wouldn't talk to you like that. She—"

"Yes, she would," he said, and dragged his nose across his sleeve. "Yes, she would."

There was something in the way he said it. Something that made Harper question what kind of state his mother had been in since losing her husband. Her youngest son.

She pulled Nick into a hug and squeezed him. "I'm so sorry."

"Nicholas, open this fucking door! You let me in right this minute!"

"Put your headphones on," Harper said.

But Nick didn't move. His tears wet her shoulder as he stayed nestled in the crook of her neck, crying softly. Eventually, she convinced him to move from the hard floor to the bed. She was hoping he would fall asleep once he was surrounded by his covers and pillows.

His mother let out another guttural moan and the bedroom door rattled on its hinges. It reminded Harper of the time she'd first asked her father about the vampires. There had been one beating on her bedroom window and she'd been terrified that the glass would break and it would come in and eat her.

They only make the noises to provoke us, her father had said.

To scare us into doing something stupid. But they can't cross the thresholds. Stay away from the thresholds, don't cave in to your fears, and you'll be all right.

"Nicholas, please!" his mother growled.

Harper pushed the hair back from Nick's face. "Put the headphones on. You don't need to listen to this."

"What about you?" he said, looking up, his eyes red.

"I'll be okay," she said.

Reluctantly, he let her pull the headphones over his ears and fix them into place. Then, for some reason she wasn't entirely sure of, she took his cheeks into her hands and kissed him. His lips were salty with his tears.

"My arm burns," he said. "What if I turn—what if—God, Harper. I don't want to hurt you. I should just let her have me and—

"No!" Harper hushed him. "That won't happen. You're staying here with me until my dad comes."

Slowly they sank beneath the covers together. She held him close with one arm, the other trailing through his hair.

"Harper."

"It's going to be okay," she said, holding him tighter.

Nick fell asleep in the crook of her arm, his head on her chest with Harper's fingers playing in his hair, tracing the line of the headphones band across his skull. When she felt his body shudder, she knew he was sobbing. She said nothing. She only held him close.

Finally, he fell asleep. Once his breath evened out, Harper reached for her phone and called her mom again.

"Harper?"

"Yeah," she said, noticing how relieved she was to hear her own mother's voice. And for it to be a kind voice, a loving voice. So different than the one shrieking outside the closed bedroom door, begging to be let in. "It's me."

"How are things now?"

"Nick's got his headphones on. I think that will help. And I have a baseball bat and a charger for my phone. But no bathroom, no food, no water. How many hours until sunrise?"

"Seven and a half. You can do this, baby. You can do this."

"It's nice to hear your voice," Harper said. "I won't keep you up or—"

"Don't be stupid. I've already made a pot of coffee."

"What about Carter and Dad?"

"They just finished dinner and now they're doing baths. Afterward, they'll head to bed without me."

"Mom, I can't keep you—"

"You listen to me, Harper Marie. This is not my first nor will it be my last all-nighter," her mom said firmly. "And there's no way I'm sleeping a wink without my girl in the house. So we're doing this."

"What the heck will we talk about for *seven* hours?" Harper asked. She talked to her mom a lot, but seven hours would be a stretch.

"I'd say boys, but I suppose he's still awake, isn't he? That poor kid. He's been through hell."

"He has," Harper said, looking at Nick. His eyes were closed, his head resting on her chest. "And he doesn't have anyone else."

"He has you. And he has us," her mother said. "Though I know it's not the same. It's not been the same for anyone for a really long time."

Harper didn't know what to say to that. It felt like her memories from before the nightmare were far and few between. Half-formed memories of the moon and starry nights. Of Halloween nights. Of coming home late and being carried in from the car by her parents—things that would never happen now in the new world.

"Why do you think this is happening?" Harper asked.

"To Nick? Bad luck. It's not like he deserves it or—"

"No, to all of us," she said. "Why is this happening to the world?"

"You'll have to ask your father about that. He's the scientist," she said. Harper heard a spoon knocking against a mug. Her mother hadn't been joking about the coffee then. She really intended to stay up the night with her.

"You're an electrician," Harper said.

"Grid operator," she corrected. "But still not a vampire specialist."

"Keeping the lights on is important."

"Keeping alive is important, and you're doing a great job of it. I'm proud of you," her mother said.

Harper's heart clenched. "You too, Mom. I'm proud of you too."

"Now," her mother said after taking another sip. "Tell me what happened to the Prius."

Harper wasn't sure when she fell asleep. But she woke to her mother screaming her name.

She sat bolt upright, looking around Nick's room with confusion. He was asleep beside her, his face a mask of calm despite the dried tears on his cheeks.

Harper picked up her phone. "Hello? Hello?"

"You're awake, good. You still okay? The door still locked tight? That banshee stopped howling thirty minutes ago."

That's when Harper noticed the quiet. "Do you think she's gone?"

"You will *not* be opening that door to find out," her mother said. "Your father is on his way."

"What time is it?"

"The sun rose six minutes ago."

"How does he know where Nick lives?"

"We used location services on your phone," she said simply.

Harper wasn't surprised. They'd agreed to get her the new phone on the condition that she left the tracker feature active at all times.

"How's Nick?" her mom asked.

"Still asleep."

"Wake him up before they get there."

"What do you mean *they*?"

"When the unit comes into the house, they'll take you, Nick, and probably his mother if they can find her."

"Will they kill her?"

"Don't ask and I won't lie to you," her mother said. "Then you won't have to lie to Nick."

Harper sat up, pushing the hair back from her face.

"They're going to take you to your father's lab and have you tested. You might have to spend the night there, but your father is going to try to get that waived. But since Nick isn't his charge, he might have to stay in the center for a couple of nights before we can get the court to sign temporary custody over to us."

"What, why?"

"You spent the night in close quarters with a vampire. You have scratches. Protocol."

"No, I meant why would they let me go and not Nick? He's seventeen."

Nick's eyes opened. He was sitting up. But before he could speak, there was a crash toward the front of the house. Harper heard the rush of feet and shouting voices.

"Wait, Mom, hold on. Something's happening."

Harper only had a moment to raise the bat before the bedroom door was thrown open.

It was her dad, in tactical anti-bite gear from the neck down. His face lit up with relief when he saw her.

"Harper." He breathed her name like a prayer. "Let's get the hell out of here."

At the facility, they were led to her father's office. Her father wore latex gloves as he inspected the cut on Harper's cheek and drew her blood. Once she was cleaned up, he turned his attention to Nick, giving him the same care.

After Nick's blood had been drawn, her father handed the vials of their blood off to a lab tech and removed his gloves.

"What's going to happen to my mom?" Nick asked.

"I don't know," her father said. The latex gloves snapped before being tossed into the trash. "She was gone when we arrived."

Nick said nothing to this.

"He can stay with us, right?" Harper asked.

"Of course. We'll figure something out. But for now, the two of you need to get some rest." He gestured at the cots against the far wall.

Harper wondered if that was where her father had slept when he missed curfew.

"I'll be right here," he said, misinterpreting her hesitation. "And your mom has already called the school. She'll pick up your homework when she gets Carter."

"Come on," Nick said, and reached for her hand.

Harper took it despite the heat in her cheeks. She felt her father's eyes on her. But they were just holding hands and they'd been through the worst night together. It wasn't like they were making out or anything.

No sooner than Harper's head hit the pillow did she fall asleep. She hadn't realized how exhausted she was until the darkness overtook her even in spite of the bright lights.

She woke to someone yelling her name.

"Harper. Harper!"

She pried her eyes open to a strange scene. Nick was being dragged away by a group of lab attendants in full hazmat suits.

"What's going on?" She pushed herself up to sit. "Dad, what's happening?"

"It's okay." Her father took a seat beside her, reaching for her hand.

She pulled away. "No, what's happening? Nick! Where are they taking him?"

They pulled him through the door and he was gone.

As soon as the door slid closed and she was alone in the lab with her father, she turned on him. "What the hell is going on? What are they doing to him?"

"He has to be moved to a quarantine room. I'm sorry," her father said.

"What? Why?"

"His blood. His blood tests weren't good, Harp."

Harper's heart sputtered in her chest. "But he was fine. He was with me all night. He didn't get bitten. He's—But it wasn't even that bad of a scratch!"

She didn't understand. Her brain struggled to make sense of what her father was telling her.

"He walked in the sunlight to the van when we came here this morning. You *saw* him."

"I know," her father said, running a hand through his hair. "We'll redo the test, but to be safe, he has to be quarantined for now."

"He was with me all night," she said again. She didn't tell him about the kiss, but she couldn't stop thinking about it. If Nick had really been one of them, he could have killed her. He could have killed her, but he didn't. She'd lain beside him all night with blood on her face and her throat inches away from him, but he hadn't hurt her.

That had to count for something. Unless…

Her guts clenched. "Am I—am I positive too?"

"No," he said. "But I do need to tell you something."

"Mom or Carter—"

He waved her fears away. "No, no. Everyone is okay."

Everyone but Nick.

"But your test did reveal something. You're like me, Harper. You're like me."

She frowned. "I don't understand."

"I can't contract the virus. I'm immune. And now we know you're immune too. In fact, you have even more immunity than I do. When I'm exposed to the virus, I get sick. Lethargic. It's like a bad cold. But your immune system is far more reactive. When I added the virus to your sample, it was eradicated. I don't think your body would even have time to register symptoms before the threat was eradicated."

"So I'm not infected. I can't be infected even if they bite me?"

"And I'm glad to hear it. Though this doesn't mean you can be reckless." Her father ran a hand through his hair. "You need to understand that immunity doesn't mean safe. They are still killers. You understand that, right? They can still *kill* you."

"What about Carter and Mom?"

"Your mom has stronger immunity than I do, but not as strong as yours," he said. "We haven't tested Carter."

"How did you find out you were immune?"

"I was bitten," he said. "Both your mother and I, early in The Event. We were attacked but not killed. But we must have already had a natural immunity before that because others in our group weren't so lucky. The immunity didn't come from surviving the attack itself. That much we know."

Early in The Event. *My god.* Harper had been close to being an orphan and hadn't even known it. Carter might never have been born at all.

"Of course, we hoped that both you and Carter would inherit our natural immunity, but there was no chance to confirm it until now. For you anyway. It remains to be seen if Carter has it as well. But it's promising that your immunity is even stronger than mine and your mother's."

Harper supposed it didn't matter if she was immune or not. Sure, it was nice to know she wouldn't turn into one of those creatures, but she didn't want to be killed. Nor did she want to lose her parents or little brother.

She clasped the back of her neck. "What about Nick? Is he going to be okay?"

"His blood is interesting. There are some markers of immunity, but more markers of infection. That's why we need to keep him for observation. We simply don't know how that will go, sweetie. I'm so sorry. I know you like him."

That was an understatement.

Harper turned and searched her father's face. "So what now?"

"We hang out here today. You can rest while I work. I know it's boring, but I want you to stay in the lab with me. Your mom will pick us up after she gets Carter."

"And Nick?"

"I've asked them to keep me in the loop. I'll let you know whatever I find out, but he'll have to remain in quarantine for observation."

"Until when?"

He didn't have an answer for her. He only said, "I'm sorry. I'm doing the best I can."

Harper couldn't fall back asleep. She spent the day on the cot, scrolling on her phone, while her father moved about the lab, shuffling from task to task. She remembered days when she'd longed for a chance to shadow him, learn what he was doing, and see him in action.

But now that she was here, all she could do was think about Nick. She was worried for him. He'd lost everything and now he might be sick too.

He might become one of them.

He must feel so alone.

She wished she could tell him he wasn't.

At four o'clock her mother picked them up outside on the curb. It was so strange standing in the bright sunlight after a day under fluorescents. Harper wondered if her father also struggled with this transition. If he felt stuck in a perpetual rotation between an oppressive night and an artificial day.

As soon as Harper saw her mother, she hugged her harder than she had in her whole life. And she hugged Carter hard too, until he gave a little squeak and she was forced to release him.

At home, no one spoke of Nick or what might happen next. Instead, they moved through the night as they always had. Homework was done. Dinner was made.

Once, her mother reached across her biology textbook and gave her hand a good squeeze.

"It'll be okay," she said, before smoothing Harper's hair away from her face. "He's safe in the lab."

"I hope you're right," she said. "I just—I just—"

"You like him," her mom said with a small smile.

"I think so," Harper sighed. "I think I do."

The first curfew siren wailed.

"Let's get the windows done," her mother said, rising from the table. "I don't know about you, but I *really* want to go to bed early tonight."

. . .

HARPER WASN'T SURE WHAT TIME SHE FELL ASLEEP, BUT SHE woke to the feeling of her mattress sinking beneath a weight. Through the haze, she thought maybe it was her mother waking her for school, or her father waking her with news about Nick.

What she hadn't expected to see when she opened her eyes was Nick.

He clamped a hand over her mouth before she could speak.

"Please don't yell," he said. "If you wake your parents, this will get ugly."

Harper's heart began to race. It wasn't that he looked dramatically different, but he did look changed somehow. There was something in his eyes that hadn't been there before. But he didn't look feral like the other creatures. Nor did he look like the ones who'd been turned first, who, over the years, had evolved to have those grotesque wings and truly monstrous features.

Mostly he looked like Nick.

It was only Harper's instinct that told her now she was in the room with something dangerous.

"How did you get in here?" she asked. "They can't cross thresholds."

"*They*," he echoed. And smiled. "Good. At least you recognize I'm not like them."

"Are you going to kill me?" she whispered.

Here, at least, he looked genuinely hurt. "I could never hurt you, Harper. That's why I came to tell you goodbye and to make you a promise."

She sat up slowly, pressing her back against her headboard. To the left were her headphones. She'd left them off in hopes she would get a message from Nick.

Careful what you wish for.

"I don't know why I'm different," he said. "I can feel the

changes. I won't lie about that. And I definitely feel hungry, and we both know for *what*. But somehow I'm still mostly me."

She searched his face but saw only the same sweet, earnest boy that she knew.

"What's the promise, Nick?"

"I'm going to make the world safe for you. I'll hunt and kill them the way they killed my family until there isn't a single one of those creatures left. I wanted you to know that you and Carter and your family will never lose each other."

"Nick, you can't—" But she wasn't sure how to finish. Can't what? Fight the monsters? Bring his family back? Make the world a better place even as it burns to the ground around them?

"I can," he said softly, and leaned toward her. "Or at least, I'm going to try."

Her heart sped up as he came closer. As his dark eyes loomed large. The first brush of his lips on hers. They were warm. Soft. Not monstrous at all.

"You can't do that," she said. "What if they hurt you?"

"I need a reason to keep going, Harper, and this is all I've got," he breathed.

She kissed him back.

He took her face in his hands. "I'll make the world safe again. I promise. I don't care how long it takes."

"Harper? Who are you talking to?" her father called down the hallway, the sound of their bedroom door creaking open.

But by the time her father came to her room, Nick was already gone.

"No one," she said.

Her father looked around as if he didn't entirely believe her. "Are you sure? Because I got a message from the lab saying Nick has escaped."

5 years later

Harper stared up at the full moon, gazing at its bright face and the stars above. Her rescued pit bull, Rainbow, strained on her leash, sniffing a low hedge.

More than once her impatience had crept in as the dog refused to choose a spot in which to relieve herself. And every time she started to get mad at the dog, she reminded herself that a few years ago, this wouldn't have been possible.

The world had changed so much. Now it felt like the whole business of vampires and curfews and sirens had been a dream she'd had a long time ago.

There hadn't been a single murder, attack, or so much as a case of infection in her city for over two years. Even the whole state had been case-free for eighteen months, and now she only heard about the occasional death in one of the larger cities far away on the coast.

They stopped using the sirens six months ago.

Harper wasn't sure if it was the vaccine that had made their lives better or whatever Nick was doing.

Nick.

She hadn't seen him once since the night he kissed her goodbye. Every once in a while, she found herself hoping he'd turn up. For a birthday. For Christmas. Hell, for Halloween night.

But last week was her college graduation and there had still been no sign of him. She was starting to wonder if maybe he couldn't find her. She had moved to an apartment across town, closer to campus.

It hadn't taken her long to realize that she missed him, that she did, in fact, still have feelings for him.

Rainbow shuffled a few feet forward, rooting deeper into a new bush.

A startled rabbit burst forth, sprinting halfway across the dark road until its gray body was spot-lit beneath the streetlamp.

Harper swore. "For the love of all that's holy, Rainbow. Please just take a piss already."

Rainbow began to growl, low in her throat. But then she whined, her tail tucking.

"It's just a rabbit. What's wrong with you?"

Then Harper saw what the dog was looking at.

It wasn't the rabbit.

It was the shadow detaching itself from the darkness and stepping into the light.

"Hi, Harris." As soon as he spoke, Harper knew who it was.

"Nick!"

He smiled, and the smile was a little sharp. Still, she held her ground as he crossed the road and approached her. He stopped a few feet short of her, just out of Rainbow's reach.

Nick, she thought. *He's just Nick.*

The dog whined. Rainbow pressed herself against Harper's legs.

"It's okay. It's okay, girl," Harper said, soothing her.

"Is it?" Nick asked.

Harper stood slowly, searching his face. "I don't know. Are you going to tear my throat out? Eat my liver?"

Nick shook his head, the smile folding into a laugh. "I already ate."

"*Oh*, that's good to know. Anyone I know?"

"No," he said. "I only eat the trouble-makers."

"You seem like a troublemaker to me."

He shrugged. "I guess I am."

She stepped toward him, looking up into his face. He went very still in front of her.

"Is this okay?" she asked. "Am I in danger?"

Will you hurt me?

She supposed every girl wanted to ask the guy she liked that.

"I would never hurt you," he said. "I promised you that, remember?"

"Will you stay then? Can you stay?"

He took a step toward her. "I'd *like* to stay. But only if I'm *invited.*"

"Vampire puns. I wonder if I'll ever get tired of those."

She came up onto her toes then and did what she'd been dreaming of doing for the last five years. She kissed him. Long, slow, and deep.

When they finally broke apart, his eyes were glassy with desire.

"I missed you," he whispered, his breath hot on her lips.

She nodded over her shoulder at the apartment building at her back. "Then come inside, vampire boy. And tell me all about where you've been."

AUTHOR'S NOTE

There are often stories *behind* every story. And in the case of the stories in this collection, here are mine:

THIRST

I was deeply affected by the novel *The Water Knife* by Paolo Bacigalupi. The story envisions a near-future American Southwest in which the water crisis begins to have dire consequences for the communities there. Even though it's fiction, it's a hauntingly realistic portrayal of how fierce competition for the control of the world's limited fresh water might play out, and how those in power might extort those resources.

I wrote *Thirst* within a year of reading *The Water Knife*, so I am sure the challenges it presented were still top of mind. *Thirst* was also the basis for my futuristic science fiction novels from The City series. *The City Below* is much farther into the future than Bacigalupi's tale, but it was still a world built around the idea of resource scarcity and just what lengths people might go to when navigating those circumstances. Because our *City Below* heroine, Grace Buteo, lives in a more prosperous zone than the characters we meet in *Thirst*, her struggles are less resource-centric. But both stories are from the same world, perhaps highlighting just how different day-to-day reality can look for resource-poor communities.

Blood & Castles

This is a story I never expected to write. Space vampires? *What?* But the opportunity presented itself in the summer of 2020. I had just completed a Kickstarter project to fund the production of three audiobooks from the Shadows in the Water series. One of the rewards was "an exclusive story written just for you!" Chris De Francisci took me up on the offer. When I asked him what he wanted his story to be, he shared his idea of a future in which humanity had left Earth for the stars, but also one in which the rich liked to buy souvenirs of our previous life—including "Dracula's Castle." *Blood & Castles* was born of that exchange with Chris, and he and I are both happy with the results. It was a fun universe to play in and I just might return to it one day. Thanks, Chris!

Seven Devils

This story is best enjoyed while listening to "Seven Devils" by Florence and The Machine. Or at least, I was certainly listening to it on repeat while writing it. This story serves as origin lore for my Castle Cove series. For that reason, Vendetta—first of her kind—is also mentioned in *Grayson's Story*, another Castle Cove tale. But I can't help but wonder if maybe it's also Vendetta who Captain Kal (from *Blood & Castles*) wakes accidentally all those centuries in the future, maybe long after Castle Cove and the earth have fallen to ruin.

V-63

During the pandemic, whenever I wore a mask, I always felt like a muzzled vampire. So much so, I often wondered who I might bite first if I took it off. This seed of an idea coupled with the pandemic experience led me to write a slice-of-life tale about an idiot too afraid to tell her crush she's in love with him as they navigate the end of the world together.

THE DARK TRICK

The phrase *the dark trick* is mentioned in Anne Rice's chronicles as the term for turning someone into a vampire. I've used it here in a similar fashion but also to suggest the cat-mouse seduction involved leading up to the exchange. This story is set in the 1870s, around the same time *Camilla* by Sheridan Le Fanu was published. In *Camilla* we have not only one of the earliest works of vampire fiction but also lesbian erotica, the tone of which is definitely mimicked here.

The story itself is also inspired by the collection's cover. When I saw the cover, immediately the details of the story began to take shape in my mind. An innocent girl, a haunting house, and who—or what—might be waiting for her inside. I also liked the idea of reversing the invitation trope, and—as was the case in this story—it was the vampire who had to invite the victim in.

A VAMPIRE CALLS

In *Interview with the Vampire* (the movie), Lestat goes to Louis de Pointe du Lac and offers him a choice. It's not a great choice, but here we first see the theme of consent in vampire fiction and how it inspired this idea of choice in many of the films, books, and stories that followed. All because Tom Cruise uttered the iconic line, "Don't be afraid. I'm going to give you the choice I never had." I'm sure Lestat was going to kill Louie either way, but I still found it interesting, the idea of a vampire stalking a particular family or victim, for reasons known only to the vampire. In the case of A Vampire Calls, I made it *my* family—the house where my mother lived just before her death. Only this time—as terrible as her life and ending was—I tried to give her something akin to a second chance.

Night Shift

As is often the case, multiple ideas came together to form this story. Here we see dramatic monologue *meets* vampires *meets* my friend is a nightshift nurse who has told me many interesting (horrifying) stories about working in a hospital at night. I'm not entirely sure why I thought it needed to be a dramatic monologue except that I'd always wanted to write something in the vein (heh) of "My Last Duchess" by Robert Browning. I wrote an entire twenty-five-page paper on it in college. Yes, that's how much I liked it. I suppose my goal is achieved at last.

Grayson's Story

I went back and forth about whether or not to include this story, since it is really just an excerpt of a longer work. But most of my vampires live in Castle Cove and so it didn't seem right not to include a story from that universe in my collection about vampires. Also, I thought this might be more reader-friendly for those who enjoy the idea of exploring a supernatural town but are intimidated by the choose-your-own-path format that *Welcome to Castle Cove* and *Night Tide* follow.

I was also leaning into the bodice-ripping aspect of vampire fiction. As most of us know, vampirism is often a metaphor for suppressed (or not so suppressed) sexual desire. That is showcased here.

Curfew

When this idea first came to me, I didn't know the story would be about vampires. I had only the idea of a disturbing siren that went off in a town every day and the way the people would rush into their houses to shelter from—whatever it was that was coming to eat them. I suspect this idea grew roots in my brain after watching *Silent Hill.*

You need not watch the movie yourself. You can simply search the internet for "Silent Hill Siren Sound" and you'll know what siren I'm talking about.

But once it became clear that I *did* have vampires on my hands, I started to draw on some of the other themes we often encounter in vampire fiction—having to invite someone in, for example. And also the idea that there's always *one* exception to the vampire rule, someone who turns but not completely (looking at you, Angel) and therefore remains just human enough to love.

DID YOU ENJOY *THIRST: NEW AND COLLECTED STORIES?* THERE are plenty more vampires where these came from in Shrum's *Welcome to Castle Cove* series. Learn more about the series **here.**

NEWSLETTER OFFER

Get Your Three Free Stories Today

Thank you so much for reading *Thirst: new and collected stories*. I hope you enjoyed the collection. If you'd like more, I have other short stories that I give away for free exclusively to newsletter subscribers—and some even have vampires.

You can sign up for my newsletter and get these free stories by visiting ➜ https://www.korymshrum.com/free-starter-library

These stories are from the other series that I write. If you've signed up for my newsletter already, no need to sign up again. You should have already received the stories from me. Check your email and make sure my emails weren't marked as spam!

Still can't find it? Email me at ➜ kory@korymshrum.com and I'll take care of it.

As to the newsletter itself, I send out 2-3 a month and host a monthly giveaway exclusive to my subscribers. The prizes are usually signed books. I also share information about my current projects, and personal anecdotes (like pictures of my dog). If you want these free stories and access to the exclusive giveaways, you can sign up for the newsletter at ➜ https://www.korymshrum.com/free-starter-library

If this is not your cup of tea (I love tea), you can follow me on social media in order to be notified of my new releases.

ACKNOWLEDGMENTS

My first short story collection! What an adventure. Hats off to my amazing production team, including The World's Best Editor: Toby Selwyn, and the Very Talented Cover Designer: Kuen Giovanni.

Of course we can never forget my ever-enthusiastic critique group, The Four Horsemen of the Bookocalypse. Katie Pendleton, Angela Roquet, and Monica La Porta. As well as a round of applause for my super fans and lovely street team. Thank you for reading the books in advance, reporting those lingering typos, and posting honest reviews. Your continued support makes the work worth it.

And no acknowledgements page would be complete without mention of my beautiful wife, Kim and my support pug Charley, who is the best writing partner in the world.

Everyone listed above is perfect and can do no wrong. Therefore, any remaining errors in the book are my own.

ALSO BY KORY M. SHRUM

Dying for a Living series

Dying for a Living

Dying by the Hour

Dying for Her: A Companion Novel

Dying Light

Worth Dying For

Dying Breath

Dying Day

Shadows in the Water: Lou Thorne Thrillers

Shadows in the Water

Under the Bones

Danse Macabre

Carnival

Devil's Luck

What Comes Around

Overkill

Silver Bullet

Hell House

One Foot in the Grave

Blood Rain

Castle Cove series

Welcome to Castle Cove

Night Tide

2603 novels

The City Below

The City Within

The City Outside

Standalone Novels

Jack and the Fire Eater

Blade Born: A Borderlands Novel

Short Fiction

Thirst: new and collected stories

Nonfiction

Who Killed My Mother? a memoir

Learn more about Kory's work at: http://www. korymshrum.com/

ABOUT THE AUTHOR

Kory M. Shrum is author of more than twenty novels, including the bestselling *Shadows in the Water* and *Dying for a Living* series. She has loved books and words all her life. She reads almost every genre you can think of, but when she writes, she writes science fiction, fantasy, and thrillers, or often something that's all of the above.

In 2020, she launched a true crime podcast *Who Killed My Mother?*, sharing the true story of her mother's tragic death. You can listen for free on YouTube or your favorite podcast app. She is now writing her new show called *A Well Cared For Human*, a mental health and wellbeing podcast.

When she's not eating, reading, writing, or indulging in her true calling as a stay-at-home dog mom, she loves to plan her next adventure. She can usually be found under thick blankets with snacks. The kettle is almost always on.

She lives in Michigan with her equally bookish wife, Kim, and their rescue pug, Charley. Learn more about Kory and her work at www.korymshrum.com